DEVOURED

DEVOURED

D. E. MEREDITH

ISIS
LARGE PRINT
Oxford

Copyright © D. E. Meredith, 2011

First published in Great Britain 2012
by
Allison & Busby Limited, 2012

Published in Large Print 2013 by ISIS Publishing Ltd.,
7 Centremead, Osney Mead, Oxford OX2 0ES
by arrangement with
Allison & Busby Limited

CIP data is available for this title from the British Library

ISBN 978–0–7531–9186–6 (hb)
ISBN 978–0–7531–9187–3 (pb)

Printed and bound in Great Britain by
T. J. International Ltd., Padstow, Cornwall

For Charlie, with love

PROLOGUE

The door creaked open as the maid stepped into the room. In a flattened jungle of leaf gold and petals of magenta, a myriad of exotic birds and flowers competed with one another. On the walls, butterflies were pinned, framed, and labelled, and all around her a dizzying quietness, except for a scratching sound made by a little finch that was kept in a cage by the window.

In the maid's hand was a key which she turned in the lock of her mistress's wardrobe, and crouching down low, she pulled out the brushing tray. The scent of lavender bags rose from the opened drawer as she lifted it up, revealing a hidden compartment and a different scent altogether. Dried ink and woody parchment. Enveloped by this scent, the maid bound the bundle of letters together with a length of rattan cord.

It was still snowing outside. Thick pelts were falling silently beyond the huge arched window which led her down into the hall. Pushing the door open, she left nothing behind, only a flurry of air and the bracing, cold bite of December.

Flora's instructions had been clear. Her mistress had been agitated, in a state of tortured indecision for over a month, pacing the floors, wringing her hands, and then she suddenly announced, in that way of hers, "I am decided at last. Make your way back to London and deliver the letters, Flora. You know where to find them. Do exactly as I have told you." And who was she to question anything? She was just the messenger, a mere servant, thought Flora, wrestling with her pocket watch, fearful that she would be late. But she needn't have worried, for here, right on time, was the regular omnibus, veering around the corner of Nightingale Walk with a deafening clatter of hooves.

Flora clambered into the coach, and holding the letters close, drifted for a while with the earliness of it all, only to be jolted back to wakefulness by the cry of, "Next stop, Great Russell Street."

Her heart pounding, Flora looked skywards at the towering Colossus before her and sprang up the steps, each bound made quiet by the falling snow. She knocked at the huge oak door with a resonating thud, to hear a shuffle and rattling of keys.

"Go easy I say, or you'll bring the house down," a voice grumbled through the grate. Flora showed the porter the scroll of letters, as he swung back the door and nodded her in.

"Sit yourself down and I'll find us a nip of something," he offered, peering at her. "It's perishing out there."

She shook her head. "I'm in a hurry," she said, and the porter shrugged.

"Dr Canning never arrives early, nor any of the other curators," he replied. "But if you like, we can go and look for him."

2

The museum was a pitch-black crypt as the pair, illuminated only by a tallow, climbed slowly up the central stairs past row upon row of shells, bones, mummified creatures. The mosaic-tiled floor clipped and echoed as they turned down a corridor, until finally the flame licked around a bend, where —

"Would you fathom it, I could have sworn . . ."

A single lamp burned, igniting a collection of minerals into a spectacular firework display. And Flora for an instant saw her fear and the scroll of letters in her hand reflected in a glass cabinet, where a flutter of tiny birds had been caught in iridescent flight. And to the left of the hummingbirds, a door with a brass nameplate that announced, "Dr John Canning, Anthropologist and Naturalist."

The door opened and a man greeted them, ruffling his hair, a half-smile upon his face.

"Ah, excellent. I've been expecting these letters for some time," Dr Canning said, as he ushered Flora into the room. He smoothed out the first of them — a scroll of golden, weather-beaten parchment — and putting on a pair of glasses, sat back in his chair and began.

Sarawak, Borneo
June 1st, 1855

To My Dear Lady Bessingham,

You know me well enough to know that I am not a man of letters. But your unstinting support for my endeavours demands that I finally put pen to paper and tell you that this world is all that you imagined. Nay,

3

madam, it is more. A country so enticing as to leave me breathless. Breathless from the sheer audacity of its mountain splendour, but perplexed because such variety disturbs me, and begs questions which cannot be easily answered. Your Council was not wanting, madam. The drumbeat of Nature beats loudly here.

By the time you receive this letter, I will be upriver near a far-flung place called Simunjan, which I'm promised will be bursting with botanical marvels. But before I elaborate, I should firstly tell you a little of my journey here.

Her Majesty's Ship The Advancement set sail for the Malay Archipelago on December 12th, 1854, a ten-gun brig, under the command of Captain Owen. Its primary object being to circumnavigate Africa and Indo-China, if the great magnitude of this journey does not defeat both ship and crew.

Before we left Dover, The Advancement was equipped to bursting. Crates crammed with every conceivable thing and, much to my delight, casks full of alcohol and spices for storing biological specimens. Some of my own finds have already been confined to the hold, and will be held there safely until the vessel eventually returns home. I only hope I shall be there to meet it.

One of my more interesting finds from this leg of the journey included a type of billfish I named Tetrapturus brodegius. It is like an Atlantic sailfish, with a great sword-like snout and a metal-grey body, as firm as a side of pork. The meaty flesh we ate for a hearty supper (leaving skin and bones for taxidermy), and I am hopeful that the fish will raise substantial funds on my return, which should please my father immensely.

In addition to Captain Owen, the crew consisted of seven officers, more than twenty English sailors, and at least ten native Malays, including Chief Petty Officer Alam.

He was a very fascinating fellow. Bedecked in a pristine English naval uniform, Alam had long since shed his native guise, but still had the athletic bearing of his Minang descendants. Heralding originally from Padang, his name meant three things, all at once. Each meaning was of equal bearing and boded well for my expedition.

"Alam", it seems, means Nature, Universe, and Teacher. Can you imagine, madam, how excited I became at this discovery? A Noble Savage made "Respectable" by our British navy and representing such a "Universal Truth". A sign, I hope, of things to come.

My other notable companion was Chief Scientist Dr Bacon. Perhaps you know of him? He has certainly heard of you. He proved to be an avid collector of sponges (genus, Porifera) and collected over fifteen fascinating examples from the rocks along the shoreline. These strange animals appear most simple, and yet, according to Dr Bacon, consist of a vast network of chambers and canals. We observed their comical habit of sucking up seawater, and spurting it out again. For what reason I cannot say, but it passed several hours of what might have been an otherwise tedious day. Indeed, these Porifera are not so unlike some people I could mention, sucking in the swell of power before it overcomes them and they are forced to retch it out.

But I digress.

Mainly, as we crossed the Mediterranean, life was quiet. The heat beat down upon the deck, and I must confess that I gave into a creeping lethargy, whiling away whole hours lolling on the deck. I still managed the odd sketch, if a gliding bird caught my eye. I would even wave my hands around frantically hollering, if a curve of flying dolphins broke the stern. But on the whole, the sea had made me listless and I longed for ground. I longed for some distinction. And we were blessed, because almost as I thought this, the softest breeze lifted and at once, sailors were shimmying up the rigging, bellowing, "Land Ahoy!"

After five long weeks at sea, Aboukir Bay. For me, the end and the beginning.

On arriving at the port, Alam shook my hand to wish me God Speed and handed me a talisman. It was an evil-looking thing, but all the time Alam was smiling as if he had given me his last guinea, so I took it just the same — this carved wooden figure with its protruding eyes, swollen belly, and reptilian claws raised as if to the heavens. He told me the carving was Dayak, from a hill tribe in Sarawak. The figure — a water spirit, he said — would ward off the bad spirits of the Underworld. I laughed, but his eyes unnerved me. But I thought nothing more of it, as I boarded the train which took me from Alexandria to Suez, keeping the talisman hidden, buried deep in my bag under a pile of drawings and instruments.

On the train I enjoyed more luxury than I deserved. Endless cups of mint tea, bowls of nuts, and hot linen towels brought by starched Egyptian servants, who called me "Master" and "Yes, sir, Mr Broderig."

The ease of this journey gave me time to drink in the desert. And it was not the arid landscape I had expected, but rather mile upon mile of luminous green. Villages made entirely of mud, crops of corn and lentils, majestic palm trees and red kites lifting in an African breeze.

The train curved along the coast towards Yemen at exhilarating speed until the line ran out, and I was forced to find another mode of transport. The most common in Egypt being straddling one's legs over some desperately overburdened donkey, as we trundled through markets with "Backsheesh, backsheesh, ingleesh man" ringing in my ears. Until at last, crumpled and exhausted, I reached the port of Aden.

The steamer which awaited took me all the way to Singapore. But I was not so happy here as on The Advancement, despite the cheering crowds and thumping bands which sent us on our way. Suffice to say, I found myself thrown in with a throng of businessmen and traders. At first, I tried to entice them by pointing out whale sharks and gliding, ghostlike manta rays, but these scurrying gentlemen were not impressed. And so I simply gave up and spent the last few weeks in my cabin, preparing for my work.

My final ship was a Chinese junk crewed entirely by Cantonese fishermen who took me to Sarawak. And for a few guineas, I had my own thatched-roof cabin with a bamboo floor, a lamp to read by, and the most comfortable little bed.

These fishermen were the very opposite to the men on The Eugene. They were enthusiastic about my work and cooked some of the finest meals I have ever tasted, and it's true to say that the last little bit of my voyage was, if not the best, certainly the most peaceful.

But I am here now in Sarawak. Ants crawl across the paper as I write. Geckoes hang, pink embryos, winking knowingly at me. For this is a world where spirits dwell in every rock and crevice. They weave in rivers and lie waiting, breathless in the ground. But the talisman sits beside my bed and I am beginning to understand its purpose. It is, I believe, benevolent and here to bring me luck.

And as for my friends from The Advancement? Their journey is still ahead of them. I often wander down to the beach and gaze out upon the South China Sea, thinking of Alam and his long journey of discovery, which will end here, where mine is just beginning, in the Malay Archipelago.

But it's late now. I must attend to my arrangements, because we have but three months before the rainy season begins. During this Season, all expedition work ceases, for the flooding is tremendous, and would make this trip upriver impossible. And so I must to my work. To collect. To understand and ask questions, madam, as you would want me to. To look at this world as a Man of Science.

Your humblest and most devoted servant,
Benjamin Broderig, esq.

CHAPTER
ONE

ST BART'S
SMITHFIELD, LONDON
1856

Professor Hatton lay slumped at his desk, his silhouette devoured by thrown shapes from an ebbing fire burning low in the grate. In the quiet chasm of the morgue, Hatton's eyes were tightly shut, shielding out the peeling walls around him. A lamp burned on his desk. He was still awake, but only just, exhausted by contemplation of the great task before him, knowing that the value of his new science, forensics, was forever in question.

"Professor Hatton. Open up, sir. There's a carriage waiting. You are needed urgently, sir."

He shuddered, gathered his thoughts, wondering what the devil time it was, but knowing Monsieur Roumande must have gone home already. Hatton found his surgical bag, and then took his coat, his hat and his cane down from one of the meat hooks and opening the mortuary door, stepped out into a moonlit yard. Lantern light illuminated folding drifts of snow as he tumbled into the waiting carriage. There was no need to find his pocket watch as a bell was chiming somewhere, three times, across the velvet skies of London.

"Good evening, Professor Hatton. My name is Inspector George Adams of Scotland Yard. Perhaps you've heard of me?"

Hatton studied the man sitting before him, who thumped the roof of the hansom with his cane and lit a penny smoke, offering one to him. Hatton shook his head, his eyes still bleary with sleep. The coach lurched off towards the river, now nothing more than a tapered line, soon lost in the swirling pall of driven snowflakes.

"All will reveal itself when we arrive in Chelsea but are you sure you won't join me, Professor? They're Turkish, you know." Hatton declined, as the Inspector shrugged and puffed on his cigarette. "This could be a very long night," he said.

"Your reputation goes before you, Inspector Adams," said Hatton finally, having taken the measure of the man. "So I presume this is a medical jurisprudence matter?"

"Yes, Professor." The Inspector was stretching his legs out, partly enclosed in a gabardine coat. "It's a case of the utmost sensitivity. But I've wanted to work with you for some time now; I'm intrigued by your new science, Professor."

Hatton nodded, curious as well for he knew a little of this man, but Albert Roumande knew more. He had heard his Chief Diener talk of Scotland Yard's celebrated new detective many times, reading snippets out of the papers about various cases.

To work with Inspector Adams? Hatton allowed himself a smile.

"As I said, I've followed your work with some interest," continued the Inspector, in what Hatton recognised was an eastern drawl, not unlike his own accent once, when he was a boy. But Adams seemed to take delight in his drawn-out vowels, whereas Hatton had long since rubbed the edges off, keen to meet society's expectations of a young professor at St Bart's, in a new position of some standing. But here was a man who clearly took no prisoners, nor apologised for what he was. A man to admire, then.

"I'm flattered," answered Hatton. "Perhaps it is the series of articles in *The Lancet* you refer to? We are so misunderstood, Inspector. Forensics needs all the friends it can get, and I understand from my fellow pathologists that you are indeed a friend. So, I'm delighted to finally make your acquaintance."

"The Yard is modernising," said the Inspector. "Look at me, for example. Do you think I would have stood a chance ten years ago? A lad from Cambridgeshire? A working man's son? An out-of-town Special? But I'm a regular hero now, if you follow the crime pages. Although, don't believe everything you read about me, Professor."

The horse whinnied as they reached their final destination.

"This way, Professor."

Hatton followed him out of the coach, briefly stamping the snow off his boots, before ascending the steps of a house on Nightingale Walk which loomed above him, its green gloss door lit by an ornate gas lamp. Hatton glanced up at the clear night sky, brilliantly lit by an arch of flickering stars, and as a flurry of snow caught his face, he relished its cold bite. It would be overbearingly warm inside.

"You should know this is the home of a bohemian, as they like to call themselves. Her taste is not the same as mine. Nor yours, I suspect," the Inspector said, as they were admitted by a constable, and Hatton was amazed to see, as they headed up the stairs, that this elegant house seemed to be crammed full of everything and anything — shelves were brimming over with a thousand books, competing for space with rocks, shells, feathers, cases of moths and butterflies. Hatton stopped in his tracks as they turned a corner into an expression of pure evil. Slashed red and black with eyes yellow rimmed and teeth as jagged as knives.

"A tribal mask, I think they call it," said the Inspector. "So, you will meet their late owner now. Prepare yourself, for there's a great deal of blood."

Stepping into the room they were greeted by more jumble still and so many policemen, doing what Professor Hatton didn't rightly know, but he could feel his temper rising as he saw all these clodhoppers poking about amongst the victim's possessions, clearly unaware that anything they moved or altered could wreck his forensic gathering.

"Please, Inspector. Would you ask your men to refrain from doing that? Yes, that!" One fellow was bending over the four-poster bed and pulling off pillows. Hatton was no novice in murder, and suddenly

"Hurry up and get Sir William a glass of brandy, Constable."

Sir William took the brandy and, recovering a little, said, "I apologise, Professor. I am out of sorts. We're most grateful for you coming here, but everything you see and hear tonight must remain between these four walls. We need your absolute discretion."

Hatton bowed. "Of course."

Sir William, knotting his brow, continued, "Lady Bessingham courted controversy before she died, as I have, Professor. She was a dear friend to me but she was also a blue stocking, a woman of learning and letters, involving herself in things which were perhaps not entirely appropriate, or this is how some might see it. But in death she deserves some dignity, surely? This brutal crime will have a thousand tongues wagging and a thousand of those Grub Street scribblers selling their lies for thru'pence. We will be awash with rumours before the sun has risen." Sir William wrung his hands. "Whatever you have to do, Professor, please do it, but I beg you, as a gentleman, proceed with the utmost discretion."

Hatton answered that he would proceed as required and turned to the Inspector. "It's a delicate question, but was she found half naked, like this?" and as he spoke, Hatton ran his eye along the lines of her hips and curves. He was already elsewhere, thinking about the cutting of her flesh which lay ahead.

Adams nodded. "There's a dress over the back of a chair in the adjoining room. There was a fire still smouldering in the grate when we found her. It's ebbing now, but the room, as you can feel, is still warm, although I doubt she slept like this. She still has her stockings and corset on. Not normal attire for bed even for a bohemian."

Hatton looked around him for some sort of clue as to what she might have been doing half dressed like this, and then made another note. Perhaps she was simply preparing for bed when somebody found her. Hatton knew little of women, especially rich ones, but he knew enough to tell him that few prepared their evening toilette without a maid to carry out their bidding. To brush their hair, to unbutton their stays, to warm and fetch a nightdress. But there was no fresh nightdress on the bed and no warming pan, either.

"She hasn't been moved or touched. She is exactly as she was found, Professor," continued Adams. "But I think we need to get her to the mortuary now. We'll follow you on with the hearse. I assume you are happy to be observed as you work?"

Hatton said that he was and if truth were known, he welcomed it. There was no opportunity here for theatrics or demonstrating his talent, as there was in the morgue. "But it's five hours till dawn, midwinter and the mortuary is gloomy at the best of times, so with your leave, I shan't start the cutting till ten o'clock. It's easier to do such work when the sun has fully risen."

The Inspector said, "But of course, Professor," before turning to Sir William and saying, "You and your son are free to go now, sir. Ah, forgive me, Professor. I should have introduced you before. This is Sir William's son, Mr Benjamin Broderig. He also knew Lady Bessingham."

Another stepped forward and shook Hatton's hand. The young man's face was weathered and bronzed by the sun, Hatton noticed, as he said, in earnest, "I believe you can help us find Lady Bessingham's killer, Professor. I've heard a great deal about your work. I'm a scientist myself and I'm honoured to make your acquaintance, but please forgive me, I must take my father home. But if I may, I will come by the mortuary room later. It would please my father knowing that one of us is with her. To the very end, if that's how I can put it."

Hatton was relieved for this support. "Of course, sir. Ask for me directly or for my Chief Diener, Monsieur Albert Roumande. I would be more than happy for you to observe. But, as I said to the Inspector, I shan't start till ten, and so perhaps, till then, you can get a little sleep?" Without another word, the younger man patted, then took his father's arm.

"Thank goodness they've gone," quipped Adams. "I can do without the relatives breathing down my neck. But Sir William's right about the press. They'll be all over this one." Inspector Adams looked at Hatton for a second, then brought out his tin of tobacco. Hatton, despite himself, said nothing.

"I prefer a cane tip. Wool gets in the teeth. Anyway, it's going to be hard to operate in this jumble, eh, Professor?" The penny smoke was lit. "It will be easier once we've moved her, but do what you can. Do whatever you like, in fact."

The Inspector smiled at Hatton as he billowed out a haze of smoke, then waved it clear again. Hatton, meanwhile, got on with his work, examining the room, a muddle of woven baskets and copper pots, fossils, lumps of crystal, and by the bay window, three little upright music chairs, covered in brocade dresses. And on a table by her bed, a gorgeous display of conches. Hatton would have loved to put one to his ear and listen to the waves. He admired the largest, *Strombus gigas*. It was pink and wet with shine.

"A regular magpie, wasn't she? No husband any more to rein her in, but plenty of money and time on her hands, I dare say, to indulge in all flights of fancy. Perhaps a flight of fancy is what got her killed, Professor?" Adams showed less deference than Hatton, picking up the shell and holding it to his ear. For a moment he seemed lost in thought. "Marvellous things. Now then, let's see what we can tell you. No sign of a struggle. No forced entry. Just the hall window slightly open to tell us someone was here that oughtn't to be. We haven't done a thorough search yet, but on the face of it and according to the servants" — he looked at his notes — "everything, more or less, as before. Apart from one thing. A missing maid. Name of Flora James, who's been in service here for three years and by all accounts was the mistress's favourite. Pretty thing, I'm told. Fair-haired. Quite ladylike in her manners, of medium height, well turned out, nineteen or thereabouts. The description is a rough one but we're putting a

18

likeness together based on what we can gather. We'll track her down, but it's odd because there's nothing of value missing, and if the little madam was a thief, well, the jewellery would be gone. Apparently, she had been sent ahead of the other staff, the day before Lady Bessingham's murder. The rest were at the country residence, at a place called Ashbourne. Flora was on an urgent errand it seems. Are you listening to me, Professor?"

But Hatton was distracted by a tiny bird, which was scratching forlornly in the bottom of its cage. How he loathed the practice of keeping birds imprisoned like this. He had a mind to let the poor thing go, but thought better than displaying such unmanly sensibility in front of Inspector Adams. The detective might misjudge him.

He looked around the room again to find something — anything — which could illuminate this crime, but there was nothing unusual. And then as his eye fell on the surface of the higly polished writing desk, it came to him, the tiniest thing, but significant.

"Are there any academic papers anywhere, Inspector? Any correspondence in the study, perhaps? Parcels waiting for despatch or post not opened?" Hatton paused waiting for a response.

"And your point, Professor? We've seen all her main correspondence, but they're innocent affairs. Mainly orders for books, bills from dressmakers, and other such daily dealings with domestic matters. There are several bundles of letters to museums and other scientific institutions, as it appears Lady Bessingham was rather doting on crusty academics. She provided some money, I understand, to several beneficiaries. I shall be investigating this further to establish any links to her death, but in my experience, Professor, the crime is often an obvious one. I suspect a lover or a thief."

There was something in his approach, so defiantly de facto, that jarred Hatton, but nevertheless, he said again, "Yes, but has anyone checked to see if there were other, perhaps unfinished letters?" His eyes travelled, scrutinising this romantic testament to art and nature. A cacophony of silks, exotica, exuberant pictures of dark bodies jostling and dancing in the clearings of far-flung places captured in oil, and iridescent beetles in graded succession imprisoned in glass. Books deftly creased, to mark a point or a query.

"Look about the room, Inspector. What do you see?"

"I see a mess, Professor."

"Well, I see something else. Something I have seen before but not in a house, rather in a University. This woman was at work in her boudoir, Inspector. At work on some intellectual pursuit, and if that's the case, then why is her desk entirely clear of papers? Where are the thoughts, the observations?" Hatton paused to make sure the Inspector was following. "There's no trace of her thinking here, at all, and you say she was a benefactor to the arts and sciences? Well, there would have been some sign of this, surely? Some scribbled notes, perhaps? Or letters pertaining to this work? So where are the letters? Her room is a jumble but it's also like a ghost. She was no recluse, surely?"

Adams flicked a little tobacco to the floor. "Do you know, I think you're right. I'm glad to have you on board, Professor. Lady Bessingham's soirees had become a regular fixture in the Society pages. Sir William told me that the great and the good dined here at least once a month. Mainly Men of Science or Philosophy. I think it's fair to suggest she courted conjecture, which in my view is but a stone's throw from controversy. Perhaps she also courted trouble."

Hatton excused himself, and as he stepped out of the boudoir, he caught a glimpse of another room at the end of the hallway, where a low lamp was throwing off a shadow. He heard childish sobbing and a voice, an old ducky one, saying, "There now, Violet, my luvvie. There now my lamb." A servant? A maid, perhaps?

CHAPTER
TWO

WESTMINSTER

The bells of Westminster rang out nine times, a sonorous chime across London, as a cold beam of light fell on the Duke of Monreith. He cleared his throat, glared at the opposition, and, addressing The House, said, "Yet again, dissenters lay down their doctrine of universal suffrage, but I deny that every man has the right to vote. What every man has the right to is to be governed by those who will ensure the status quo. They who propose change will lead us into barbarism, Frenchyism, anarchy. My Lord Speaker, we, its leaders, have been ordained the responsibility to ensure everything must remain true to God, Church, and Monarchy and that England remains, forever, immutable."

Men jumped to their feet, waving their papers in thunderous approval as the Duke looked around triumphant. But others, towards the back, were slipping out, their words drowned out. Their "Shame, shame on you" a dull echo but, yet unknown to them, a shadow of the future.

The Duke, however, was nowhere near finished on matters of parliament. There was a long day ahead with a night sitting in The Lords, and so he swept up the central stairs, past a labyrinth of corridors, then through an arched door to where an old man was sitting hunched over a pile of papers.

"Good God, a little speed if you will. Haven't you finished the speech yet for tonight, Ashby? Another hour at the most or I'll set the dogs on you."

The Duke settled his rump on a leather chair by the fire, a glass of malt in his hand, whilst the recipient of this usual abuse let the wave of animosity wash over him. Because thirty years of scratching, scribbling, hurrying, and carrying had taught Arnold Ashby that duty was an onerous thing, but that order must prevail. The clerk finished scribing the last of his master's words, then pushed his glasses back onto the bridge of a bony nose; forever sliding down again, these accursed glasses, but without them, where would he be? His eyesight, he'd noticed, as did Mrs Ashby, had started to fail him, even with the help of spectacles. Lord knows, there was no money left to buy a new pair, so he must make do.

Thinking on money, Arnold Ashby sighed. He had so little left to pawn these days, or offer those greasy fingers, the latest in a long line of lenders who had counted out the money, muttering barely above a whisper, "You still owes me for the last lot I gives you. Interest is mounting, but it's a pretty ring. A little thing, but little things are often precious. Shame, ain't it? But a man must eat."

"Just the money, sir." Though it bothered Ashby to call the lender that, for he wasn't worth the title of a gentleman. But there was no choice because Madame Martineau had whispered that everything was at stake.

The Duke's reputation and with it all that Ashby was, all that he believed in, the very air around him, the roof over his head. Madame Martineau had been very clear about the latter. "Do as I say and bring me the money, or it will be more than just his head that'll roll. It'll be the workhouse for you, old man." So, Ashby had no choice. He had to protect his master as well as himself, so the money was needed and the ring had to go.

Rising up from his workbench, Ashby enquired about the diagrams which should accompany tonight's speech. "Lord knows but I need maps, you cloth head, clearly depicting the various trade routes."

Ashby bowed dutifully to the Duke, his bows shallower with each passing year, arthritis interfering with deference. Somewhere in the vast rooms a clock ticked. The crackling timber in the hearth burned.

The Duke of Monreith put his whisky down and stretched out a liver-spotted hand for his coat, and as he did so said, "I'll be back from my club after lunch, and then we'll head to the docks. I have business matters to attend to which are in need of a clerk." He continued talking, as if to an infant.

"The East is troublesome. A whole consignment of spice has failed to reach us, again. And the reasons given? Trouble with the natives, of course. Well, my speech tonight will make reference to this, and all that's required for the sound running of the Empire, because, mark me, Ashby, this is no time for treachery, for uprisings, for even a sniff of sedition."

Ashby bowed this time lower than before, to signify his absolute understanding. He had, only a few hours

24

earlier, sat with his quill, scratching out the words which appeared in all of the Duke's parliamentary work. Delivered in bombastic tones, as the Duke stood, pipe lit, smoking jacket on, spouting his usual, "Country, nation, class. Church, party, monarchy . . . are you listening, Ashby? Are you getting all of this down?"

Yes, of course he had. His vowels, spider's legs; his consonants worse, and the black ink a permanent stain on his fingertips, as Ashby drafted, corrected, copied, but rarely embellished, taking some comfort in the endless repetition, with the promise that everything that was would always be, now and forever, the same.

"And Ashby," the Duke barked at his obedient dog. "Don't forget that Joseph Hooker has another paper out, circulating amongst those sacrilegious Athenaeum members. He talks about flowers and the distribution of seeds, but I know where it's leading. He's an atheist. All those botanicals are. Secure a copy, Ashby."

The old man scratched his head. "Secure a copy, Ashby." A command which meant having to trudge along icy streets, his head down, the wind up, to be met by the porter of the Linnean Society with a glare and, "Your master ain't a member, is he? What's he want with it, anyway? Ah, well, since you've come all this way. 'The Distribution of Arctic Flowers' by J. Hooker. Is that the one?"

Ashby looked out of the mullion window across the frozen river, where the late morning light was half drawn — an angel breath of citrus, a rush of lilac. A thick fog was rising and out across the city, an eagle's view warranted him a vista of winter-clad people, horses and carriages. He shuddered as he watched skeletal elms bend and twist against the ferocious weather. The snow couldn't lie and cover it up, he thought, as Ashby watched a mud lark, a mere child, chipping the icy Thames for bones, pennies, fish heads, bits of this and that.

Ashby crossed the floor to an oversized drawer and stopping at "B" he took out, then unrolled, a map. Smoothing it, he ran his finger across a coast rendered gold, a mighty river, ultramarine, wide at first, then breaking out into a cobweb of azure tributaries. And as he did, revelled in the faraway lines imagining the waves, the sand, and the busting fecundity. There was a time once when he would have fancied himself as a mapmaker who travelled on a brig, the captain's personal cartographer, charting the lines and dips of South America. An artist of form and definition, of exact measurements and tidy summations.

But he'd better get on with the work, he supposed, and so rolled up the map and, picking up the papers, scurried along till he found himself in The House, where Ashby looked up at a sky-high monster of panelled wood and iridescent glass.

The sweet, pungent scent of beeswax and linseed oil filled the old man's nostrils, because even in the depths of winter, the workings of government ground on. The great heart of politics kept pulsating by a thousand clerks like Ashby. The lucky ones pouring in from the suburbs, and like many men, Ashby dreamt of a time when he, too, might get away from the city before it consumed him. More fantasy again, which this time had a garden, a privet hedge, and an abundance of sweet-smelling flowers. He put his hand to the place where he kept a cameo hidden from view, on a cheap silver chain, because his mother had loved flowers, too. And told himself, that a clerk on fifty pounds a year was not nothing. That it was something to relish, and tell his children and grandchildren one day.

"I met the Prime Minister. And the Queen. Stood as close to me as you are now."

"And what did they say to you, Father?" would come the reply.

"Well, naturally, was I well and content? And I answered that I was and settled in my station."

Ashby did what he had to do in The House, then made his way back again along the winding corridors to the Duke's vast rooms, which were lined with generations of oils. Their eyes seemed to follow him, but he shrugged the feeling off, ignoring the portraits, and got back to shuffling this pile here and that pile there. To his right were logbooks pertaining to trade. To his left, hidden under a pile of papers, was Madame Martineau's money.

According to his pocket watch, it was just past three o'clock when the barouche came to fetch him. Ashby had waited in the porchway reserved for servants, glad to be out of the cold. The walk to the Linnean Society had been a wasted one. "The arctic flowers paper ain't ready. Come back in a month. Mr Hooker still has facts to verify."

Ashby knew better than to offer up failure, and so quickly got into the carriage and said nothing. The Duke belched onion breath, and kicked Ashby sharply on the ankle, saying, "Pay attention and have a look at these figures, old man. By my own reading, I believe our exports of Machars whisky needs beefing up. Our jute consignments, as well."

The barouche hurtled along until they reached the Isle of Dogs, where they got out of the carriage and fell into a great hubbub of screaming and shouting. All around Ashby was a wall of sound and a swell of multicoloured people, to which the Duke of Monreith paid no notice, using a cane to part the wave, Moses-like. Ashby followed and at last the two men reached the warehouse door of the Machars Trading Company.

Ashby looked up at the mighty stag, the company's emblem, cast in weather-beaten iron, bellowing at nothing. Inside the building, Monreith's arrival was like that of a king. More men, who looked exactly like Ashby, ran forward to greet the Duke. Monreith marched forward as if into battle, deaf to the chatter all about him, through the vast warehouse, where all the wares bore the proud announcement "Made in Great Britain by the Machars Trading Company", including a nod to the Duke's Scottish heritage — bottles and bottles of single malt.

"Business is booming, sir. We can hardly keep pace," said one worn-out-looking clerk.

"Give the ledger to Mr Ashby." Monreith was direct and to the point. The Duke paid an active interest in the profit line, but the rest ran itself, to way back when Monreith traded in other things, no longer permitted. But Monreith had said his piece on that. He had talked till The House had groaned from his endless rationales about the benefits of the slave trade, till it had yawned wide open at his arguments. That battle was long since lost. But there were other fights he could take on.

"Did you get the Hooker paper, Ashby?"

Ashby paled, studying the ledger. Monreith took out his snuffbox, unperturbed, just pleased to listen to himself. "I am sick of those collectors and their so-called theorising, with their reckless ideas about how the world was made. Starting with that rag, *Vestiges*. So ashamed was the author, such a coward, that he wouldn't even put his name to it. Calling into question as it did the very existence of God. And I hear the sound of the botanical's geological hammers knocking in my head, knowing it is the death knell of everything we know. And let me tell you that it's getting worse. There are more of these botanicals every day, it seems." The Duke took a snort of his snuff. "Even women, dammit. But I'll soon put a stop to it." The Duke sneezed and put his snuffbox back in his pocket.

Ashby handed the ledger back. "Everything is in order, sir. You are on track to make an excellent profit, and it's the whisky, I believe, that's making the difference. It seems to be very popular, especially with our eastern customers. May I be so bold as to suggest you could perhaps refer to this in your speech, tonight?"

"If you say so, Ashby." Monreith was distracted because the clock on the wall told him it was getting late and he had another place to go.

"Come along. It's gone five. My barouche will drop you at The Strand. I'm going to a bookshop on Millford Lane and then perhaps to Clunns for an early supper, but I'll be back in good time for my speech. Hopefully, if all goes well, which it should at The Lords, we'll be finished by midnight. In fact, I'm rather looking forward to it. There will be no opposition and no radicals there to contend with. It'll be home from home."

The barouche took off and Ashby was dropped at the far end towards The Aldwych. Ashby braced himself against the chilly air as he stood in a flurry of snow and watched the Duke's barouche heading down Millford Lane. He lowered his head and walked on.

CHAPTER
THREE

SMITHFIELD

Earlier that day, in the eastern part of the city, Hatton had started his morning with no coffee and no respite. Two constables and some ad hoc mortuary assistants loitered in the putrid stink of the embalming fluid. The ripe mixture of various preservatives barely disguised the faecal matter and vomit which was the backdrop to Professor Hatton's work. Stomaching the stench was the first hurdle to conquer for any young physician considering a career in the area of medical jurisprudence. That and its paltry pay.

Hatton looked at his filigree pocket watch to check that it was indeed ten o'clock and time to start the cutting. Despite the morning hour, the morgue was still gloomy. Lamps had been lit and flickered around the walls, still splattered with the yellowing body fluids from yesterday's post-mortem. A young girl, barely twelve, who had been stitched back together with due attention by Monsieur Roumande.

"Bludgeoned to death, then dumped in an alley off Joiners Street." Roumande spoke to the young man, who stood next to him and asked for her name. The man stepped away distraught, but Roumande continued. "There have been at least two others like this, with the same marks. But like the others, none have claimed her, and so she ends up here. Naked, wrapped in a cloth, and labelled as 'pork'. Sorry to be so brutal, sir, but since you asked."

"Let me introduce you to my right-hand man, Mr Broderig," Hatton was quick to intervene, with a flourish of his hand. "My Chief Diener, Monsieur Albert Roumande." Roumande bowed as Hatton continued, lowering his voice a little, "I don't think Mr Broderig needs any more detail on a nameless cadaver. He's just lost a loved one and has volunteered to attend this morning's autopsy. So go easy on him, Albert. This is his first cutting." But the young man said he was perfectly well, and to please continue.

Roumande shrugged. "Well, all I can tell you is her skull was smashed, her throat slashed. See here." He pointed with the tip of his scalpel. "The lower part of her body, from her abdomen down, bludgeoned to a pulp. Her arms were bruised and cut, as you can see on inspecting her wrists." Roumande brushed the spindly arms lightly with his fingertips. "Strange pricks, as if by a bodkin."

"She was abused, then?" asked Benjamin Broderig.

"Abused and murdered, though for some reason Scotland Yard seems happy to part with this one, without even a delivery note." Roumande looked over at Hatton. "Perhaps I'll ask Inspector Adams when he gets here, because it seems out of sorts. It is Inspector Adams, isn't it? Inspector Adams of Scotland Yard?"

"The very same, Albert." Hatton smiled at Roumande, because they were friends. "We'll start very

32

shortly, Mr Broderig, but remember, if at any point you cannot bear it, we will have an assistant take you out. There's nothing to be ashamed of."

"I haven't offered my presence here lightly," Broderig said, his eyes gold in the light of the mortuary's lamps. "But I'm used to cutting. I'm a specimen collector, although my dissection is of a different nature. For scientific research, cataloguing and so forth." Hatton looked up from polishing his knife, thinking it was good to have another Man of Science in their midst. But this thought was cut short by a rapping at the door.

"Good morning, gentlemen. The bulldogs said I had to come round the back. Not the response I would normally expect for a man in my position, but apparently your Hospital Director insists upon it." Inspector Adams hurriedly took off his coat and continued, "So, tell me, where the devil are we, exactly? Is this the basement? Or a store cupboard?"

The Inspector laughed, but Hatton frowned, feeling the insult, because the cutting room had long been designated the stealthiest position at St Bart's, far removed from the rest of the hospital. His life's work still held by many with a mixture of disgust and loathing. Pathologists like Hatton remaining hidden, often left to struggle alone or, in his case, helped by a diener, as Albert Roumande insisted he still be called, although Roumande was far from being a mere servant of the morgue.

It irked Professor Hatton that he should be shut off in this way, and he didn't feel better by having it pointed out. Especially when his hours were long and his income little, but today was an opportunity to impress. To prove himself. And Hatton had noticed, recently, that requests to attend his autopsies were increasing. This was the fifth cutting this month which had involved a small audience. Did he dare hope that interest was growing? Hatton narrowed his eyes and reached for his knife; there was never any question that this was simply his calling. His affinity with the exact science of forensics was something which had surprised him once, but now his life would be wholly meaningless without it.

"Do we have a jug of porter available, Professor? Or some salts?" Inspector Adams didn't wait for an answer, catching sight of the Chief Diener. "Ah! You must be Monsieur Roumande. I've heard of you, sir. Every mortuary room I have ever had the misfortune to grace speaks of you, if I may say, in a hushed tone of admiration. And of course," the Inspector smiled broadly, "you're a man of many letters."

Monsieur Roumande gave a curt bow. "I've heard of you, too, Inspector Adams. And yes, I'm in regular correspondence with The Yard about various concerns of mine. Vice, crime, felons, and the murder of prostitutes. Perhaps it's because I'm from Spitalfields and feel an affinity for such things. We are one up from the rookeries at Fleur de Lys, but if my wife heard me say that, she would murder me herself. Your reputation goes before you, Inspector." The two shook each other's hands.

Hatton called Roumande over to wipe down the dissecting table, and then with the help of others, lifted the cadaver onto the slab.

"Monsieur Roumande, if you please."

Albert Roumande was a head taller than Hatton. More bear-like in stature than the Professor's medium frame, and with the gruff voice of a man who liked to make his presence felt. And to Hatton, he was more than a friend. Roumande was an able, exacting, acutely intelligent observer without whom no post-mortem would be entirely accurate. Despite Hatton's elevated position, the younger man, at thirty-three, still felt firmly under Roumande's tutelage, because they had worked little more than a year together, and Hatton was not so arrogant to assume anything.

The dissection table played centre stage, the cadaver now its focus. Roumande lifted the shroud. The gathering stepped forward to see thick, chestnut hair coiled around delicate shoulders. Her hands were long, her fingers tapering. Hatton noted Lady Bessingham's status — a ring of gold on the wedding finger. But turning her hand over like an attentive suitor, a more intriguing detail. A briar ran up the middle of her ring finger, at the bottom of which was a tiny star and at the top, a rose-like flower. So delicate, the adornment would have easily been hidden by a pair of gloves and only noticed, Hatton was sure, by those whose eyes were as observant as his own. This smallest and most delicate of tattoos confirming what they already knew. That this lady was, or had been, independently minded.

Hatton lifted the hair to make his first incision. Blood. Thick, black and coagulated but he wanted her on her front, because it was clear where he needed to look. Roumande tipped the body sideways, revealing a fist-sized hole, a mangle of tissue and bone. On first impression, what looked like tiny chips of stone were embedded in the skull, and as Hatton began to pick his way through her sodden locks, he could clearly see sharp fragments framing the gaping wound. Bigger lumps lurked within.

"An extremely heavy blow to the back of the head resulting in direct trauma to the brain."

Hours had passed since they had moved Lady Bessingham from Chelsea, and the blue marbling of livor mortis had spread across her body like a map. Hatton lifted her hand once more. It was as he thought. "Take a skin sample from the index finger please, Roumande. There's ink here." She had been writing. He said as much and a nod came from Inspector Adams as another note was written down.

"We'll have to shave these locks, Professor, at least at the back where the wound lies," answered Roumande, already busy cutting great tangles of chestnut locks away from her skull. The cutting finished, Hatton took each tiny shard from the wound and Roumande transferred them to a tray. "The fragments appear to be from a brownish-grey stone. She was either hit with a large rock, thus," Hatton brought his hand down, fist clenched white to the back of Roumande's head, stopping before any possible impact, "or with another instrument and then she hit the ground. But the floor in her bedroom was oak and the hearth Italian marble." There were secrets to unlock here, Hatton was sure of it.

"Gentlemen, I should warn you." Hatton looked at the young man who had stayed deathly quiet throughout. "A full removal of the back of her head will be necessary for me to see the full extent of her injuries, but it's safe to say she died from cerebral contusion."

Heads were normally removed using only a knife, chisel, and handheld saw, requiring two men to do the work, and the hacking of heads from torsos was time consuming. But Roumande had recently managed to obtain an oscillating saw from a fellow diener working in Germany. It had taken Roumande a month of letters to secure the funding.

Roumande bent over it, almost lovingly, and started the rotation. He'd spent hours already, oiling the wheels and checking the rivets. The saw shuddered and whirred, the instrument astounding the two men with its accuracy and speed. The noise was deafening as Hatton locked eyes with Roumande, and for a moment, he saw the flicker of shared excitement. Their work was entering a new age. Their time of hiding away drawing to an end. Bone chips went flying and the two men working like dervishes. Together, they moved around the head with proficiency, peeling back the fat encasing the skull, cutting through veins, hacking further and deeper.

"I have it," Hatton muttered, as he wrenched the object from its burial place. Covered in a mess of blood and tissue, Roumande held it up towards the gas lamp anchored over the end of the dissecting table.

"What the devil is that?" Adams's eastern drawl.

Roumande held the object nearer to the light. Jagged edged, roughly hewn, and dripping with blood, there was no question of the murder weapon. Hatton recognised it instantly. He had a collection back in Gower Street along with his shells and feathers. An ammonite. Perfectly formed, a magnificent specimen, and as a crushing instrument of death, fatal.

"Well?" asked the Inspector again.

Hatton spoke, delivering only the facts. "Subclass *ammonoidea*. It's a fossil, Inspector, from an animal which, like the dinosaurs, many believe became extinct millions of years ago. There are a number of equally impressive specimens at the British Museum. Lady Bessingham would have paid a considerable amount of money for this."

"It's clearly the murder weapon. Using your forensics, do you think you can get traces of anything useful off it?" Adams's questioning was quick and to the point. Hatton shook his head.

"I don't know, Inspector. We're not so advanced. We will do whatever tests we have, but looking at her body, I can see there are no bruises to her wrists or hands, no scratches to her face. The assailant came from behind or she knew him or her well, suggesting the maid. There's also a slightly odd odour about her skin. This we can test. She had either been drugged or she used an opiate. And of her more intimate details? There are no bruises to her inner thighs. We have removed her stockings and her undergarments and already examined them carefully. None of them were ripped to suggest rape or anything of a sexual nature." Hatton turned to a nearby neat pile of French lace and the finest of English corsetry to underline his point. "Soiled only with light splashes of her own blood. The worst of the blood was absorbed by the thick rug on the bedroom floor. But I'll need to finish the autopsy to know any more."

As Hatton talked, Roumande had dried his hands and was now sitting at a trestle table making notes. Roumande wrote quickly and fluently, embellishing facts with his own comments. He sometimes observed what Hatton's eyes missed, so intently was the Professor delving into the crevices and cavities.

"So, Inspector, she was definitely murdered. But the ammonite is a strange choice, don't you think? There was a poker in the grate, and also on her desk I noticed a huge glass ball, used as a paperweight."

Adams was pensive. "It may have been the nearest thing to hand, if the murderer was disturbed. It's blunt, heavy, and would have been easy for a woman to grab. But it would have required some strength to crush a skull like that. And Lady Bessingham didn't cry out. Perhaps she knew her attacker, as you say? All grist for the mill, Professor. But can I light up now, or would you prefer I went outside? I think Mr Broderig could do with a puff."

Broderig smiled weakly at the Inspector. Hatton nodded that they could go ahead, knowing more tests would be required, and at this, his heart began to pound. Not because ideas immediately formed. But because they might. Was this the chance to prove without doubt the power of forensics?

Because for too long now, life in the pathology department had been a struggle. But he saw the opportunity for improvement all about him. Not for nothing had he spent years away from friends and family. Edinburgh first, to train in the rudiments of medicine. Three years as a physician, with his father's blessing, but then his bolder switch to surgeon, which did not rest so well.

"Butchers! That's what your mother would say if she were still alive. One up from a meat shop."

"For pity's sake, Father."

"And why Scotland, for heaven's sake? We are not averse to self-improvement, but a surgeon, Adolphus? There are better opportunities in medicine. Lucy's Jeremiah, for example . . ."

Hatton had shaken his head as they'd walked the lanes in Hampshire. Yes, he knew his sister was engaged to what his family thought to be a proper doctor, but his mind was made up. The intricacies of muscle, organs, sinews which made up the molecular puzzle of Man was all he was intent on. Forensics, a word barely understood outside the mortuary room, would come later.

Roumande walked briskly to a large enamel sink at the back of the mortuary room, where he picked up the bar of carbolic and lathered his hands, the acidic stink rising up into the air. Taking a nail brush, he carefully scrubbed away any traces of the victim's flesh from his fingers. He'd hung a shaving mirror, at the request of Professor Hatton, and peered at himself.

Unlike Hatton, not so young any more, and he was tired. But he knew this was where he belonged. This was where he was most himself, if he could dare think such a thing. Madame Roumande would have laughed at such thoughts, and as he looked at the little cadaver now, just a calico form, he felt chastened, thinking of his own five children. And though he had jested about it, his lodging rooms were a long way from the rookeries. Not geographically speaking, granted, but in every other way. His house was cosy and paid for on time, once a month, every month, and had been for years. His oldest boy was twelve. His eldest daughter, barely ten. He shook his head in disgust and reminded himself to ask Adams why the child had come here yesterday with not even a question. And she was not the first they'd seen like this. Unlike this Lady Bessingham, whose death would be more than noted. She would be investigated, contemplated, eulogised even.

"Are you coming out into the yard, Albert?"

"Like you, Professor, I'm not a great partaker of tobacco, but I could do with some air. By the way, I'm interested to know what you make of our Inspector."

Hatton smiled, indulging his friend. "I think he'll do well enough, and more importantly, we'll earn some badly needed guineas for our coffers. Who knows? An annual income of five hundred a year? Perhaps, even a Scotland Yard retainer?"

"So, you think a permanent contract with The Yard is possible, then?" Roumande turned the collar up on his coat. "It would certainly help. Our supplies are as low as ever. But do you know, Professor, his face is familiar to me. I'm sure he used to work in Spitalfields, though perhaps it's just his likeness I remember from the crime pages. Do you sometimes get that sensation, Adolphus? Of thinking you have met someone before, but cannot place them?"

"Every time I look in the mirror, Albert. But come, you'll scrub your face away. Did you hear Mr Broderig say he's a collector? Can you imagine? He must have seen some incredible things. He must have travelled far and wide."

"Indeed," said Roumande, "I wasn't aware it was a profession, but thought it more of a hobby. But then, unlike you, Adolphus, I'm not an educated man. I know little of that science."

Outside the air hummed and the yard gate moaned. The four men gathered in a round, stamped their feet, and kept their heads down, shielded by their hats from icy blasts.

"Aaah, Professor," Adams spoke first. "If you don't want baccy, have a nip of this. Mister Broderig brought it."

Broderig, still pale from the autopsy, said, "Go ahead, Professor. In Dayak, it's called *tuak*. Rice wine."

Hatton was intrigued and took a gulp from the hip flask thrust towards him. "It's the right stuff in this weather. Thank you, Mr Broderig." Broderig nodded and beckoned Roumande to take some.

"I hear you're a specimen collector, Mr Broderig," said Roumande. "I was saying to the Professor that I didn't know it was an actual profession."

"It's my chosen vocation. I've recently returned from Borneo, less than a month ago. Lady Bessingham was one of my principal patrons." Broderig knocked back a slug. "We wrote to each other when I was on my travels. Our correspondence should be somewhere in the house. Perhaps you have seen these particular letters, Inspector? They are very personal to me, and they were distinctive, written on parchment from the depths of a tropical forest."

The Inspector shook his head at this. "No, Mr Broderig. We found nothing along those lines. Parchment, you say?"

Broderig, his face clouding with thought, repeated, a little more agitated, "As I said, they are private and all that I have left of her. I will want them back again, as soon as possible. Are you sure you have looked everywhere?" He bit his bottom lip, clearly worried as to their whereabouts. "Searched every nook and cranny of the house?"

"You'll get them back if we find them, Mr Broderig. But speaking of correspondence, do you know if she wrote to any other scientists? I understand she courted controversy when it came to ideas. Do you know a little more of what your father referred to last night?"

But Broderig had turned away and was looking back towards the morgue, lost for a moment before shaking his head and saying, "I really do want those letters back, Inspector. She would have wanted me to have them. My poor Katherine . . ." He pushed his hand towards his mouth, his lip trembling, his voice lowered. "I have dissected many things. I have seen death, but what we have just witnessed . . ."

"We can talk later, Mr Broderig. If this pains you."

He shook his head. "No, Inspector, I'm here for this. But please . . ." He gathered himself and turned back to face them. "You asked me, did Lady Bessingham court controversy? There was one piece of work, but I was abroad at the time. It involved a Dr Ignatius Finch and the topic was the Nature of Man. His conclusions upset her, but controversy is a debatable thing, because it really depends which side of the fence you sit on."

"You mean Science or Religion, Mr Broderig?" Hatton was beginning to think he understood this man.

"Exactly, Professor. He's based in Cambridge now. I've never been to any of his lectures, although rumour has it, like me, he's an avid collector of butterflies. I had a mind to show him one or two of my specimens, but I'm in no mood for it now. I don't have the heart."

"Please, Mr Broderig, come out of the wind, sir." Adams steered him towards a small outhouse used for stacking tools. Hatton and Roumande followed and the four men huddled even closer.

"I'm uncomfortable offering an opinion on a man I barely know, but Katherine often had soirees when she

44

was in London, scientific gatherings, and I understand he attended one or two."

The Inspector lit a cigarette. Hatton, intrigued by this talk of science, urged him, "Please, Mr Broderig. Tell us all you know."

"Very well, Professor, but it's little. Dr Finch, I believe, is working on a radical theory of transmutation. The idea being that we are all animal. That we share the same instincts, good and bad. His theorising is, of course, an extension of other people's work, but apparently going a great deal further than many would dare. Lady Bessingham wrote to me in Borneo and made mention of his thinking, which I understand saw him drummed out of University College. Katherine was rarely shocked but she seemed greatly upset. I suggested that if she was unenamoured with his thinking, she should simply cut him off. After all, it's the patron's prerogative."

Hatton nodded, feeling his face redden, because the same had occurred to his work in forensics, many times.

The Inspector randomly lit a Swan. "Well then, perhaps we should see this Dr Finch, if he's as controversial as you say he is. And to Cambridge, of all places. My old stomping ground, but we cannot just go hurtling into a college, unannounced. Perhaps, Mr Broderig, you would be prepared to take us there and make a formal introduction? As Lady Bessingham's friend?"

The young man nodded. "I studied at Trinity and I would be happy to help."

The Inspector sucked up the last dregs of his tobacco. "I'd better get back to The Yard. The Commissioner's already on my back about this missing maid, and there's work to do if we're going to keep this out of the press." He turned to Hatton. "Report on my desk tomorrow, Professor. I have more than my superiors to answer to on a case like this." Adams pulled his coat around himself a little tighter against the bitter chill. "And perhaps you would like to join us on a short trip to Cambridge, if Mr Broderig can arrange it? It would be a good opportunity for us to get to know each other a little better."

And heaving the whining gate open, Adams and Broderig headed off down the road, soon disappearing into a flurry of white.

Hatton turned to Roumande, peering under his frosty brim. "That gate needs oiling, Albert. Perhaps another one of your begging letters wouldn't go amiss? We could do with a new one, frankly. It's embarrassing, and hardly demonstrates us at the helm of our profession. Well, never mind. It's almost noon and we've a heap of work to do, but we've been offered an opportunity here. I really think so."

The day in the cutting room was finally over and Professor Hatton's walk was against the wind. Up ahead, the lights at Number 14 Gower Street were welcoming as Hatton looked at his pocket watch again. The filigree face of his gold Swiss timer said it was just gone ten and that Mrs Gallant would still be up waiting for him, although her other tenants would be out in restaurants, gentlemen's clubs, or already asleep. Hatton sometimes wished for a life that was more conventional than the one pathology afforded. Or so he told himself on these long walks back from the morgue. He could have taken a carriage, but walking allowed time for contemplation and reminded him that there was indeed a world outside St Bart's, where people lived. Where they argued, laughed, raised families, had passions. He saw the results, but did he really live that life himself? Not yet, he thought. But maybe one day, soon.

He turned the key in the lock to be met by the usual greeting of Mrs Gallant's King Charles spaniel baring its teeth and snarling at him.

"He likes you. He really does, Professor. Shall I take your coat, sir? I've got some soup ready. Stop it, Archie. Really, the dog is very bad. Aren't you, Archie, dear?"

Hatton's smile was weak and he often gave the dog a sharp kick, but not in full view of the owner, who this evening was wearing a full-skirted brocade of orange tartan. She'd worn it specially, because Mrs Gallant loved Professor Hatton only second to her dog, and often wondered to herself that if she was ten years younger, or perhaps twenty, and a dress size smaller, or perhaps several, he might one day sweep her up into his arms and declare, "Mrs Gallant, it's more than your economical soup I'm after." But luckily for Hatton, no such thought had ever occurred to him. He was oblivious to her head tilts, her dips, her special favours, and the jealous stares of the older tenants at the lodging house, who he thought were very welcome to her.

"No soup, Mrs Gallant. Not tonight. I ate at the morgue."

Professor Hatton went upstairs and closed the door behind him. Somewhere along the corridor a piano could be heard. Keys played, off scale.

His bachelor rooms were comfortable enough. One room adjoining another, the latter room benefiting from a huge sash window, a desk, an easy chair, but very little else save his medical journals.

He ran his finger along a shelf until he found the thing he was looking for, which was a small wooden box. No *Strombus gigas* or anything so impressive, but to Hatton this box had no need for grand dimensions to be of value. It simply was so.

He opened it to reveal a shell, too delicate for words. Too delicate for touch. Nestled in cloth, an angel coloured nautilus which, with barely a thumb press, would shatter into a thousand pieces. A crystalline wafer, gone. Dead, like the creature who had once lived there, and beneath the shell, a small piece of paper. Not a love letter, but a list of facts, written in the bold hand of a child. Not much older than the girl today in the mortuary he'd been, when on a glorious day one summer, he'd found the shell washed up on Wittering Beach. Professor Hatton smiled to himself at the memory, but at the same time was troubled. To smash a woman's skull? To hear it shatter? And for what? Hatton knew the dangers of being a freethinker. Lady Bessingham had been writing before she died; forensics had proven it. And Mr Broderig had grown so agitated when he spoke of their correspondence. He'd been pale

48

from the autopsy, of course, but it was more than that. Broderig seemed worried, a little desperate even. So, thought Hatton, putting the nautilus back in the box, where were the letters now?

Sarawak

June 4th, 1855

Dear Lady Bessingham,

The mail boat arrives this afternoon and so I decided to sit down once more and put pen to paper. Suffice to say, you would not recognise me, dear lady. I am already liberally freckled and my hair is turning blond. I have grown a fine set of burnished whiskers to give the impression that I know more of this collector's trade than is entirely true. Whiskers, the longer the better it seems, have two excellent uses in this climate. Firstly, they impress upon the Dayaks that I have some age and some authority. The men are practically hairless and cannot grow a beard. Secondly, the whiskers keep the bugs and flies off my chin. Because if there is one thing I cannot get used to, it is the biting and infernal scratching which is part of my life here along the marshy banks of the Sarawak River. And I have been warned, if one does not take the right precautions, the impact on my body can be grave indeed. I have therefore followed the advice of my friend and companion Mr Emmerich Mann (who, by the way, is a very erudite German) and taken to swallowing quantities of powdered quinine, washed down with generous amounts of rice wine.

Perhaps I should describe this place to you? My house is quite basic. Built on stilts to keep the rains out, its sides are made of ironwood. The floor creaks deliciously under my bare feet as I pad about, and as this hut was once a rice store, it is embellished with some wondrous carvings. The Dayaks believe that rice has a soul and that they must worship it to keep evil spirits away, and so you see, I am protected not just by my little talisman but also by the twisted serpents which curl around the roof.

The hut sits on the edge of a forest by a river which curls towards a pearl-white beach. And what better place to immerse the intellect and soul? The river gives me endless pleasure, and I often sit here and watch bright-green butterflies settle on the ground fluttering their petrol wings in unison, like some orchestra of colour. There are ancient turtles in the river and dolphins which rise and click, as if they're laughing at my open-mouthed amazement.

But perhaps the most bizarre of my neighbours, Mr Mann aside (I jest here, madam), are the mudskippers (Periophthalmodon schlosseri). Are they fish? Or are they lizards? They have gills but live above the water, and astonishingly walk along the land. They are fish that walk. This is the truth, and it is a truth which begs a question. When God created the mudskipper, could he not make up his mind?

And I wonder if these little fellows would travel well, for I'd love to take them back to England so that we could all admire their qualities. They are four inches long, or thereabouts, and have the face of a fish. Their bodies are slimy and wet, and they have fins and tails, but spend much of their time hopping from place to place or wiggling through primordial splendour.

Nature isn't tamed here, as it is in Ashbourne. It bursts out and clamours. It creeps, weaves, and glistens.

From time to time, I wander the mile into Sarawak, a great sprawling stretch of bustling buildings and people, so different from my forest. And it's here that I get my provisions and have been able to build up quite a comprehensive collection of equipment which I will be taking on to Simunjan. I have now in my possession a sturdy camp bed, a compass, a selection of fish hooks, a barometer, ammunition, a gun, and, of course, spirits for preserving the specimens I hope to capture upriver.

Armed with your letters of introduction, I was invited to a party held at the gardens of the British Consul. The gathering was most enjoyable — delicious pastries, English tea, dainty sandwiches, ladies dressed in flounces beguiling one with idle chit-chat. Pleasant enough but more interesting, a small, rather ramshackle collection of Dutchmen caught my eye, for they were scribbling in their notebooks and chattering animatedly about something in the foliage.

I went up to them and made an introduction. Firstly, a Mr Banta most politely tipped his hat. Whilst another introduced himself as Mr Demarest and explained that his colleagues had noticed a very unusual and quite new beetle (Cyphogastra calepyga) in the undergrowth. Well, as you can imagine this was my opportunity to explain to them my purpose and, at once, much discussion then took flight on the various components of our trade.

And the very next day, they invited me to town for a game of chess, and it was while playing that I discovered that their best player, a Mr Christiaan Ackerman, is more of a businessman than the others and has strong views on the trade of collecting. He had a ledger with him but was not inclined to share its details, which I can fully understand. What he did tell me is that he works for a number of trading companies, as well as individuals, and specialises in the more unusual specimens. He quite plainly ridiculed my interest in insects and reptiles, telling me emphatically that what wealthy buyers wanted was the Beast.

Because if money was a concern, he stressed the word again, bearing down on me with his mesmerising eyes, then it was the Magnificent, the Mighty, the Stupendous, and the Monstrous that we collectors must provide.

And Mr Ackerman spoke quite vocally about his concern that with so many new Naturalists arriving, men such as himself were feeling the pressure to produce increasingly impressive finds. Therefore, the results of any expedition, he stressed, given the great costs in organising such a venture, should be significant.

And so after a week or more worth of chess playing and entomological discussions, zoological transgressions, philosophical digressions, and economic ramblings, I am sharing my journey with these Dutchmen, and it seems, aside from embarking on a collection of reptiles and beetles, shall be going on an ape hunt.

Your dutiful servant,
Benjamin Broderig, etc.

CHAPTER
FOUR

THE BOROUGH

It was past midnight when Ashby finally left Westminster, the Duke's speech on trade delivered to no one much, the audience a paltry collection of the dead and the dug up. The Lords was not The Commons, but it was still an opportunity to show off, without any of the bother of intelligent argument.

At the late-night sitting, the Duke had snatched the speech from Ashby's hands, declaring that he would not offer up anything tangential, but would stick to the point. Ashby bowed, noticing an odd scent which sometimes clung to the Duke's clothes. The Duke smelt of sweat and cigar smoke but also of something else, something which was hard to put a name to. Ashby pondered on it as he sat at the back of the chamber listening to his master's drone, slightly distracted. His eyes were dimming, and as they did so, other senses rose to the fore. His imagination, his sense of touch, his sensitivity to smell. There was a tap on his shoulder. A manservant in liveried clothes, interrupting these thoughts.

"Oi, Ashby. The Duke's in need of his snuffbox. Fingersmith's been at 'im. Says you carries a spare one."

Ashby delved into his pocket and found the silver one he carried for the Duke, which had no jewelled edges but would do perfectly well, and ensure that all went smoothly tonight and that, as ever, order prevailed.

The speech over, Ashby headed out into the ink of midnight, bent double by the snow. He trudged along, keeping his eyes to the ground, an acid light thrown from the gas lamps, spacing out farther and farther until there was but one solitary beam, positioned on a corner where alley met alley, which said Welcome to The Borough.

Checking in his pockets with fumbling fingers, the old man remembered Madame Martineau's words, which had festered in his mind for over a week now.

"Oh yes. What I have is worth a pretty penny, alright. So you get the money, Mr Ashby, if you know what's good for you. Because what's good for you is good for the Duke of Monreith."

She'd stepped out of the dark, not far from where Ashby stood now, almost as a spectre might. A chimera of silk, a vapour of perfume, as she tucked her arm around his and drew him into her, her jutting hip like a knife, her fingers like daggers, as she repeated, "And make sure the money's clean. I don't want anything grimy. I won't put a figure on it, but let me tell you, what I have to offer is security. We don't want the whole apple cart upturned, do we now? We don't want turmoil. We want everything to stay just as it was, a world which is immutable. Like my heart," and she'd laughed. "Like stone, Mr Ashby. But stone can change given the right conditions. Situations can shift and in your case, perhaps not for the better. Haven't you read Charles Lyell? I thought you were an educated man, Mr Ashby. I thought you were the king's own clerk." And yes, of course he had read Charles Lyell and his *Principles of Geology*. How the earth had evolved over millions of years. How the present was the key to the past. But what had that got to do with the Duke of Monreith? But before Ashby could ask, she had already gone.

But what to do about it? Only one thing it seemed, so he'd rifled through his mother's things and pawned the ring. Isn't that what was demanded? Isn't that what he did? Tidy things up for the Duke? Do as he was told? And now do as she said. And understanding all the time the nub of it: that money was key to this transaction.

The entrance to the old house, a shoddy pile of dirty brick and fallen timbers, was down an unlit alley, off Weavers Lane. A bundle of dirty rags was piled up in the snow outside the doorway. He wrinkled his nose, stepping over the moaning heap of soiled clothes which begged him, "Luvvie, spare a coin," and stepped into a passageway, more black than the alley he'd left.

The instructions he'd received had been clear. The money was to be polished, and to a figure of his choice. Ashby gritted his chattering teeth against the death chill of December. A perishing month if you suffered, as he did. But still, press on, he thought, press on.

"Is anybody there?" hissed Ashby.

No answer came, but Ashby could hear a faint scratching sound so he carried on down what he thought must be a narrow hall, feeling his way like a mole with hands against the walls. The scurrying seemed to be ahead. And whispers? Yes, whispering. And a whirring sound and click, click, click and a clack, clack, clack.

The clacking sounds grew louder as Ashby stumbled his way on through the winding passage until he saw a chink of furtive light, a thin shard, nothing more. Pushing against what Ashby felt must be a door, he stepped inside a room stuffed to the brim with a myriad of colours. The peacock splendour of it all whirled around him in iridescent flashes, as the whispering and the clacking grew louder. Ashby had never seen anything like it before in his drab little life, but he'd read of these places in books which he'd devoured as a boy. Like some Indian bazaar or Egyptian palace, this room was exotica. He found his voice. "Are you there, Madame Martineau? It's Ashby."

Stepping into the storeroom, a figure in black stood silently for what felt like an age, before answering him in the faintest of accents, "I was expecting you at least an hour ago. Have you got my money?"

Madame Martineau arched a black brow, questioning. Her jet hair almost entirely hidden by a white cap, etched either side with cascading ribbons. Her dark eyes staring, unblinking, and nestled under long, thick lashes. In one hand she held a sharp pair of scissors. In the other hand, nothing.

"I decided on a single payment of ten guineas. It's all here, Madame. Please check if you like."

"Indeed, Ashby, I shall if I like. The figure you have selected seems appropriate and I see you have polished the guineas. Well done!" And she laughed as she took the coins from his hands.

"So, Madame. Where are these letters you promised me?"

"You shall have them, but come, Mr Ashby. Follow me. I need to rest a little. I'm not my usual self."

The sylphlike woman turned her back on the scribe, swishing her skirt behind her, and Ashby followed, meek as a lamb. At a series of long trestle tables sat a bevy of girls, heads down, hands busy at work. None looked up, because they feared their mistress, but Ashby knew now where the whispering and whirring came from. Each girl was sewing or cutting. One dark creature with bony shoulders sat hunched over a strange contraption, her little foot pumping up and down. Ashby spied what he thought must be a needle, winking silver, which bounced up and down on violet brocade. The other girls stitched by hand, as high fashion demanded. The faces of the girls, though lowered, looked little more than children.

"This way," commanded the dressmaker, ushering Ashby into a tiny side room decorated with an elaborate collage in the shape of dragonfly wings splayed across the wall. Madame Martineau had partitioned this place off from her workforce to create a kind of boudoir.

"Please, monsieur. I shall count the money, if you don't mind. It's not that I don't trust you, but I have plans to spend this tomorrow. Perhaps I can offer you some coffee?"

Ashby hid his astonishment at her inappropriate politeness but he obeyed and sat down on a chair. It was midnight. He was tired. He wanted the letters, not coffee. He could feel a wave of irritation rising in his gut. Press on, woman, press on.

But when not in the servitude of others, Madame Martineau took her time, and she sat down opposite him with a smile, placing her scissors down on a table. Although not one normally to notice such things, Ashby was struck by her beauty.

"You have honoured our agreement, which is good, because I place great sway by it." She sat back, rubbing her flank. "I have been ill this past week, as women often are, but unlike the ladies we stitch for, there's no lounging on cushions for working girls. Even now in such a state of nerves, I must work through the night for my customers. They make such demands, but miss an order? Never." She poured a whisky, creasing her eyes in pain. "At least sixteen gowns to be delivered by dawn. These ladies know no bounds. The flimflam of the fashion world, monsieur."

She leant forward and poured herself a coffee, then passed another one to Ashby. Neither tasting the drink nor rejecting it, he pleaded, "You know it's not coffee I've come for. The letters please, Madame, which you say are so very delicate. I must make haste. It's already midnight and I must rise early tomorrow."

Madame Martineau stood up, flattening her dress as she did, and reaching up high to a shelf, took down a neat bundle of letters which were tied with a bright-blue ribbon. The paper was flesh-coloured, flocked, and with a highly distinctive monogram shot through with gold, like a crest. The monogram said simply, "M", but the pattern it made on the paper wasn't simple at all. The monogram was voluptuous in its curves, almost Romanesque in its ambitions. Ashby paled because he recognised the paper at once. It was the Duke's personal notepaper, of that there was no doubt.

"You know, monsieur, I run a number of other services which many of the parliamentarians are only too pleased to use. Perhaps you, too, sir, have needs? You only have to say the word." Her pause was complacent as she sat down again. Ashby watched the letters still clutched to her bosom. She leant over and took a little nub of sealing wax she kept on a table, along with stamps and string, and rolled it between her finger and thumb, as if a lady of leisure.

"Despite our best endeavours, it's strange how little things can unsettle a man, and it's these unsettling things that I, or for that matter any of my girls, can soothe away, and I offer variety." She attempted a smile, but it was barely that.

Ashby thrust out his hand. "The letters are all that's required, madam, I can assure you."

"No matter, old man. Calm yourself, for you have grown quite pale. As I said, I never let a customer down." She laughed and held out the little bundle for the old man to take, and as he leant forward, she snatched it back.

"Not so fast, monsieur, pretty please and you shall have them. Indeed, you are a clerk, *n'est ce pas?* A little bow would be nice."

Ashby stood up, slammed the coffee cup down, which went crashing off the tray, and wrenched the letters from her.

"Why, monsieur." Madame Martineau tilted her head to the side with a pout. "Why so rough? You had only to ask, *et voilà!*"

That does it, impudent, insufferable wretch, he thought. Leaping off the chair, he thrust his bony face close to her dewy skin and hissed in her ear, "Go easy, Madame. Go easy with your hateful taunts and your foul, unnatural suggestions. I need nothing more from you. You breathe a word of this to the Duke, a word, I say. You have no understanding of anything, do you? We have order here, madam, not anarchy. Another word, I say . . ."

"Or you'll what? You think you know who I am? Where I come from? What drives me? I'm not some silly English girl come up from the country. I know more than you think." Her face flashed with anger as she grabbed the old man's wrist and twisted his arm up behind his back. Ashby heard himself yelp, but she kept twisting, her voice no longer quiet. "You've got what you came for, and I promise, when you read them, you won't be disappointed." She twisted his bony arm a little further. "Now, monsieur, I've grown tired of your doglike company and would ask you to leave."

She let go of his wrist. Ashby felt sick. His arm was searing.

He stumbled out of her room, and as he did heard her calling after him, "And don't think this is the end, old man. Ten guineas is just the beginning."

Rubbing his wrist, he stumbled past the dressmakers, the folds of silk, back through the darkened hall till he found himself breathless, out in the cold, her words banging against his temples. Not the end of this? He tottered on the ice a little, his arm limp and heavy. His writing arm. Damn that whore. Damn her to hell. Flickers fell about him. Rats scuttled in front of his way. Stumbling on through the stinking allies and narrow lanes, he pounded through the snow, mentally shaking off the weakness he had displayed to that, that *magaziniere*, that mantuamaker. Isn't that what they called themselves?

Ashby wound his way round passages and corners, lit by the moon, and then up into Bermondsey Street. Far behind him, the great chimer of St Saviour's struck one. At a pace, crossing Tyers Gate into Leathermarket Street. Home.

The street where he lived stunk of cabbages. Debris belched out and discarded by the market traders, whose stalls stood like miniature shipwrecks, half erected, half taken down. Night creatures picked over the frosted scrapings of carrots, skins of onions. Ashby shuddered. The wind was up and sending great flurries of icy flakes into his eyes, blinding him to this poverty, this human flotsam, and still he pressed on. At the end of Leathermarket Street, the clerk opened a door and climbed up the stairs.

No Mrs Ashby or any children, as such. But the clerk often thought there were. And so he said his hellos to his wife and the little ones, and patted them on the head saying, "Oh yes. I've had a regular day of it, Mrs A. How's the baby? He don't look too well. Wrap him up, woman. It's perishing outside. And little Johnny? Reading already? Just like his father, eh? A right little scholar. Well, my sweet, I'm somewhat exhausted so I must be to bed. I've an early start in the morning."

And so Ashby, alone in his bachelor's lodgings, kissed good night to his armchair and patted his table on the head. He hugged the old pillow and after chatting away to his rickety wardrobe, peeled off his snow-clad coat. Lighting the grate, he stared at the flames.

The room was bare of ornament save one picture and a fine rosewood cabinet. The cabinet had been his mother's and had come, like the picture on the wall, from a fine house, far away and long ago. A gift from her employees on starting a new situation in London. It was, he believed, what an auction house would call a secretaire. In the top drawer the clerk kept some odd cutlery, a sharpened knife for fruit peeling, a nut cracker. In the other drawers, all manner of things.

Opening the top, he took out the knife and cut open an orange with the precision of a surgeon. The flesh tasted sweet and refreshing. He nibbled on a crust of dry bread and, supper finished, got into bed. Despite his exhaustion, Ashby took up the letters, untying the bright-blue ribbon.

The flesh-coloured paper had an odd scent, which was rank like the workhouse. On some pages the writing was small and ill-formed. Just a few pages, he thought, to see what they said. Her words had suggested a sensation and the "M" taunted him even more than her words. What had she said? Oh yes, "An upsetting of the apple cart, Mr Ashby, and the end of your world. It'll be the workhouse for you, unless you pay me the money."

The inked words blurred across the sheets. They rushed around his head. A great, single tear lolled down his face and he mumbled something about "God" and "God's mercy". He pulled a worn blanket over his head, shut his eyes, and eventually, fitfully, the old man slept.

Madame Martineau counted her money again. It was barely worth bothering with, but she opened the box anyway, which was decorated with pearly blossoms and butterflies flitting about in jewelled colours. She sat down and shifted her dress a little, unfastening the hooks at the waist, the pain in her pelvis like a vice. Old wives said she needed to rest at this time of the month, but she instead found the tiny pots of herbs she kept for her girls, the older ones, which if she doubled the dose would do the trick for her as well. She could feel swelling at her temples again, the headache gathering a storm.

She measured out the salicene, two drops of laudanum, and the rest a mixture of dried-out, sage-coloured dust steeped in hot water. Ten minutes she would give it, but when the moment passed, still the gnaw in her belly. She picked up a little hand mirror and looked at herself. Yes, she was drawn. By the pressure of it all? Perhaps, or the passing of another unborn. She hated anything leaving her, but mostly it was the girls, and she forbade it. There were lines around her mouth but they were fine. She hauled her frame up and wrapped her coat around herself, and on top of that, a fur-lined shawl. She found a muffler and an outdoor hat. She chose black bombazine framed with red-dyed rabbit.

Then, she went into the sewing room and spoke sharply to the girls. None looked up. She told the tawny one at the machine, "Hide that colour from me. You know I detest it. Why must the ladies insist on purple? It's a reminder. Cover it." The sallow little girl knew a bit of what madam said and why, and so splayed her hand across it realising the colour was a reminder of treachery, because the colour wasn't strictly purple at all. It was violet.

"I'll be back at dawn," Madame Martineau said. "Make sure you are finished by then, because I'll want to pack the gowns myself. My ladies like the personal touch, and as for the gentlemen . . ." She looked at the girls and her eyes fell on a little one. "Yes, you girl. Tabitha, I think he likes to call you. There'll be a job for you and I tomorrow."

None of the girls asked her where she was going, because these night saunters were not uncommon.

So Madam Martineau left The Borough, cutting through the skeletal dockyards and iced jetties. The freezing air was doing the trick and she felt better for the movement. If she hurried, she could find a little skiff before the clock struck two. Spectre-like, she wheeled down to the portside where she heard men hollering and the sound of creaking ropes. She found a solitary boatman and gave him a shilling and told him, "Put your back into it, sir." But if truth were known, she was not in a hurry, and despite the aching damp of the timber, she let the river envelope her.

The boat was lit by a single lamp and cracked through the ice. She listened to the sound of the melting underneath her and felt the pull of the oar and let her head tilt a little onto the ruff which she had made into a pillow, recalling the old looms of Spitalfields, long fallen still. Her family dead and gone. To the wall, they called it. But she could remember her life before she was this. Hanging silks on tenterhooks and her love of bright colours which had stayed with her. A picture book of memories of the fields beyond the slums where they pegged out the yarns, the colours flapping like spun gold, the flags of some ancient emperor's palace. But then the ice water sprinkled her from the tip of an overeager oar and the boatman said, "Sorry Miss," and the shock of it woke her.

She could see the islands up ahead and the looming warehouses. The boatman held the lamp aloft and helped her up the frost-grazed steps. Nightmen looked up from their work as she glided past and tried to catch her attention and call after her.

"Heh, my pretty? Don't leave me, my heart is breaking." They laughed.

"Lord, what a beauty. Come back, angel. We loves you, we do."

She smiled back, black ice glinting in the moonlight, but she knew there were bridges up ahead. Pushing her svelte frame against the chill, she swished on. And there along a lane by the river, an entrance brick plain, and above, a stag bellowing in pain.

She looked at the creature briefly, then turned away, reminding herself that she would speak to the Duke tomorrow. Make a visit to where the rich people lived. She despised all of them and would soon topple their empire, but not yet. She knew she had to wait. Sedition was a piece-by-piece endeavour. Revolution a misnomer in this country, not helped by the view of fools like Ashby, that with hard work and deference something good might happen. But Madame Martineau was not of this opinion. Her vision for the future was bigger and bolder, but ambition, she had learnt, like the clothes she stitched, often came with a snag. And her snag was money. Money to keep all of this going. Hadn't she learnt that from the king himself? The Duke of Monreith, her most loyal customer.

She turned on her heels, knowing that a deal was a deal, whoever the player. She would honour their original agreement. And Monreith would pay her. Every damn guinea for this one. She felt cold, and began to shiver and pulled her stole around her, but then changed her mind, and using nimble fingers, loosened it a little. Yes, he would pay her, she thought. Or he'd hang with her, as well.

Her printing rooms were just along a bit from the Machars Trading Company. She lit a candle and the room flickered into life, illuminating her weapon store, which was not stuffed to the gill with cudgels, pickaxes, and swords but with an artillery of papers, illustrations, and all manner of seditious material. And in the centre of the room, a printing press, which wasn't the latest or the fastest but would do the job well enough. The Chartists with their demonstrations and calls for justice had failed. But words circulated. Periodicals were debated. Ideas stimulated. Even here in England, Madam Martineau was certain, there was still a chance.

And how ironic that her secret printing press was just a spit away from Monreith's sprawling empire, and how he didn't know that this was how she spent the money he paid her. Not on bottles of rum or shots of opium, or the curse of gin which so many women in her predicament favoured, but words. Superheated words which promised to ignite everything, because all around her was the grinding poverty of labour. Long ago, Madame Martineau had vowed, that come what may, she would play her part. And that these nightmen and watchmen, these sailors and rope makers, would be grateful for her. They would rise to the occasion, lit by her words. They would bring the Duke of Monreith, and all like him — the dogs and their bitches — down to the same level as she was.

And it would be worth it. The pain of keeping all of this going. Madame Martineau ran her hand along the silenced machinery and picked up one of the many periodicals she favoured. The periodical fluttered in the tallow light, the sedition so deep inside the pages, so enticing she could taste it. She held the periodical to her mouth, pressed her lips upon the pages, and as she did so, felt the pain ebbing away. Madame Martineau sighed, tucked a little lock of hair behind a dainty ear, and put the periodical down. Knowing it was just around the corner. Her time would come.

CHAPTER
FIVE

SMITHFIELD

Hatton was back in the morgue and examining the body, to see Roumande had done the most excellent work. Lady Bessingham's skull had been pieced back together like a jigsaw puzzle, whilst the skin on the back of her head was plumped out and re-configured with the usual concoction of wax, gelatine and isinglass. Meanwhile, the stitching around the top of her ears and down to the back of her neck had been wrought in an almost invisible cross-cross of linen thread.

"Exquisite," said Hatton, fingering the thread as Roumande leant forward, taking Lady Bessingham's hand in his as if he might kiss it. Hatton took a sharp intake of breath, confused for a moment as to his diener's intention, but then remembering immediately the skin sample from the index finger he'd insisted upon earlier. Roumande twisted the hand around and reading Hatton's mind said, "I have the skin sample ready as you requested, Professor, but I've also been intrigued by this tattoo on her ring finger. The flower looks like a rose, but I think it's more exotic. Do you think it's from the East?"

"Perhaps, Albert. I don't know why I didn't ask Mr Broderig at the time. It's certainly unusual, but since the Exhibition so many ladies' fashions seem to draw their inspiration from the colonies. Did you go to it, Albert?"

"I took my whole family and we made a day of it. It was unbearably warm inside and we all had ices. In my opinion, the glass house was the most impressive construction. It's up at Sydenham now, I believe."

"Yes, but we digress and I need to look at the skin sample."

Roumande held a square of laboratory glass towards Hatton. "When I was preparing her body yesterday, I re-examined her hands. There's ink, but also something else. I don't want to influence your observation, Adolphus, so you look, and we'll see if we concur."

The shard of flesh was no bigger than a shilling. A smudge of indigo lifted from her index finger.

Roumande positioned the gas lamp over a magnificent microscope. A Zeiss imported from Jena in Germany and a make, in Roumande's opinion, without a competitor, such was its optical quality. The Zeiss reduced spherical aberration to a minimum and almost did away with the colour distortions Hatton had come to expect and to work around. The aperture of its lens was more accurate than any other instrument in its class. It stood up on its well-hinged, mahogany frame.

Hatton peered down the binocular columns, adjusting the turning wheels so that the image blurred then expanded again to crystal clear. Roumande was good and, so often, almost irritatingly right. But any professional jealousy was wiped away in an instant with the mounting excitement of what Hatton's eyes saw now.

There was wax. The merest trace of it.

"So she wrote a letter and sent it, using a seal perhaps? She was at work on the very day she died. I think we can say this without question. A Zeiss cannot lie, Roumande. But it could be she had just lit a candle."

Roumande shook his head. "It's blue wax, Professor. Your first impulse is the correct one. It's sealing wax. Given her love of tattoos, I suspect the Penny Post was not sufficiently distinctive for Lady Bessingham."

Hatton moved over to his desk and took a quill and handed it to Roumande. "Your illustrations are far more delicate than mine. I think I'll go and see Mr Broderig and ask him to tell us a little more about our victim, and while I'm in Chelsea, I'll double check for traces of wax. Inspector Adams will have to wait a little for his report because without these *i*'s dotted, the autopsy conclusions aren't complete. Do you mind, friend?"

Roumande smiled. "Perhaps pass me a finer quill, Professor? If he's a collector, he'll know the flora. It's certainly worth a try."

Roumande penned a perfect copy of the tattoo. A briar, a roselike flower, a star.

Hatton rolled the piece of paper up, taking his coat down from the meat hook, and made his way to the house, which was easily found, having the biggest plot and positioned directly opposite Chelsea Physics Gardens. He checked the brass plate to make sure he wasn't wrong, but etched in metal, Sir William's name and title. Hatton rang the bell.

A servant said that he would see if the master was available. Hatton waited in the drawing room, admiring a miniature clock topped by a tiny Indian prince resplendent with a turban and an umbrella carved from solid gold. The face was set to the right time — eleven-thirty in the morning. The servant came back and announced, "Mr Broderig will see you now, sir."

Benjamin Broderig was at his desk and dressed in black. He looked up from a map opened before him, a large green ledger to his left, and said, "Good morning, Professor. Can I offer you some coffee or a sherry, perhaps? We have a fine Manzanilla."

Hatton smiled and said Manzanilla sounded exactly right for this weather. "I have been up all night again, so please forgive my not making an appointment with you, Mr Broderig, but I have come on spec. I think you might be able to help me."

"Not at all, Professor. Please, sit by the fire. I've been up all night myself, because my mind is so restless here in London. There's a great deal of administration, when death comes. But forgive me, as you can see, I'm not busy with the details of Lady Bessingham's estate just at the moment." He patted the map. "An obsession of mine . . ." Hatton looked at what appeared to be an island.

"Is that Borneo, Mr Broderig?"

"No, it isn't, but you're very close. It's where I intend to travel next if I can raise enough capital. I met a man from Usk who by now will be collecting birds of paradise in the Aru Islands. This is the largest of the Arus, Tanahbesar. It's my intention to join him. Perhaps you have heard of him? His name is Alfred Russel Wallace."

Hatton shook his head.

"Well, he's not so celebrated as Mr Darwin but he shares a patron with me. Dr Joseph Hooker of the Linnean Society." Broderig paused. "I can see already by your face, Professor, that you've heard of him."

"Dr Hooker. But, of course. He's a very eminent man."

"Yes," answered Broderig, taking a little key and placing his ledger into a drawer, before turning the lock and saying, "And by what the Inspector said to me, you'll soon be joining Dr Hooker in the Hall of Fame. He's very impressed with you."

Hatton was delighted to hear such praise. "I've done very little so far, but yes, forensics I believe is the way forward, although it's very early days. And Inspector Adams seems to want to understand my work and be prepared to listen, to take advice, or that is my impression."

Broderig nodded, enthused by this company. "I think he does, Professor. And to have one's ideas listened to. Isn't that what we Men of Science all desire? But come, how exactly can I help you?"

Hatton took Roumande's sketch from his doctor's bag and placed it over the map of the Arus. Broderig nodded. "It's the tattoo, isn't it? It's a very good likeness." The young man sighed. "Lady Bessingham was a very strong-willed woman. It's *Paphiopedilum katheriniadum*. I discovered the flower and named it after her, and so I suppose she took it as a little symbol of her own and added the star, which is also Dayak."

Hatton looked puzzled. "Ah, sorry, Professor. Dayak. I think I mentioned the term yesterday. It's the name of the forest people in Borneo."

Hatton listened, mystified, and at the same time excited, but a servant appeared at the door and set the cups and glasses down, all jangling together on a silver tray, an unwanted interruption. Broderig waited till the drinks were poured and, ignoring the coffee, knocked back the sherry. Hatton did the same.

Broderig continued, "Now let me see, I have a book somewhere." He crossed the room and climbed up a ladder, which was leaning against a wall stacked with shelves of books. "I can show you more examples, but there are better pictures in the British Museum. My collection of anthropology is very poor, I'm afraid. There's a specialist you could talk to who could tell you more. His name is Dr John Canning. He is a botanist by training but has long since veered off and is interested in the native savage, whereas I stick with my lizards and butterflies." Broderig opened the book.

"Here's the meaning of it." He read it out, his voice cracking slightly. "The star is to light the way to the next world. I'm sorry, Professor." He took the bottle of sherry and poured himself another. "I don't wish to vex you with my unmanly sentiment. To light her way, Professor? She'll need it now."

Hatton rested his hand on Broderig's shoulder and waited for the weight of grief to pass. Broderig sat down again. "But tell me, on another subject entirely. What will happen to the girl?"

"The girl in the mortuary?"

"Perhaps you are inured to such sights in your work and I shouldn't have looked I suppose."

Hatton shook his head. What could he say? "We've had girls like her before and Roumande gets incensed by it. They are gay girls, Mr Broderig, there's no delicate way to put it and we are men of the world, are we not? Girls who lift their petticoats to make a living. It's a dangerous profession."

"But she was a child? Can The Yard do nothing about it?"

"The police do what they can, which is to move the girls on from place to place, though it achieves little. Roumande is planning to speak to Adams about her, much good it will do."

"And you sleep at night? Knowing this, Professor?"

"It's absolutely necessary to be objective in my profession. As with all science, Mr Broderig."

"Do you play chess, Professor?"

Hatton smiled, relieved at the change of direction. "A little. Do you?"

"It passed the time in Borneo during the rainy season. Perhaps you would care to join me one evening? I've been playing with my father since I returned, but he's not the queen slayer he used to be."

"I would be delighted to," answered Hatton.

The clock struck twelve. "Would you join me for lunch, Professor? You'd be very welcome."

Hatton shook his head. "Another time, sir."

Leaving Broderig, Hatton walked along the river for a bit. Chelsea riverside was bustling and, for a second, he watched the queue of passengers attempting to take the paddle boat to the city. There were arguments brewing with the steamer's captain shaking his head and pointing at the ice. Hatton looked away from the ship and back towards the house on Nightingale Walk, which had taken on a melancholy air. He'd take the traces quickly, he told himself. He had no desire to linger there.

He knocked on the door which was opened by a dishevelled footman, his jacket half on and half off. Hatton went straight upstairs and into the room he had been in the night before. There were traces of the wax just along the sides of her desk. Hatton scraped them and bagged them, then went back down the stairs eager to visit the morning room, but found himself stopped on the stairs by a woman who had a rolling pin in one hand and a knife in the other. "The footman shouldn't have let you just glide in here, sir. Why, you could have been anyone."

Hatton was impatient to get on. "I'm working alongside Inspector Adams. I'm here on police work."

"I know who you are, sir. You're the doctor of death, aren't you? I have heard all sorts of things about your black art, and it's not right, I say. Not right at all that our lady is being . . . no I shall not say it, for it sickens me. Isn't it enough that I have all of this to deal with?" She waved the knife around in a terrifying fashion and Hatton, not normally a man to shirk a blade, stepped back a little, for the tip was close enough to shave what little whiskers he had, which was hardly any.

"Please, Mrs . . ."

"Cook will do. I don't go by any other title. I don't mean to be rude, sir. Just to the point. Are you finished up then with whatever you were doing?"

Hatton shook his head at her and then dared to creep down a little further, sensing that her mood was softening, because the blade had come down to the starch of her apron.

"I have to check the morning room, so if you would be so kind to show me the way. I have an important report to conclude." The cook flinched again but Hatton kept on anyway, because he had become tired of this so-called sensitivity to his work, which he saw as nothing more than hypocrisy. Society used his science, but they didn't want to acknowledge it.

"Well, if you must, it's not my business to say if you can or cannot. And I suppose you'll be wanting something?"

Hatton answered quickly, before she changed her mind, "Tea would be good. Thank you, Cook."

"I'll send a maid up with it. The morning room is one door along."

He found the room easily, opened the curtains, and looked about the place. Bills and an appointment book on the desk, dressmakers' patterns left piled high. A mannequin for alterations, and to his left, positioned on its own embossed cherrywood table, a magnificent globe. He pushed his finger hard along the curve, admiring its spherical richness. Hatton smiled to himself, and was just about to look at the place chosen for him by the spinning orb when presto, there was a rap at the door.

He cleared his throat with a stern, "Enter."

The maid was rickets-crooked with poxy skin. She begged his pardon and set the tea tray down clumsily and asked if he wanted milk with it. And as she poured, she sniffled to such an extent that there was nothing to do but to offer her a handkerchief, and tell her to blow. "Thank you, sir. I'm not myself and this is not usual my work. Cook told me to do it cos the housemaid, her name's Emma, she's off polishing the drawing room . . ." And at once the sobbing started. Hatton could do without this interruption to his work, but ordered her to sit down for a bit, saying that he was a doctor and she was to do as she was told.

"I'm fine now, sir. Really I am. Cook will want me back in the scullery. I've got work to do."

"Very well, so long as you are completely composed. Tell her to give you some tea with two sugars in it. You're very pale, my dear. Tell Cook I insist on it. Do you have a name, child?"

The girl looked at him, her big eyes swelling again. "Yes, sir. I have a name, sir."

Hatton was not without humanity. "Well, my dear, what is it?"

"My name is Violet, sir. Violet. I don't really have a second name, but when Cook took me in, well, I am

79

like a daughter to her she says, so she's given me hers. She calls me Violet Jennings, cos she says it's no way for a girl like me to be without a family name even if you've got none, so to speak. She says, Nightingale House is my family now, sir."

"Indeed." Hatton was bemused by this broken creature. "And the other maid, Violet. Was she like a daughter, too? The maid who has fled?"

The maid's eyes widened. "Flora ain't like me. She's regular educated and was Madam's favourite. And before you asks me, I don't know where she's gone."

The Professor smiled, and touched her arm, but she pulled it back, embarrassed. "But I ain't no snitch. She ain't so bad. She took me to a museum once. But now she's gone, and I must work twice as hard. It ain't considerate of her."

"So you don't think Flora ran away, then? You don't think there's a connection with what's happened here? There're no valuables gone. Do you think anything's missing, Violet? I bet you're a really clever girl who notices everything."

The maid moved towards the door, but not before saying, "Flora's a good girl, sir, just a bit la-di-dah, with her gloves and her ladylike manners, but that ain't a crime, is it? Flora came and went as she pleased. Cook says Madam indulged her. But I'm not supposed to discuss nothing with no one, 'cept the coppers. I told them everything, which is nothing, sir."

The maid gone, Hatton took what other traces of wax he could find about the place and then, leaving the house, hailed a carriage back to St Bart's thinking, so

Violet must have been the one that found the body and who he heard sobbing last night. What a shock for her. No wonder she was pale.

When Hatton arrived at the mortuary, Roumande was writing, muttering French expletives.

"Is something bothering you, Albert?"

"I have damned well put the wrong detail down on this bit of the form." He crossed out a line with something sounding like a snort.

"Is that Lady Bessingham's autopsy report?"

"No, Professor. No, this is the little girl's." He flicked his quill over to the smaller cadaver.

"No one asked you to do that, Albert. Why in heaven's name do you bother?" Hatton despaired of Roumande's overzealousness. An autopsy report for a pauper?

"Well, I understand you are going to Cambridge, Professor," Roumande replied curtly. "Would it be too much trouble to give this to him?"

"Give it to Inspector Adams, you mean?"

"Is the little girl's murder really worth less of our time than Lady Bessingham's? Of course, it's meant for Scotland Yard. It's his responsibility, and Inspector Adams, it's coming back to me now, I'm sure he worked in the slums before he become so celebrated." His lips curled round the word. "It's the least we can do for the child. And I shall pay to bury her. She's not going in the incinerator. I'll not stand for it."

"Calm yourself, Albert. Please, I don't disagree with you. We'll go halves. We'll have a proper burial, a lined coffin, we'll do her hair, we'll lace her shroud, I'll visit the grave myself . . ."

"Thank you, Adolphus. I'm overwhelmed a little." Roumande gestured at the huge pile of work on their desk. "There's never any end to it, is there?"

"Work is work, Albert. Don't let it get on top of you."

"That's easy to say, Adolphus, but you forget it's my responsibility to make ends meet here. There is so little response to our pleas, so little interest."

Hatton was sick of the subject. Money, or the lack of it. "Send another letter, Albert. You managed to get the saw, didn't you? And the microscope? There are people out there who want to support us. Just keep going. Leave the letters on my desk and I'll sign them when I get back. I need to drop in on The Yard."

"With all due respect, Professor . . ."

Hatton rolled his eyes. He knew what was coming. "Then sign them yourself, Albert. For heaven's sake man, you've done it before. Just write the damn letters."

CHAPTER
SIX

BLOOMSBURY

Flora James pulled the blanket up over her lap, shivering a little. She still wasn't convinced they hadn't been followed. Moving shadows, when they first came here, looming out on the street and odd noises down the stairwell. Whatever Dr Canning had said to comfort her, it didn't matter. She was still afraid.

"Miss James, you're imagining it. Is it any wonder that your mind should play tricks on you, after all that has happened? Don't forget that I've barely left your side. But you cannot hide in this room forever. I think the sooner we go to the police and explain everything, the better." Dr Canning looked at the girl, who was instantly a mass of heaving sobs again.

"Don't start up again, please, Miss James. I'm expected back at the museum for a lecture, but I'll see to it that the doors are securely locked behind me. And tonight I'll do what your mistress would have wanted. I'll get the letters to Babbage." Canning patted the scroll of letters and smiled. "I'll be back as soon as I can."

They were five flights up in a flat-fronted terraced house in Gordon Square. Flora stood up and moved towards the mantel, taking the invitation down again. It was black rimmed.

"I don't even have any mourning clothes, Dr Canning. No crepe. Not even a veil." Flora put the funeral invitation, which was addressed to Dr John Canning of 10 Gordon Square, Bloomsbury, back in its place. It had arrived today in the morning post. The funeral was to be held in a few days time. She would make do with her fawn dress and her drab winter coat. Perhaps Violet or Cook would have something for her when she got to Ashbourne, a sash or a swathe of sombre bombazine, because go there she would, invited or not.

Dr Canning shut the door firmly behind him, and she listened to his brisk footstep disappearing like a fading echo. She poured herself a little drop of porter and thought of him, this man she barely knew. Her position in his lodging house was not appropriate.

She had tapped on the door that morning in the British Museum, two days ago now, and he'd looked up and smiled, sending the porter away. What a wreck she must have looked. But he didn't seem to notice and welcomed her in and she had told him everything her mistress had said.

"Please, Miss James. Sit yourself down because I've been expecting you."

She had rambled a little about what her mistress had said needed checking, which sections needed verifying, before the letters could go to their real destination, the *Westminster Review*.

He'd read them initially in silence then suddenly smiling, or sighing or saying out loud, "I couldn't agree with you more" and then towards the end ringing entire paragraphs. It was beyond her, although Lady Bessingham had warned her that the ideas contained within would cause a storm.

"Just think. Little Flora delivering a sensation, and myself at the centre. What a commotion we'll cause. I'm glad I've finally made my decision to share them. They're my letters, after all." And her mistress had laughed as she had said it, and asked for the green dress with the jet sash.

Dr Canning's room at the museum had been crammed with bones, arrows, and masks. The type Flora saw that day she came to the museum as a visitor once. But these artefacts were not for public display, but rather strewn about in corners, or teetering precariously on piles of books.

There were compasses and strange instruments and pictures on the walls of native people. Savage men with haircuts which looked like the latest gentlemen's fashion for bowler hats. And those monstrous holes in their lobes. Why did they do that?

Dr Canning had caught her staring and had asked if she would like to see the pictures better. Had she actually nodded? She had, and he'd taken a book down from one of the shelves. The image that stuck in her mind was a drawing of a young woman covered from head to foot in swirling tattoos. She had a little star and a flower like the one her mistress favoured, but these were not tiny, delicate things. These were enormous, and curled up the young woman's hip and spread out like branches or creeping ivy across her breasts.

Flora had shut the book, crimson-faced. She'd forgotten herself. Dr Canning had carried on making notes once again in determined silence and then finally, when he spoke, there was a look on his face, a look of such astonishment it made Flora fear for them both. He shook his head, as if the letters were a burden, but then stood up, ran his hands through his hair, turned to her, and said, "They are as I suspected. The ideas in the letters are embryonic but they question all that we know, everything we believe in. She is right. They will set the world on fire, and in the wrong hands could be extremely dangerous. I suspect your mistress wants Mister Babbage to see them as 'a shot across the bows' to a bigger debate which must follow. And it will, Miss James, because we're just the beginning. Tell me, Miss James, there was a publication ten years ago called *Vestiges*. Perhaps you have heard of it?"

Flora blushed. She had read it under cover at night, but she knew the penalty for a girl like her reading such seditious material openly. The Church had condemned it, vicars crying from their pulpits that it was the devil's work. Saying it was the work of an atheist, a radical, someone who wanted to destroy everything, the natural order of things. Nevertheless, its ideas about how the world was made had bewitched her. But Flora said nothing of this to Dr Canning.

He smiled. "Well, *Vestiges* was nothing, my dear, to the outcry these letters will cause. They will upset the whole apple cart and cause a right old commotion in

The House, but it's just what I would expect from your mistress. I don't speak ill of her, not at all. I admire her. She's a fine woman and, it goes without saying, pays for all of this," and he'd waved his arms around his pokey little room, as if it was a palace.

A bigger debate, he'd said. Madam loved debates, and that whole day went by in a whirl of ink, jugs of porter, blotting paper, corrections, and comments. Verification, he called it. And added with a smile, "Before I arrange to take these to the *Westminster Review*, would you like me to read you the letters, Flora? So that you know what they contain? You see, my dear, ideas are a dangerous thing." Flora had nodded, terrified, not able to resist. She'd shut her eyes, and felt a breeze rustling through a far-flung forest.

June 21st, 1855

My dearest Lady Bessingham,

I am writing these words upriver, far into the dense jungles of Simunjan. I was hoping that I might have received a word from you on life in England, but alas the mail boat arrived with nothing for me, save a few notes from my father who is such a sparse and unemotive writer. Father, as ever, discussed the current state of play in Westminster. I must confess, being here a million miles away, I find it all, dare I say, irrelevant. I suppose I should pretend to be a little more attuned to the Great Acts of Parliament, but it seems to me that there is more to learn here about the governance of life than is ever found in politics.

For as I lie here, a thousand tiny creatures go about their infinite work. Ants march in line and the sky seems lost to me. I crane my eyes up above the looming canopy. It glints, a gesture of the world outside the forest. But it's never peaceful here. It's deafening. Everywhere I look and listen, I am spellbound, intoxicated, drowned in and drowned out, by the onslaught of Nature.

We left Sarawak on June 9th, giving us just a few months before the rains are due. Alongside my Dutch companions, my friend Emmerich decided to join us, tempted by the call of rare and undiscovered pitcher plants. Emmerich not only speaks excellent Malay but also, most impressively, some Dayak dialect.

He is an amusing fellow, both entertaining and highly informative. There's not a fern, a palm, a root, or a bud that defeats him. He has been in East Asia for five years wandering the islands as far as Aru, collecting only plants. Quite rotund and short, he has a kind face and a gentle, studious manner, as you might perhaps expect a man obsessed with botany. The day I first met him, I was haggling over the price of butterfly nets when he sprang to my aid and secured a price of three shillings for half a dozen. We quickly fell into an animated discussion about where we had come from and where we hoped to go, and after a breakfast of mangosteen and coffee, Emmerich soon had me under his wing.

Our party numbers five collectors (including myself, the novice) and our native helpers. The boats had been hewn from the enormous tapang trees (Koompassia excelsa), and as we moved along the river, within a day from Sarawak, we were soon in virgin forest. The banks began to slide away and enclosed us in a silent, trickling, half-light place. Nature folded in around us, monkeys hollered, holding sway with fallen trees, branches, roots, and creepers delaying our onward journey. But the helmsmen pushed on through the floating grass and giant lilies till the gullies of tawny water ran like veins.

Our general servant, Uman, is efficient and helpful. He is a bullseye shot and, like my German friend, speaks the hill tribes' dialects. His English is faultless and despite his lack of any formal education, he burns with an impressive intellect. I know he is our servant, but there is something in his manner which absolutely confirms him as more than my equal. Uman is aided by a young companion, who I believe is some sort of cousin to his family. This rascally slip of a boy is called San and he cannot be more than nine. His voice flitters round the boat like music. He hops from task to task, and if we do not keep a regular watch on him, is often slurping back the arak that I keep for my specimens, but when we catch him it's hard to be angry for long. He looks at me, as if to dare a beating, then dives off the boat down to the bottom of the river, his lithe body twisting coppery like weeds. And when he rises up again (we are all with bated breath, for he has been down for far too long), he spits out the water like a little whale and I think to myself, how very like the animals we are!

This is a tight little community, confined as we are to camping on odd patches of earth between the mangroves, but despite our containment, we are getting along. For example, Mr Banta is a fine fellow. His laugh is infectious and just the slightest quip can set him off. We all laugh with him when this happens, except Ackerman, who seems to find Mr Banta less amusing. He only looks at us with a faint, but just detectable, mocking in his face.

But Mr Banta is a brilliant ornithologist and has won quite a reputation for his cataloguing of hornbills. He and Uman draw great flocks in towards our dugouts with near perfect mimicry. Uman has a little whistle made of reed which he puts to his lips, and when he blows it, the air fills with a flurry of gregarious birds.

I like to think myself a taxidermist, but the speed at which Uman strips these brilliant feathers is extraordinary. His fingers fly across the bird until the skin is bare. The bones are boiled, dried out, tagged, and boxed. The flesh is cut up into little chunks and skewered in an oily marinade. One thing is for sure. Nothing is wasted here and everything feels connected.

So on the whole I am very happy in the company of these men, but there's one, I must confess, who irks me. He is Mr Ackerman, the chess player. I cannot say exactly why, Lady Bessingham, and I am sure you would urge me patience, but something in his nature unsettles me.

Perhaps I am judging him too harshly, for he's done nothing to warrant this dislike, but if I was to put him in a category it would be insectile. His classification would be Brunneria borealis. He is like a praying mantis. Bent over, hands clasped together, blank of eye as if waiting for something to happen, for one of us to make a false move, whereupon he can swoop upon us like the predator. He suffers from a heat rash and so his skin is scaly, but he's stoical and never scratches like the rest of us. He rarely smiles except when playing chess (which is not a time when most men smile), but it is clear to me why Mr Ackerman smiles. He is beating us.

Ackerman gives little of himself. He seems to be distracted and rarely joins in with our conversations about Nature. His passion is his gun, his Machars whisky, and, it seems to me, his damn ledger, which he forever has his nose in, making copious notes, but he gives nothing away as to its content. I do not know who he really is, or where he's from. He's clearly well connected in the world of trade and I understand he even works in England when the promise of money takes him there.

Emmerich thinks he is from Vlissingen on the coast of Holland, and like the boatmen, knows the water. If he does, he doesn't show it and seems intent on nothing but his gun. Even in the dugouts, he's forever oiling it or taking it apart, examining every hinge and bolt. In silence. He is readying it for hunting.

Madam, forgive me. I am rambling, but is it any wonder that in this forest, one becomes jumbled and confused? Of course, I am fine here and have already collected over twenty specimens of butterflies, including the common birdwing (Troides helena) and common tree nymph (Idea stolli), and identified more than five types of orchid, guided by the knowledge of Emmerich. Tomorrow we are heading for Empugan, a small village, where we will stay for a while and are promised many pitcher plants (for Emmerich) and for the rest of us, orang — meaning man — utan.

I will put this letter to rest now with the others. Who knows when I shall next see a mail boat.

Your servant etc.

Dr Canning took off his reading glasses and lay the letters down, but left Flora wanting more. More of Borneo, of its secrets, and for Dr Canning to look at her again for just a second longer, but then came the message from Violet.

Violet didn't come herself but had sent the footman. Her so-called beau, as Violet foolishly liked to call him. The knock when it came was a harsh interruption. Flora went quickly to the door, telling Dr Canning she'd only be a minute, and stepped out into the hummingbird corridor, where the footman grabbed her by the arm and hissed in her ear, "Where the hell have you been? Lady Bessingham died last night. Her head crushed in by that bloody great fossil. You know the one, Flora . . ." And then he said that everyone was looking for her, and that she'd better "hop it" or she would "cop it", unless of course, he added with a lascivious wink, "You'd like to do a little favour for me, nice little chit like you . . ." These last words delivered as he scrunched a note into her face, whilst clinching her waist and trying to kiss her. A sharp stamp with her boot was all it took to make him let her go and Dr

Canning must have heard the blood curdling yelp, because he was quick to the door with, "What the devil's going on out here?" but the footman had already gone.

Back in the room, they examined the note.

"The writing is poor," she said. "There is an attempt here at an *h* and another at *d* and *e*. She must be telling me to hide."

Canning tried to persuade her otherwise. "But how did she know you were here? I thought your mistress told you to tell no one you were coming to the museum."

Flora was as pale, visibly shaking as she admitted, "I mentioned my errand for Lady Bessingham to another maid called Violet, but she's a meek little thing and would never say anything to anyone. She must think we're in some kind of danger or she wouldn't have sent a warning."

"Well, this is a matter for the police, Miss James. They'll want to talk to us and your friend might be right. We could be in danger. These letters? Who else knows of their existence? Are you absolutely sure you've spoken to no one else? Miss James? Are you listening to me? Miss James?"

Dr Canning caught her as she fell. He rushed to get brandy and held a glass to her lips but she pushed it away.

"We need to leave here, sir," she begged.

"This is against my better judgement," he muttered to himself but ten minutes later they were walking quickly through the snowy streets of London, Dr

Canning knowing she was right and that they needed to go somewhere private, somewhere he could think a little more clearly.

Home, he thought. Home is where they needed to be.

And home was Gordon Square, just a quick hop from Great Russell Street. His rooms were in a house on the corner, opposite a monstrous church, and as they reached his door, the bells rang out, a great peel of chimes calling the faithful to prayer.

The sky was tin metal with great puffing clouds, and Flora was glad to be inside the narrow stairwell because she couldn't help thinking they were being followed. But there was nothing, of course. And no one.

Dr Canning had busied himself arranging the furnishings to ensure she had some privacy; this simple act of kindness to her, a maid and nothing more, not unnoticed, and Flora stayed in this little room of his for what felt like for ever.

She sighed remembering all that had passed. It seemed like an age but was only two days ago. She swayed as she stood, the funeral card still in her hand.

But then a tread on the stairs. A little tread and a creaking sound. Was it near, or far away? Her heart stood still. Her blood ran cold. There was nowhere to hide. She'd been right. Someone had followed them. How foolish. How ridiculously foolish to think they could pass unnoticed, for there is always someone prepared to sell a stranger's life for practically nothing.

94

The card dropped to the floor. She listened. Steps quite heavy coming up the stairs, nearer and nearer. She was panicking, but where could she go?

When the bang on the door to the room came, it was loud. Like a hammer. Did they hammer her mistress's head in? Is that what the footman said?

Quick, think, for heaven's sake, Flora, she begged herself, then, wild-eyed, looked at the window, pressing her face against it, knowing she could fit through, yes, but fall to her death? There were up five flights. It was certain. So instead, she simply waited. Until she heard the person move away again with a clack, clack, clack down the stairs.

CHAPTER
SEVEN

BLOOMSBURY

The banging at the front door was insistent, but it was
the yapping which probably disturbed him. It was only
seven o'clock in the evening but it was not uncommon
for Professor Hatton to take to his bed by this time, if
he'd been up all night. Perhaps it was his country
upbringing which gave him the constitution of a larger
man, because Hatton wasn't robust-looking. He was
sinewy, sharp featured, milk-pale. But despite his
catatonic stupor, he sprang up fully dressed, already
sensing the knock was for him, and headed down the
stairs to see his friend, Roumande, patting the King
Charles spaniel which was wagging its tail.

"Forgive me, Adolphus. But something peculiar has
happened. I waited an hour before I decided that it
would be best to fetch you. I'm deeply troubled by
something."

Hatton, asking nothing, immediately took his cane,
his thick coat, and a derby, hoping that at least his
friend had brought a carriage. But he hadn't. "Are we
walking then, Albert?"

"I went round the block twice. I went in and out of a
tavern, but it was no good. My mind wouldn't settle.
We've had a delivery, Professor."

"And will you tell me, in heaven's name, what of? Or I am to be suspended in aspic, like one of your organs, Albert?"

Roumande laughed and let the snow settle on his nose and his lashes, looking skywards. A cold beam from an ornate gas lamp highlighted the spot where he stood, a circle of white. A shimmer of ice.

"Round and round the block, but nothing, and so I thought a puzzle is a puzzle. And I know how you love a puzzle, and Mr Broderig isn't the only fellow in London with a hip flask." Roumande tapped the side of his coat. "She's just along here a bit. The body collectors wouldn't bring her all the way. Said they were unnerved by her."

"She? What sort of she?" asked Hatton.

"Another girl, Professor. From her ragged clothes, clearly a pauper."

By now, the two men were on the corner of Charterhouse Street. Roumande took Hatton by the arm and guided him down an alley. "It's not much farther," he said, his voice thick, until they reached a little hump in the road and beyond that, a girl. Professor Hatton could see it was a girl before he even looked at her. Her childlike hands just visible, ghostly in the moonlight.

"Here, Adolphus. You might want a slug, first?"

Hatton looked in Roumande's eyes to catch a glimpse of what lay ahead, taking the flask from his friend's hand, grateful for it.

"Do you want to see her?"

How odd the question felt. It hung, dead in the air.

"Do you want me to do the honours, Professor?"

Roumande seemed a little lost, a little hesitant, a little unsure of himself, and so Hatton, resolute, stepped forward.

Her hair was damp but she lay on a soft down pillow as if slumbering, tucked under a woollen blanket and placed in an orange box. She was dead; dead girls were two a penny around here, but still the questions came to him at once. Who was she? Where was her family? Did she have any? And how did she end up here and like this? As a boy Hatton had watched, with some amusement, his sister Lucy tucking up her treasured doll exactly like this little girl. And this child seemed unreal, like a doll, but perhaps it was just the moonlight.

Yet it was clear to Hatton at once that at some point she'd been in the river. Hatton gently pulled back the blanket to see wet, barely formed breasts and a child's mouth agape, and around her mouth and in her hair a few souvenirs from the Thames. The tiniest shreds of flotsam. He checked her hands but there were no pebbles or rocks which might have been present if she had grabbed at the banks whilst trying to cling to life. But he was sure her death had been by drowning.

"Look at her wrists, Adolphus."

Pinpricks, but not random slashes and scars as with the previous girls. They were neatly done and barely touched the skin, more like bee stings or the imprint of kisses. "Does it remind you of the girls we already have? The pauper girls, Adolphus?"

"Cover her." Hatton pushed his hand in his mouth. "Do as I say, Albert. Cover her, for pity's sake." And for a second he thought of Flora James — the missing maid. Could it be her? But no, that thought was gone in an instant. Inspector Adams had been very clear that the missing maid was ladylike and nearly twenty.

"She's perfect, Professor. Like an angel, but barely twelve is my guess."

"I can do very little here. It's the light, the snow, the temperature, but I think she drowned. We'll take her back to the morgue to be sure. But she hasn't been beaten, Albert. She's as you say. Apart from death, she's perfect."

Roumande nodded. "Foundlings are often left like this. Lost children. But you're right, she's definitely been pulled out of the river. I had a closer look before I came to get you, Professor. My guess, she's been here a couple of hours. Most of her hair's still damp to the touch, but some of the strands near her face are beginning to harden with frost. Two hours, best guess. Maybe three at the most. The body collectors did the usual rounds to Coram's Fields and to several of the workhouses, but no joy. I should give you this, Adolphus."

Hatton was shaken, but why he didn't know. She was not the worst cadaver he had ever laid his eyes on. She was eerily beautiful. He opened the note, which said, "Metropolitan Police Delivery Note/ For the Urgent Attention of Professor Hatton, St Bart's Pathology Department."

"It looks official enough. But don't the Specials normally bring corpses to the mortuary yard themselves, if it's a suspicious death? It's not our normal procedure."

Roumande shrugged. "Methods are sometimes slapdash between the workings of The Yard and the body collectors. You've heard me say it, many times. The body collectors had a tip-off. They've labelled her as 'pork', but she's more than that, isn't she, Adolphus? She seems cared for, cherished almost. She seems as if she died but minutes ago, and that if I picked her up and carried her home I could warm her by the fire. That she would yawn and stir herself."

Hatton nodded, and helped Roumande with the crate, thinking of the chicks he used to catch as a child. The sick ones put in a tin, wrapped in calico, and left near the hearth. A trick of his father's, who would promise the boy that they'd be better in the morning, and sometimes they were. Other times, little eyes shut, warm still from the nearness of the fire, but their short life brutally over. His father's hand, steady on his shoulders. "*They are not meant to live, son, if God has ordained it so.*"

"Have the men at least left us a wagon, somewhere?" Hatton beckoned again for the brandy flask.

Roumande stamped his feet. "They said she had a ghost upon her. They said they didn't want to touch her. Off to Newgate by now most likely, or the rookeries. But don't worry, she'll be as light as a feather. At least the Specials had the decency to label her this time. But even so, it's a paltry amount of

100

information offered. We should get her back, and then perhaps you could bring this up with the Inspector. Surely, this one he can't ignore?"

Hatton pulled out his pocket watch. An hour, maybe two, and they would be done. Dinner by eight. He agreed with Roumande. "Let's make it a quick autopsy, Albert, and I'll speak to the Inspector tomorrow."

In the morgue, the lamps were on. It seemed, unlike the other girls who had been beaten to a pulp, that his initial impression had been right — this child had died simply by drowning. Hatton stood over her, inspecting her organs. "Trauma to the sinuses and the lungs, considerable debris in her throat, and substantial haemorrhaging, suggesting that she struggled, sucking in the water before she succumbed. Pinpricks on one arm but nowhere else. Her body, malnourished, which is to be expected, although oddly it appears her hair has been brushed. What do you think, Albert? Her locks should be tangled, full of debris, but there's only a little. The river has been frozen for a month. Not solid granted, but I think by the state of her, she's been dead a day or so. But her cadaver kept in abeyance, helped by the freezing temperatures. Would you agree?"

Roumande nodded. "I agree with everything you suggest, Professor. Her locks are smooth, brushed, as if she was on her way somewhere."

Hatton was troubled. "How many does that make now, Albert? Two? Three? Four girls? It's not the same cause of death, but it's the same sort of age and the pricks have definitely been done by a needle of some description; they have barely scratched the skin, as if the pricks were made after she was dragged from the river. And this narrows it down to what? Maybe a seamstress or a bookbinder? The sweatshops are notorious for child labour. The binding industry, not a whole heap better. But it is a very odd sort of person who would mark a cadaver."

Roumande shrugged, finished up writing their notes. Hatton washed himself down and lay his hand on Roumande's shoulder.

"It's almost ten, Albert. Are you hungry? And would Madame Roumande forgive me, if you missed supper at home tonight? Because I could do with a drink."

Roumande looked up at the Professor from his notes. "I'll put her back in her box and leave her by the hearth. It's foolish, I know. Sentimental, even."

Hatton shook his head. "You know we can't do that, Albert. She's possibly a murder victim. We can't warm the body. We need to preserve her."

"We have the details in the report, Adolphus. Would one night of comfort really matter? I'll not leave her near the fire. I'll put her at the end of the passageway. It's cold as ice there, but she'll be near the other cadavers and have some company."

Hatton nodded and poured himself a glass of porter and watched Roumande scoop the little girl up and place her back in the orange box.

"Did you check the box she came in, Professor?"

Hatton shook his head. "No, just the girl. We were both out of sorts this evening, Albert, so forgive me. Why? Is there something wrong?"

Roumande bent down, the girl still in his arms. "There's a book in here, Professor, beneath the pillow."

Roumande picked it up and read out its title, *"Flora and Fauna of Great Britain*, by D.W.R. Dodds, with a Foreword by Sir Joseph Dalton Hooker, Botanist, Biogeographer, Traveller."

Hatton took the book from Roumande, flicking from front to back to see a number of pages tagged and marked. The birds were done as simple line drawings, but beautifully wrought, depicting nature at its most varied. Hatton turned to the last page, to find an inked stamp, which he read out, knowing that Roumande was hanging on his every word. "Write this down, Albert, then call a cab. Property of: Mr Daniel Dodds, Purveyor of Fine Books, Number 202, The Strand."

"I'm just telling you what I knows. Ain't never been no Numbers Two Hundred and Two, on this road. Number One Hundred and Ninety is as far as I can take you. So that'll be two shillings, if you please, and two shillings if you don't."

Hatton fumbled for his money but, as ever, had forgotten to bring his purse. And so Roumande did the honours, jumping out with a thud into a drift of snow.

Despite the inclement weather, The Strand was full of people. A number of fine restaurants were still offering excellent dinners. The sweet, pungent smells of cooking filled the air, but there was no time for eateries, reasonably priced or otherwise. And the cab driver was right. The Strand had no Number 202. It stopped before it hit these digits, the last even-numbered building being a rather tatty musical hall.

"Wait for me here, Albert. I'll ask someone."

Hatton was out of the music hall quicker than he went in it, but this time with two half-dressed ladies on his arms, both of whom he attempted to shake off, but who were clinging to him limpet-like, and one of the ladies, puckering up and slurring, "You is gorgeous, sir. Ain't he gorgeous, Rose? My friend thinks you is gorgeous, as well. Ow's about both of us, for half a guinea."

"Please, ladies, desist. Albert, be a good fellow. Help me out here?"

Roumande wondered if he would just let his friend struggle for a minute longer before he interceded, because it was rare to see the Professor with any kind of woman on his arm, but pity got the better of him. He released Hatton, being charm itself to the ladies, hat doffed, and giving them both a shilling, asked, "Two more, if you can tell us the whereabouts of a bookseller?"

"Don't read, luvvie. None of us does."

Roumande brought out a half a guinea. "Name of Dodds. Daniel Dodds? A purveyor of fine books."

The girls looked at the money.

One of them put out a hand but Roumande took the money back and repeated, "You had better be honest with me, girls."

The girls looked at each other before one of them spoke.

"Dodds, you say? I know 'im. Quiet as a mouse. Wouldn't say boo to a goose. Purveyor of fine books? Purveyor? What sort of word is that when it's about? But he does 'ave a shop. It's along a bit, down Millford Lane. There's those round 'ere says The Strand, cos it sounds better but 'e's no better than us. Can't miss it. Great big bloody bird in the window. Stuffed, ain't it?"

"Thank you, ladies. You've been most helpful," and Roumande bowed again, a little lower, as the girls giggled and nudged each other. And although Hatton was glad that he didn't have the ways of the street, on occasions like this he could definitely see the benefits of having a little Metropolitan *je ne sais quoi*, when it came to detective work.

They made their way quickly, taking a street to the right which appeared to be mainly ladies for sale, but at the end, the sound of hammers against leather, people talking, spilling out on the streets. Not drinking, but talking. Mainly foreign voices, Italian and other things. A young man with a cap hissed at the two men as they walked up towards a sign, which flapped in the chill, announcing, "Purveyor of Fine Books, D.W.R. Dodds Esq."

"Anarchists. All Italians are, Professor," Roumande mumbled in Hatton's ear. "Knife you in the back, soon as look at you."

Hatton nodded, knowing his friend was right because London had had an influx recently and they were up to no good. Hanging around on the street corners, and their leader, Giuseppe Mazzini, widely reported to be attempting revolution at home, but for some reason,

105

holed up here, the least radical city on earth, stirring up sedition from the library of the British Museum with his absurd notion of Giovine Italia.

Hatton had little time for it. He pulled on the bell of the shop, noting the stuffed bird, a large black crow with a nut in its bill. In the window were books. Mainly scientific journals and back copies of the radical journal the *Westminster Review*, which was edited just around the corner. Hatton pulled the bell again, impatiently this time, and turned to Roumande ready to say it had been a wasted journey. But Roumande had crouched down and was busy at the lock.

"There's more than one use for a scalpel, Adolphus. Jimmying, it's called. Nimble fingers required. Ah, there you go."

The lock clicked. The door opened.

And splayed out on the floor, hammered to the ground and pinned like a moth — a man.

"Mother of God."

"He's dead, Professor."

"Yes, Albert. I can see that."

Mr Dodds was wearing only his nightshirt, which had been pinned up so his penis hung out, a flaccid lump. The foreskin had been stretched and pinned to the skin on his thighs. His fingers pinned to the floor, along with his earlobes. His hair had been pulled into strands. His ankle skin pinched and nailed.

"He looks like Gulliver, Professor. When the traveller falls asleep and wakes in Lilliput and is pinned down by the little people."

Hatton nodded, slightly nauseous from the sight, thinking that yes, Mr Dodds was like a picture in a book. But not a perfect replica of Gulliver, because the man's heart had been cut out and sat near the body on a white plate, shining like jelly.

Roumande spoke, "Property of D.W.R. Dodds. We're quite a hike from Charterhouse Street where we found our little angel, and there're no family portraits on the walls, just moths and butterflies."

Hatton bent down and felt the man's temperature. "There's no wedding ring here and I can tell you that he's freshly done. Hours, I'd say."

"He was gagged first," said Roumande. "And the noise outside might have masked the culprit, but the cutting would have made a mess. It's a bodge job. Still, they knew where to look."

Hatton shook his head. "Any man knows where his own heart is and where to find another's. He may have been strangled first. Gagged, tied, throttled with a rope, and then cut. There are abrasions around the neck."

Hatton stood up and looked at the books on the shelf. "All these are mainly pertaining to natural science, but then we are not so far from the University."

Hatton turned a handle to an adjoining room but it was locked. He walked over to the desk, which had a ledger for customers, and looked for the till, but there was none, just a tin box which he shook and then opened. "Well, whoever did this wasn't here for the money. There's fifty guineas plus a heap of change in here. Another person of means. Another botanical, pinned like a moth, but the book which led us here suggests this Mr Dodds had his mind on higher things. He was probably a collector once and ends up here, which is odd. But many start off in one profession and then end up in another. But I think we have a clue, Albert." Hatton put the money box down and went back over to the book they had brought with them, found in the orange box. "These pages have been tagged to mark the birds. But we shouldn't touch anything else because police procedures are very clear on this. We need to fetch Inspector Adams."

And Hatton was right to be of that mind. To call a cab and head straight to Number 2 Whitehall and demand that Adams come with them immediately, because the link was clear. The title of the book was *Flora and Fauna*. The maid was called Flora, wasn't she? And the pictures of the birds? On closer inspection, the book was nothing but a hodgepodge, a mere vanity thing. The Foreword had spelling mistakes and was clearly not written by Hooker at all. Had Dodds, Hatton wondered, made the book himself? Using a needle, a bodkin, and inserting into the middle, not British birds at all, but plates which had been widely circulated. Hatton knew these pictures well. Everybody did, because they were finches from the great expedition by Mr Charles Darwin to the Galapagos Islands. They had been torn from *The Zoology of the Voyage of HMS Beagle*.

Adams was at his desk smoking and he continued to light penny smoke after penny smoke in the carriage to Millford Lane and to continue puffing, despite

108

Hatton's protestations, as the Inspector peered closely at the body of Mr Dodds.

Finally, stubbing out his cigarette, Adams took the bird book and handed it to one of his Specials, saying, "Bag it." And then turning to Roumande, who was speaking at great length, cut him off mid sentence, impatiently with, "I hear you, monsieur. I promise you, we will investigate the girls you speak of. Perhaps they are all connected, but probably not. And this new girl you found this evening? This angel, you describe? I know nothing of her, Scotland Yard delivery note or not. However, this man's death . . ." Adams bent down to further inspect the corpse, then stood up and scratched his head. "Flora and fauna, eh? Very clever, and points directly to our maid. Perhaps she's what mind doctors call an hysteric? A mad girl, who hated her mistress and wanted all like her to suffer? Or perhaps, she works for another? Or has some bizarre connection to Mr Dodds, and has now dealt with him, too? It makes no sense to me. Well, whatever the reasons, I'll have someone interview all the staff at Nightingale Walk again. There's more to wheedle out of them, I'm sure of it."

Hatton went to speak, then shook his head.

"What's that, Professor? Something I've said? Or have you got a theory of your own? Don't hold back, Professor. We're short on ideas here and the Commissioner's breathing down my neck as it is, so please, sir, share it."

Hatton waved the smoke away. "I think Dr Finch is the key. Our academic in Cambridge, Inspector? The man Mr Broderig mentioned. Don't you think so? Because the pages marked in the book clearly depict finches, and in my opinion, no woman could have committed this terrible crime. This act is monstrous. To cut a heart out? To pin a man like this? Women use poison, stealth. This is a maniac at work."

The Inspector said, "I think you're right, but still it's strange that your discovery of a pauper girl should lead us here." Adams pointed at the walls, where displays of Merveille du Jour and common emeralds were framed in gilt.

But Hatton's mind was on words and writing again, not moths and butterflies. "I've been thinking, Inspector, about Mr Broderig's letters. He was pale when he spoke of them, more than a little agitated. Could they contain something so dangerous that people are being killed for them? Perhaps the letters are of some value? Perhaps Flora James brought them here to sell them to Mr Dodds and someone followed her? Which means if Mr Broderig knows the content of whatever these letters say, he could also be in danger."

Adams nodded. "Or perhaps he's got something to hide? I worry about the letters, too. We've done a search again, and there's nothing like them in Lady Bessingham's house. As to Mr Broderig's safety, I have two Specials I can assign to Swan Walk, but we need to talk to this Dr Finch, sooner rather than later. We'll leave for Cambridge tomorrow and I'll keep a close eye on Mr Broderig, myself."

"But what about Mr Dodds, Inspector? I'd like to inspect the crime scene properly. It's often the tiniest

110

detail that can illuminate something vital. Subtle signs and traces which tell us more about our victim. Who he was. What he knew. And why someone might want to kill him."

The Inspector stepped back from the corpse. "I don't want to dampen your enthusiasm, Professor, but I give the orders round here. My superiors will want containment, so when we make an arrest, it sticks. I want to proceed carefully, go step by step. My men will seal off this place. Nothing will be touched or tampered with, rest assured. You'll get to do your forensic sweep, but not tonight."

Hatton was not a "by the book man", but nevertheless, to leave a crime scene so quickly didn't feel right, and there was a locked door to another room which might tell them something. He said as much to the Inspector, who only shrugged. "If we find anything, I'll tell you. I think I've made myself clear."

It was unusual and not police procedure, but Hatton complied. "Very well, but no one should be allowed to cross the threshold until I return, and as for the cadaver, I suppose it can wait. But surely you want to check for a list of customers or suppliers? Perhaps Lady Bessingham was a regular here, or even Dr Finch? There's a ledger over by his money box."

The Inspector nodded. "Good thinking, Professor. Leave it with me. There's also the matter of this damn maid. Downstairs staff mixed up with wealthy botanicals. When this gets out, the press will have a field day."

He then turned away and started barking orders. Hatton watched Adams for a moment. He was commanding, resilient — his eyes on the body as if it was nothing unusual. A problem to be solved, cleared up, dealt with as efficiently as possible, so he could move on to the next thing. Yes, thought Hatton, he made an excellent policeman, but the Inspector was not, in the Professor's opinion, what he would call inherently interesting, and, thinking to himself, he was glad Mr Broderig would be going to Cambridge, too. He was better company, with more about him than Inspector Adams — celebrity detective or not.

The crime scene marked, the area sealed off with ropes and "Keep Out/Metropolitan Police Crime Scene" erected in what felt like seconds, Hatton stood with Roumande on the icy pavers, watching the Inspector hare off to interview suspects.

They trudged off to a local tavern together as the night folded in around them, and it was there they supped their ale, staring into space, neither of them uttering a word but both knowing what the other one was thinking. And they had been like this, in synergy, since the very first day they met, on a night very similar to this. A night which was unforgiving, bleak and ending in violence. Knowing that they shared something which could not easily be captured with words. It was more than a feeling. It was more than pushing back boundaries. It was more than science. It was the mystery of death itself, and the draw of imminent danger.

CHAPTER
EIGHT

THE STRAND

Flimflam and fripperies. Olinthus Babbage was the very opposite of grubby. Now there are plenty of folk that thought the common trade of journalism was the lowest of the low. Grub Street, full of grubs and lying creatures. But Mr Babbage certainly wasn't one of them. For despite growing up in the scribbling trade as a purveyor of half-truths for the lurid penny dreadfuls, Babbage had come up smelling of roses. Discovering, as he did, that what the readers really wanted was sensation thinly disguised as news. The longer the words, the bigger the scandal, the better.

Babbage had learnt his trade from the bottom up. Starting with local reports about all manner of things. His own personal favourites being "Scandal — Man of God Kicks Dog" and "Justice! Deaf Mute Gets Hearing." And after a number of years, Babbage found a new job, sidestepping any more hanging out at Newgate or dropping in at The Marshelsea. This job was a plum duff, a real honey pudding of a job. A weekly opinion column situated at the *Westminster Review*, 142 The Strand. An address, most radical, where he plonked himself down and looked at his watch. Five-thirty. What time did Dr Canning say they would meet? Seven o'clock, or thereabouts.

Always a late riser, he had already penned his "Comments on the Day" at home, and along the way to The Strand, via one or two gin palaces, had commissioned several other thinkers, essentially strangers, to "Go on, sir, have a go! My round!" and say what they really thought, not holding back, about the Great Universal Questions. About Rocks, Fossils, and Stones. About Who Was the Real Author of *Vestiges?* "No, sir! Not I," he would say, laughing his great fat head off, but pleased that his gin-soaked companions thought he might be.

But the pubs had closed till opening time again, so here he was, watching the clock and intrigued as to what sensation might be offered tonight. Because he had an appointment with Dr John Canning, who was well known amongst learned circles as having Opinions on the State of The Native Savage and to back up the arguments with apparently enticing pictures to match.

And sensations were just his thing. They were weapons of destruction. Bullet-like, shot out into a searing current of chatter, down The Strand, around Trafalgar Square, along Pall Mall taking a sharp left, then a right and thwack — straight into the heart of Government. Babbage had seen the effect of the *Westminster Review*'s sensations, many times.

And Babbage surmised that this journal was definitely one of the best places to find women, because they flitted in and out of here all day long. Some pretty, some plain, but all, he thought as he chomped on a piece of buttered toast, all a delightful distraction from his very heavy workload.

Because the *Review*, though prestigious, hardly paid Babbage enough to cover his rent, never mind his dinner. Only last month he'd penned for the *Man in Moon*, *Chat*, and *Punchinello*, plus the *London Journal*, the *Illustrated London News*, *The Times* . . . to name but a few. But still he worried, especially in the winter when his feet were freezing and his teeth chattering, that he might go out of fashion. And a tale haunted him of another writer, who was found in a soiled and grubby chamber in Johnson's Court, just a hair's breadth from The Strand, starved to death surrounded by his Notes and his Comments, unread and unpublished. And his body nibbled by vermin.

But enough of that. Babbage took his quill and with a flourish wrote: "Notes on the Rights and Liberties of the Working Man." That done, he started another: "Notes on Man. In His Physical, Social, Moral and Economic Relations with Society." It was warm at 142 The Strand, so he kept up the scribbling and two Notes finished, it was ten to seven and time to meet Dr Canning.

A good early dinner was all that he needed and it was vital, imperative, to feed this intellectual because this evening he must tackle another greater task. An essay. This time an essay on . . . Well, he wasn't going to give it away now, was he? But rumour had it, though not confirmed by The Yard, that one botanical was already dead and rumour had it these letters to be presented tonight would cause a storm and set the world alight.

He rubbed his hands in anticipation and, putting his coat on, stepped out into The Strand and turned towards Fleet Street, walking towards The Old Cheshire Cheese.

No pea souper, no swirling mist or phantasmagorical shadows. Nothing to confuse his journey, only a fluttering of snow. He shivered and walked a tad quicker, until he saw the welcoming lights of the tavern.

Inside the smoky hubbub, Babbage quickly spied who he needed to speak to, because Dr Canning stood up — a distinguished young man — and beckoned him over.

"It's good to meet you, Mr Babbage," Canning said, offering his hand. "And at such short notice, which I am grateful to you for, because a man in your position must be very busy. But I think what I've got to offer you will make your journey, even in this weather, worth the bother."

Babbage swelled with pride, buoyant with, "No need to thank me, good fellow. I'm delighted. Delighted, if a scoop's in play. Always love to hear from the scientific community, especially these days, Dr Canning. As a species, you are so rarely out and about!"

But Canning wasn't laughing; rather he grew furtive, checking over his shoulder. But there was only the usual chatter of a pub and nothing untoward. Flora's habits were infectious. And as he thought on her, he muttered, "Yes, we're holed up with our books and our theories. I rarely get out of the museum, but the suggestions in these letters, and their implications, need to be shared with those who may be sympathetic to such thoughts. But as to the contents? Well, I will say nothing more. My work was only to read them, verify the facts, and pass them on to a credible source. The letters will speak for themselves."

Babbage looked at the scroll on the table, which was tightly bound in rattan. He patted it and said, "First things first. Are you hungry?" and without waiting for a reply, demanded pints of ale to be brought and some of his favourite grub. A supper of chops finished, Babbage slowly uncurled the golden parchment, which no longer smelt of the sea but the headier scent of power and money.

"So these are the famous letters then from Lady Bessingham, Dr Canning? You see, I already knew she had them. Lady Bessingham has favoured me before. But is it true what I've heard? Did they bash her head in with a fossil? Do you know anything more on that?"

Dr Canning shook his head. "Read the letters, Mr Babbage, and you can ask your questions later."

Babbage's eyes widened a little as he looked about the tavern, then back to Dr Canning and dropping his voice said, "Well, if I were you, I'd be careful young man. I've been involved in scoops before. You need to mind where you go and who you talk to. Lady Bessingham trusted us. Are you sure there's no one else she spoke to? And you definitely haven't been followed?"

Canning shook his head, knowing he would move Flora tonight, before the letters were made public. He looked at his pocket watch. Two hours from now, they could be in a carriage and safely gone from London.

But he said nothing to the hack about his fears. He pushed the scroll back towards Mr Babbage and insisted, "As a botanist and anthropologist, a member of the Royal Society etc. etc., I can guarantee you, sir, that you won't be disappointed. But please, delay no longer. The letters, Mr Babbage. Read them, sir."

July 1st, 1855

Dearest Lady Bessingham,

We are now in Empugan. A small Dayak village at the foot of a great mountain on the Simunjan river.

It is a relief to be here amongst the villagers. The walk was hard. My boots filled with leeches and palms tore my hands as we pushed on through the undergrowth. Uman used his parang, a Dayak machete, to hack through the lines of screw pine and rattan which blocked our route to the village. Only Emmerich took delight in this strangling labyrinth.

"Wait a moment. A brief moment, gentlemen." We all had to stop while Emmerich bent down to the ground. "Some fine examples of the yellow Coelogynes." Uman smiled at me as Emmerich lost his great bulbous nose in his treasured petals. "This is extraordinary. Vanda lowii. It grows on the small branches of a tree and its pendant flower reaches the ground. It must be six, no eight foot long. What a marvellous specimen."

And so his chatter continued, as the leaf-strewn floor began to clear, the trees and shrubs began to thin a little, the matted roots abated, and great, lemony beams of light shone down upon our weary bodies, like a sign from Heaven.

Uman told us it was not much farther. That we would soon reach the foot of Ular Mountain and be back near a bend of the Simunjan river. And as he spoke, I felt ready for whatever might lie ahead.

That was a day ago. Never, Lady Bessingham, have I been so glad to see other people. As we made our final push, like a mirage or a waking dream, the pleasant sound of laughing children carried through the shafts of space between the trees. And I will always carry in my heart the sight of San at that moment. He was ecstatic as he called out, as clear and loud as a hornbill, "Selamat petang! Selamat petang pade!" Suddenly the shapes moved in the trees before us. "Selamat petang. Selamat petang pade." This time Uman was speaking. Steady and calm.

At once, the shapes became forms. Before, all had been shadows. I blinked hard, for I did not trust my senses, but the forms were people — a small group of hill Dayaks.

You cannot believe, Lady Bessingham, how glorious these people are. They are not like us. They are taut, sinewy, and bedecked with beads and a blaze of feathers. And swirling all across their bodies, a maze of stars, serpents, angels, and crosses. Twisting tattoos. I have drawn the best and enclose them with this letter. At first, on my first sight of the tribe, I could not take their beauty in. "Selamat petang. Selamat petang, abang." Abang, meaning brother. They are our brothers but we have left this world of Nature far behind in our vast metropolis. We have buried ourselves in hats, gloves, and manners. The Dayak call us orang putus. White man.

Uman and Emmerich spoke batang lupor, the hill tribe dialect, and we soon formed a little party on the forest floor, handing over beads and folds of calico, drinking cups of arak, and showing willing, by chewing betel.

The little party over, we followed the group of Dayaks to their village. And what became apparent was that though he has not said so, I believe Mr Ackerman has been here before. The village heads shook his hand firmly and nodded to him as if there was already some agreement. If this is the case, Katherine, how odd of him not to mention it. I saw him just an hour ago, handing out cigars to a number of local tribesmen and laughing together like they were old friends. It is the first time I have seen Ackerman share anything, and that alone is strange.

Each of my party have been given a bilik, and what luxury it is after the crushing closeness of camping in the forest. San whimpered a little, so he is sharing with his uncle, who seemed keen to watch over the boy, which is only natural, for this is a strange place and we should remember that San is very young. He's not shown such shyness before, but here in Empugan he seems a little nervous. He jumps at the screeching sounds of the jungle and does not play with the other children, who anyway are hidden away from us by their mothers. It is the custom here, I think.

Tomorrow we have an early start. The tuai rumah, the tribal chief, will take us a mile by foot, up into the mountains, where durian fruit are plentiful. This is where the Mias live. The orang-utan. Their name so close to ours here, so that even through words I feel connected. That we are all as one. That we were not created in seven days, as those blinkered priests would have it. That there was no Fall nor Flood but, somehow, we are like the rocks. Do you remember, Katherine, chipping the cliffs in Kent? Do you remember that blustery day, and what we discovered? The fossils and ammonites?

The planet is spinning in space. The earth, trees, rocks, and flowers. Orang-utan. Orang putus. These words so close and our link with the natural world, so dangerously intimate. But these thoughts are sacrilege, Katherine, and I must whisper them because those bigots in the pulpits would shake their fists, insisting that Man was made in His Likeness and the animals were created instantly, as God's miracles. "Let there be light," they cry but forgive me, madam, because I do not think it is light Convention wants, but the darkness of ignorance.

I know you have warned me. And I know how upset you become when arguments about Man are manipulated for different purposes. So you are right to tell me to be careful.

In your last letter, Katherine, you sounded upset. But do not let that unnatural man trouble you. He sounds like a brute, and does not deserve your ear. Perhaps you should ask my father about this Dr Finch, before making any final decision on his future.

But enough of my sage advice! It's so hot here. I must rest now, and lay down this pen. I miss you, Katherine. Can I tell you that? I miss your laughter and your company. I miss your mind. I miss having another person who, like me, is prepared to think the unthinkable and is prepared to delve. And when I think of you, I remember the day you came on a different journey with me. I can recall every detail as if it was yesterday. The corsage you wore. Our picnic on The Backs. Cambridge had never looked so splendid and yet, even there, a shadow loomed, but we would not have our Paradise ruined. I was younger then. Oblivious to the harsh world around me and only intent on the beauty before me. You blinded me, Katherine. You blind me still. And I know when you read these words you will laugh and quip that my head is full of foolish, romantic nonsense. But I will tell you with all my heart, that as I lie here, the image of your face has never been clearer, and that I have never felt so far away from home.

Your faithful etc.

Benjamin Broderig

CHAPTER
NINE

BLOOMSBURY

Unbeknown to Dr Canning, he had indeed been followed. And how did Madame Martineau do it? Well, she'd done a tad of snooping a little earlier round Chelsea way, which is but a hop from The Borough. And the footman at Nightingale Walk had taken her round the back and told her for half a guinea and a little lift of petticoat, a maid had gone missing.

"But chasing maids is an easy occupation, if you've got a nose for it." He'd winked. "Flora James she's called. Right little tease, and when I caught up with her to warn her to scamper, she was holed up at the British Museum in a room with a name plate on which said, 'Dr John Canning'. Bold as brass, she was. I warned her that everyone was looking for her and that she'd better hop it or she would cop it."

Madame Martineau had purred, "Go on . . ."

"She'd been running errands for Lady Bessingham the day before she died, and rumour had it that her and this Dr Canning had been reading letters and calling for jugs of porter, scribbling things and whispering. Not that I told the coppers any of this. Downstairs staff should stick together, unless there's money in it."

And locating Dr Canning had been easy. At the British Museum, it had been the work of a moment to wheedle information from a porter, and only a few moments more to find his lodging rooms in nearby Gordon Square. And when there was no answer at his door on the fifth floor up, she suddenly realised her folly, because only moments earlier hadn't she just passed a gentleman academic who appeared in a hurry? He'd been in the road outside faffing with something. *Merde*. How could she be so stupid? She'd been so intent on finding the lodging rooms, she hadn't noticed, until now, that he'd been carrying letters. Letters! A scroll of golden letters! And so turning on her heels and flying down the stairs and out the door, Madame Martineau was just in time to catch sight of him turning the far corner of the Square.

She followed him back to the museum and it had taken an age until he re-emerged, his head down against the wind. The sun was gone and it was dark as she followed her quarry, her boots making no sound in the snow, even though she was wearing the high stacked ones, which was vain of her. Her armour against the fear of something loathsome, and as she thought on the risks, she put her gloved hands around her throat. By now, she was not far from Newgate and the Old Bailey was just up ahead of her as she followed him into Fleet Street.

But where was he going? She'd looked at the tavern sign, which said The Old Cheshire Cheese. She'd hesitated for a second, and as she did, saw a wave of men come crashing down the road. They were lit by lanterns, shouting obscenities, and a couple of Specials were blowing whistles at them, but it was over in the wink of any eye. A young man wrestled to the ground for demanding something. Some shouting, a punch, a black eye.

What wasted effort, she thought. Did the working man still not realise that sedition was a step-by-step endeavour? That the right words would change everything. She'd heard the speakers in Victoria Park promise it — Giuseppe Mazzini, Marx, and all the others. Their words like fire and she'd clapped, whistled, and shouted that words could indeed bring the rich man down. Her station was settled, was it? Her place determined? Had God stuck a needle in her hand? Had God ordained her place, kneeling at the crotch of a rich man? She shook her little bonnet and the red rabbit fur caught in her mouth.

Inside the tavern, her quarry was over in a corner, and for a moment it was so very tormenting. Should she snatch the letters now and run? Because she was as swift as a breeze when she wanted to be. But the old windbag had been very specific with her that morning, in more ways than one, and after he had finished with her, he'd said, "Madame. Whatever you do, do it quickly, because for each passing minute that you waste of my time, I shall deduct a guinea. And when you come here next time, use the servants' entrance."

"I don't like the dogs," she had pleaded, and she didn't. She hated them.

125

The Duke of Monreith had laughed at her, saying, "Just get the fucking letters, Madame, without the mess and the risks this time. Oh, and before you go . . ."

He had pushed her down and clamped her to him and run his hands over her breasts, but she felt nothing, except the ache of her knees and a pair of frightened eyes that had watched them from a corner of the room. Her pupil, the little one, Tabitha, and they'd done what he wanted. Called him Papa.

She'd spat the word, rancid and bitter, and when it was all finished, she'd looked at herself in a gilt mirror, wiping her mouth. Then turned around and saw the coins as they scattered all about her. He'd call her a filthy whore, but she picked up every one.

And there were more coins to be won here in The Old Cheshire Cheese, she was sure of it, and this work was sweet-smelling. In the tavern, the golden parchment was spread out across a table and she was so close. But then who was this? A great big fat thing who had joined her quarry and was talking to the younger man, pointing at the letters and asking him questions. She watched them all the time, her head down, sipping her gin as they were eating, chatting, laughing even. And when they'd finished, the great lard arse wobbled up, shook the younger man's hand, and she noted that he had the letters now, all of them tied together with rattan, a parchment of gold, just as they were when Madame Martineau had first discovered them under the brushing drawer, a month ago. She cursed herself that she hadn't snatched them when she'd had the

126

chance. But there was no use crying over spilt milk now. She must simply secure the letters, whatever the risk, and be done with it.

Madame Martineau followed her new quarry, but the fat man seemed to notice that something was wrong, and turned round a few times, but then thought better of it and kept on going. My goodness, she thought, but he was an oaf. And talking to himself, she didn't wonder? Yes, his lips were moving but her eyes were on his clothes thinking how many acres of gabardine did it make to finish that pattern? How many buttons? How much snipping . . . and as for the thread?

She would get ahead of him. She was fast, and moved along the alley like a cat, and then went back on herself. The iced sleet cut her face, but in her belly was a fire of such torching anger that she didn't care about the weather, only getting what she needed.

Babbage had glanced quickly at the parchment scroll in his hand thinking "Writer-in-Chief". How grand that sounded. Perhaps, when this was finished, any title would be possible. Why not? Sensations of the scientific kind were just his thing and this one was a corker; a meal ticket to a whole round of parties promising outrage, adulation, applause, and other more enticing rewards.

Ah, yes. How quickly his mind turned to ladies swirling in damask, enticing ankles and domed décolletage. Babbage walked along briskly, smacking his lips. He sneaked the little golden scroll up under his coat and hugged it to his breast, because it was a real sensation. If he cracked through at a pace, he could be finished by midnight, leaving plenty of time for a quick hop over to Granby Street for some gentlemen's entertainment. Now *that* put a spring in his step.

She watched him coming up the alley towards her. What a fine lump of roast pork he'd make. She'd shut him up alright. He was so fat the coat flapped open so that she could see the bulge in his breeches, pathetically small, and that made her laugh a little and so, why not? Why not do it properly this time? A little flimflam of her own?

She stepped out of her corner and hissed, "Fancy a saunter, sir?" And then, before he could take in her waist and say, "Yes please, missy," all was blanking out for Olinthus Babbage, Opinion Writer and Commentator of the *Westminster Review*, with a mind so full, so overflowing, so palpitating with the scoop before him, that he barely noticed her booted ankle and the patch of ice which sent him falling over like a skittle. He didn't feel the gripping and digging which dragged him, groggy and moaning. He barely felt the weight which pressed him down and placed the gag around his mouth. Or the linen thread unravelling which wrapped him tight.

But he saw the bone folder which keeps the seams flat. It was glinting in the moonlight. Carved and pretty and made from horn. Babbage was choking. He was spluttering. Not words like he was used to, but blood.

The thread was so strong, five-ply Irish stuff, the thickest and the best. An awl came next, and was pushed against his neck, searing through his skin,

128

making puncture marks and holes. Followed quickly by the thread because here was a real artisan at work. Babbage had recently written admiringly about them in an article entitled "An Essay on the Rights of the Working Man".

And he didn't know then that it was to be his last social commentary, because his papers were being lifted from him. His headlines and essays snubbed out, and never written. The flattening blade worked quickly. Snow fell. Vermin scuttled.

And when she had finished her work, she sat down in the snow for a second, exhausted, but then found a place to shelter. Because the wind was really whipping and the soughing hurt her ears, but in this little brick and mortar dell, she nestled down. Just a little look to make sure. To taste that taste again. Madame Martineau opened up the scroll and up rose that delicious scent of pressed orchids and heady, tropical rain and fecundity, the type she had only ever dreamt of. Because she did have dreams, helped by salicene to escape the city which hemmed her in.

August 1st, 1855

Lady Bessingham,

I should have read the sign better, for it was there. On the morning of the hunt, one of our party had taken to his bed in a state of mild delirium. I thought little of it at the time and Mr Ackerman was adamant, saying it was nothing more than a passing tropical sickness. But I can still hear Mr Demarest now, as I write, moaning in the hut next to mine.

Before we left him behind, we gave him quinine. The villagers put little wooden figures all about to drive the evil spirits back down into the Underworld, which they said were infecting him, but perhaps they drove the spirits upwards and they followed us, along the mountain trail. But how should I write this? And what should I tell you? I still do not really know what happened out there in the forest, but I am altered and I am not the same. You must hear my story, Katherine. It is a confession.

As we set off, Ackerman took the lead, and as we walked, lectured me on the trade of specimen collecting. "Supply and demand, that's what you need to understand, ja? This work's not about pretty pictures and Latin classification. It's about survival, but then you would hardly know what that means, would you?" I couldn't argue that I wasn't rich. I could see that some of us were here in Borneo to pursue something like a hobby whilst Mr Ackerman with his shabby breeches and worn-down boots was in many ways no better than a workhorse. But he was not without luxuries. He had a fine French gun, a belt of English leather, and an endless supply of whisky, which he didn't share with the rest of us. A gift from a grateful client, he liked to boast.

"You can have anything you want in this country if you are prepared to work, ja? Why, I could buy ten of these boys," a wave at San, who cowered from him, "for a box of cigars."

130

I gave him short shift but he continued. "And don't think I haven't noticed you peering at my ledger trying to see what names I have in there, but I can assure you, it's none of your damn business."

"Settle down now, Mr Ackerman," despaired Emmerich. "Mr Broderig hasn't been anywhere near your ledger. None of us would dream of being so presumptuous."

Mr Ackerman shot everything that moved, even if the creature was not worth the ammunition. I watched him eyeing a sick Presbytis rubicunda which I would normally have shot myself, its skin being a glorious auburn colour, but this one was shabby, dragging its feet, its life almost over. We all knew that it would disappear into the depths of the forest to die quietly, its final resting place a nest of leaves.

Bang. One shot. A brutish laugh, then up hopped Ackerman and seized the dead monkey with his hands and tossed it into the bushes. San and Uman were silent, but I read their eyes. This is not how we treat Nature. This is not the way. But I said nothing, nothing at all.

Emmerich had no interest in catching the mighty Mias. It was a creature, he said, that when you looked in its eyes, looked back at you pleading for its life. Instead, he came only for plants and flowers.

"Benjamin, stay close to me and learn. Mr Ackerman would choose to walk past this little botanical treasure but he would be foolish, for this, gentlemen . . ." We all stopped in our tracks as he pointed at a hideous plant.

"Nepenthes villosa. Extremely rare. Prise it open, Uman. That's right, slowly does it." Uman slid the blade between the teeth. The plant opened, revealing two scaly bodies, blank eyes.

"Are those lizards inside?" I asked, astonished.

"It's not just the mighty that's king in this forest, Benjamin. This plant doesn't need to beat its chest or break a neck. It merely opens its mouth, thus." He prized the pitcher plant open further. "A lizard climbs in and das schmeckt gut, ja?"

A slow and menacing "clap . . . clap . . . clap" came from the wings. "I think you have made your point, Professor Mann. Now gather up your little pets because some of us have a living to make."

Emmerich smiled as if to say "Take no notice of him," but something about Ackerman's manner troubled me. Even little San looked anxious and sprang to Emmerich's help to gather up the pitcher plants. Five boxes filled and we started up again.

It was only a few minutes of trekking back along the mountain trail when I heard a distinctive rustling in a tree above my head. "Mias," whispered the tribal chief. He waved us to lie down, stay silent, as a fully grown male crashed through the canopy showering us with leaves. I glanced back at Emmerich who smiled, nodded.

The crack of the gun twisted in my stomach, like a knife. Ackerman. I didn't see him keel up and point the barrel of the gun, but without a flicker of hesitation, I knew the shot was his.

The great beast fell to the ground and the jungle roared its disapproval. Birds screeched and monkeys howled as the dust rose up into the air, then all was deadly silent.

"Bullseye. Straight through the heart. My aim is getting better, ja?" The others held back for a moment, afraid the sleeping giant would stir, but Ackerman was right about death. And I asked myself, could I really shoot these creatures? Bringing down a hornbill or a squirrel was easy. But something made me ache in the pit of my belly. Was it guilt? Mourning is too strong a word, but it was loss. And yet this was the work we were here for.

Ackerman gave the ape a kick. "It's dead. No question." He was still panting from the kill. "What are you waiting for? Hurry yourselves. I want at a whole troop before the sun is down. Amsterdam Museum will pay a fortune for these skins. We'll leave this one by this myrtle till we have finished the hunt." Ackerman continued haranguing the servants. San scurried around, avoiding Ackerman's odd swipe at his head as he went about his tasks.

"Maaf, tuai rumah. Maaf, maaf." Over and over poor San muttered, pleading his apologies to the dead ape for doing the white man's bidding. And as I watched them, I saw Uman stroke the creature's hair then crouch down and listen to its heart, his head cocked like a bird. "Its spirit hasn't left," Uman said, and then began to hum a low long chant. "Ummmm toh Urang. Ummm toh Urang."

Ackerman hissed in my ear, "You see why Orang Putus is Master here, Mr Broderig? Still, we have to let the Natives have their mumbo jumbo nonsense. But tell the chief we need to find another now. Make haste or I shall leave the lot of you behind." But before we all moved on, I looked back at the great ape. Its brown eyes staring out into its forest kingdom, lost forever.

We shot the apes all day, as Ackerman insisted. Five in as many hours. I took a young female down from the trees with a single shot. She limped away, howling, as Ackerman rasped in my ear, "Finish her off. Did you see the baby clinging to her back? Finish her, Broderig, before I do."

I shot again. Another crack and I reloaded for a third. But someone pulled my gun down. "It's enough, Mr Broderig." It was Uman. "The Mias is dead."

I peeled the baby off its dead mother and it gave out such a yell I almost dropped the creature. I gave the little Mias over to San, who held it tight.

"It won't live," said Ackerman. "Shoot it now. It will only sicken and then the skin's worth nothing. Here, give me the Mias and I'll deal with it." But the little boy was too quick for the Dutchman, and in a flash he had shimmied up a tree with the Mias clinging to him.

"Leave him alone, Mr Ackerman." It was Uman who stood directly in front of Ackerman, neither threatening nor afraid. And for a fleeting moment, I think Ackerman saw what I saw. If there was a hierarchy on this trip, it wasn't simple.

We piled up the bodies and built a fire. San sat playing quietly with the infant, whispering, "Maaf, maaf," meaning sorry. Ackerman skinned his prizes. Orang-utans are magnificent creatures even in death.

Mine was left till last. I worked the skin myself. I felt murderous, but still I scraped. The skin was a good one. I boiled the bones. I asked San to leave the baby and help me finish my work, but when the boy tried to prise the clinging Mias off, it gave out such a scream, I told San not to bother. Ackerman scowled at me, and I believe he would have hit the boy, but tropical nights are sudden, and this one fell before the deed was done. And so, we burrowed down to sleep. The little creature had tucked itself into the boy's arms and they curled together, like innocents, their faces gently lit by the dying embers until the darkness took them.

The crack of the whip brought me to my senses. I opened my eyes to see Ackerman, standing over me like some vile prison warden. I'd noticed his whip the day we left Sarawak. He hadn't touched it until now, but as I cursed him and staggered to my feet, I sensed his mounting agitation.

"Our guide here," the towering Ackerman embraced the tuai rumah in a menacing grip, "has just informed us that he wishes to return to Empugan, giving us only one day's more hunting. So, English boy, if it's not too much trouble?"

Uman and the others were already up finishing the skinning and tagging. Emmerich was squatting by the fire. I smiled at my benevolent botanist, surrounded as he was by a cluster of orchids. "I gathered these this morning. The forest is full of them. Mr Banta knows more about my chosen field than he would at first let on, isn't that right Mr Banta?"

135

"I bow to your superior knowledge, Professor Mann, but what do you think we should call this?" asked Mr Banta, looking at me for an answer. The orchid in his hand was spectral white and covered with flecks of silver. We named it there and then. An incomparable beauty. Paphiopedilum katheriniadum. Your namesake, Katherine, and as I held the petals in my hand, a damsel fly weaved above my outstretched palm. Its needle body a flash of violent, brilliant blue, its wings crossed with a labyrinth of ebony veins. And at that very moment, a stream, a beam, a thread of gold pierced down and lit the insect from the sky and it cast a tiny, hovering shadow across the luminous flower. And then the fly lifted its membrane wings and, in a flutter, was gone.

"San. Get here, now boy. We'll tag and measure in Empugan." Ackerman sweated as he loaded his gun. "The sun is rising fast and I have a hoard of creditors to pay."

Packing up our kit and picking up our boxes, we moved off.

For three hours we moved liked ghosts. Ackerman went ahead of us, sprung like a coil, his gun pointing this way and that. San clutched the baby Mias, which was sucking his thumb, keeping it quiet. For three weary hours we followed the guide who urged us onwards, hold back, lie down, with just a show of his hand. But there was nothing except empty forest. The Mias had gone.

"Evil spirits," whispered Uman.

I could see the sky begin to darken. A crack of lightning. A rumbling answer.

"A storm is coming, the spirits are unhappy. We must say a prayer, or turn back," said Uman.

"No." Ackerman spun around, his face smouldering anger. "I say we go on. My only master, and yours may I remind you, is money. I need another beast to make it worth my while. Large or small. Young or old. It doesn't matter. The baby would do it. What do you say, San? A child and his little monkey. Yes, I'll take the pair of them together. You're very quiet San. Lost your tongue?"

San shrunk back, away from Ackerman's leer, shielding the infant Mias, but Ackerman grabbed him by the arm, stroking his hair, his eyes all the time on Uman.

"What do you think, Mr Broderig? I know the English are very keen on children."

Uman grabbed the boy back and shouted at the frightened child, "Get on with your work and stay away from the white man."

The boy obeyed his uncle, wiping back his tears.

"Leave the boy alone, Mr Ackerman. We understand your meaning and it's very badly done. You can make up your catch near Empugan. Show some respect, sir, and leave the child alone."

Emmerich was shaking as he spoke. His hat askew, his face furrowed by years in the eastern tropics. But despite this sorry appearance, Emmerich moved himself solidly between the malevolent hunter and his latest prey.

"You foolish old man," said Ackerman. "And what have you contributed to this trip, I'd like to know? I suspect your decision to join this merry throng was not altogether for scientific reasons. Am I right or am I wrong, Professor Mann? Are you not married to a very Christian lady who is waiting vainly for her husband to return? But who needs religious devotion when you can have a beauty like our little San? These dark fellows know what I'm talking about. Heh, I'm speaking to you . . ."

Uman looked quickly across at the boy. But Ackerman hadn't finished.

"So, Mr Broderig? Perhaps you were not aware of Professor Mann's little . . . let's just call it an arrangement, ja? He keeps her quiet, this little beauty, but not quiet enough." Ackerman threw back his head and laughed. "I'll wager you didn't discuss that over cribbage, when you persuaded Broderig to hire you as his botanical chaperone. How much you, and so many others, like to lift a bit of petticoat."

It was at precisely those words, Katherine, that I brought him down with one blow. Ackerman fingered his whip but he read the group well. Five men against one. He stumbled away muttering and every now and then spat out gobs of blood, as the rest of us fell quiet. Above our heads, the clouds thickened and another crack shattered across a burnished orange sky. The chief made his offerings but then another crack — nearer this time. The Mias chattered and bore its teeth, grabbing San's hair. San grinned at me and shrugged his shoulders.

"The storm is getting closer."

Uman started hacking down great umbrella leaves to shield us from the rain. The sky blazed cinnabar. A million dying embers trailed across the sky. "It won't last," shouted Emmerich above the pounding din. I smiled at the others in camaraderie, but our group, despite the storm, was already splintered. Ackerman stood apart, letting the rain drench him to the skin. Was it a show of bravado? Or something else? The only thing he had bothered to cover was his gun. He had placed it in one of the storage boxes, his heavy boot upon it. Then suddenly, as it had begun, the rain stopped. The sun broke out beams of yellow through the blackened clouds, which shifted into whispers, then disappeared. The storm was over.

After the rains had gone, we settled down for the night, and I must have slept for hours. When I woke, San's hand was shaking me gently. "Mr Broderig. The Mias." His eyes had filled with tears.

"Your baby, San? Is that what you mean?"

"It's gone, Mr Broderig."

"It can't have gone, San. Let's try the riverbank. There are jack there and durian. Maybe your little pet is down there stuffing himself to the brim?"

It was the earliest point of dawn, when the air is fresh and cool. Basking lizards shot like skirmishes into the pools of circling water.

"We'll find him, San. I promise." The boy looked up at me with half a smile.

It was a little in the distance but I knew what we'd found. Up ahead, at first all I could see was a curtain of insects, hovering around the drooping branch of a belian tree. I swept the flies back with my hand not caring if they bit or poisoned me. The body hung limp from the tree. The little Mias had been slit from ear to ear. Its dead head lolled to one side. He had hung the baby, Katherine. Not content with slicing the ape's throat, he had hung it from a branch with a rope of rattan. I took my knife and cut the Mias down. And I knew who'd done this. It was Ackerman.

I took the boy's hand and, stumbling, we wandered back together. Along the way, I found some fallen leaves and wrapped the Mias in a shroud and as we made our way back to the camp, I saw Ackerman still lying on his pua-kumbu and I readied myself.

"Get up." My anger needed no announcement. "Get up and tell the others what you did. Get up, Mr Ackerman, or God knows, I'll get you up myself."

Ackerman stirred. I raised my voice again.

"Get up you coward, for here he is, gentlemen, the Great White Hunter, and look what he got, a real prize catch. Ah, yes, there's the knife. Why, you couldn't even be bothered to clean it and cover your tracks. You are a damned coward, sir. Get up, I say."

Ackerman pulled himself up. "I was doing it a favour, putting it out of its misery, ja? But what do you know about this world? You're just a passing visitor to Borneo. Has your aristocratic family ordered you here to make your way? To check on the colonies? To prove yourself a man? Some of us have a real living to make. The skin will fetch a bit. The bones, too."

"Get up, damn you" was all I could say. His bravado was beyond me.

The rest of the camp was awake now and I could feel their questioning eyes following me as I lifted my gun.

"For the last time, Ackerman, get up and tell us what you meant by this. The boy has done nothing to you. The skin of this Mias is worthless. This was spite and nothing more."

Ackerman swaggered before me, the butt of the rifle jutting ready under his chin, his finger on the trigger. He took a step forward. "I wouldn't point your rifle at me, English boy. I think we both know who's the better shot. It's just payment for what you did, Broderig. You might well have slit the beast yourself."

"Please, Mr Broderig." It was San, pleading with me. "Please, let's just bury the Mias."

I could have shot Ackerman there and then but something held me back. I knew, when it came to guns, it was an unequal match. That he was the better shot. For all my desire to punish the man, I failed to do it.

"Come, Benjamin. He isn't worth it."

It was Emmerich and I felt my anger abating. It ebbed away like a tide, but something else flooded in to replace it. This was not the trip I had planned. This was not the adventure I had dreamt of when I crossed the seas on The Advancement. I hadn't come to Borneo to prove myself to the likes of Ackerman. An ill-educated lout brought up by some washerwoman stinking of fish in Holland. I was losing myself in the forest, Katherine. I was losing my sense of self-worth.

Uman meanwhile was busying himself, cutting up long pieces of coppery bark, which lay scattered all around our camp. Soon there was enough to make a little box. We laid the Mias inside the coffin, and that done, San placed a little carving on the top. A wooden hornbill, to ward off evil spirits, which were now circling all around us.

"He'll not have the baby's skin," whispered Uman. "But no good will come of more bad words. The orang putus is powerful. We need his work to feed our families. You will go back to England, Mr Broderig, and we will not see you again. But Mr Ackerman will always need us. We must accept that."

Of that, I couldn't argue. I knew that England would always be my home and that this time in the forest was fleeting. That it was men like Ackerman that ruled the day. So there was nothing else for it. We buried the creature and packed up the camp and set off back to Empugan.

This time, the chief followed the bend of the river. The mighty Simunjan roared. We kept to the high banks above it, slowly and silently, allowing the sound of the jungle to be our words. I was lulled by it. Soothed by it. Admonished by it. Melodic gibbons hurled themselves in acrobatic delight, warning us to stay out of their sight. Proboscis monkeys growled their disapproval. They seemed to know everything, Katherine. What had gone and what would come.

No good comes of evil. And evil was in the air. It smelt stale and bitter and it had rancour on its face. Now the Mias was gone, San was the weakest, and more than once on that walk, I noticed Ackerman finger his whip and curse under his breath if the child fell behind or stumbled.

But then a strange thing happened.

142

Somehow, we seemed to find ourselves back in the very spot where I had shot my first and last orang-utan. The ground was still crushed from the weight of our boots, and there was a stunted myrtle tree where we had stacked the cadavers. Nothing had changed here, despite all that had changed for us.

San was the first this time to hear it. The faintest rustle. And then a crack and falling branches, just up ahead of us. Orang-utan. But why this part of the forest, where their brothers and cousins had been slain? Why had they come back here when they were kings of the forest and could go where they pleased?

"The tuai rumah says no more killing today. We must return to Empugan." I quite clearly saw Mr Banta nod in agreement and Emmerich bow his head in respect. But before any of us could stop him, Ackerman had pushed past us, gun loaded. He moved like lightning, the fusil de chasse cocked and ready. A gentleman's gun, in a murderer's hand.

This time I didn't wait motionless, but as quick as Ackerman, I was after him. I had a plan. I moved with speed. I had two shots. So had he. I think I heard the others calling after me, but the voices soon faded to whispers.

The forest was suddenly dense. I could still hear crashing ahead of me. It was the Mias, I was sure of it. "Ackerman," I hissed through the spaces in the branches. "Ackerman, leave the beast." Another rustle, then a foot tread. Orang-utans don't walk. They stay above the ground and swing through branches. "Ackerman," this time louder. "It's Broderig." No answer came but more rustling. Ape or man? I couldn't be sure. My head was spinning and then through the dense foliage I saw something move.

A huge male. One shot in the right place and it would be over. This was dangerous and I knew it, but I had hunted at Ashbourne and seen what could happen with two in the fray, guns loaded. Accidents happen and the Mias had to be saved, at any cost, can you see that, Katherine?

I fired my first shot in the air. Howls and shrieks rose into the canopied treetops. The Mias had sprung away from me, which is what I intended, but I kept on going, knowing my real purpose. And then beyond a pile of fallen tree, I saw Ackerman. I saw his gun glinting, its pin-thin shadow taunting me as he aimed straight ahead. "Ackerman. Enough." He caught my eye and I'm sure he smiled, but then he was gone.

I had one more shot. Breaking back rapier branches with my arms and the butt of my gun, inured to the tears at my skin, springing over roots like a civet. The steaming jungle urging me on. Breathless, I stopped. A rustle again, so close I could smell him. Yes, it was Ackerman, his back to me, readying himself. One more crack and it was certain death for the ape, but I had made my decision. I pulled back the trigger and focused my eyes through the sighting of the gun.

For a split fraction of time, I tasted triumph. But then I tasted dread. I knew what I had done. I had shot a man, in cold blood, to save the Mias.

I stood for just a moment longer but the moaning grew louder. Ackerman had been blasted to hell, a ball

144

through his gut. There in the forest, looking at me, his eyes seeing what I had seen, knowing what I knew. The Mias had been in his view, I am sure of it, but I had been quicker this time. I had been the better shot.

He was spilling out on the reddening earth, still full, I thought, of marble cake and Machars whisky, for I had watched Ackerman this morning, as the rest of us buried the baby. He was happily swigging single malt and chomping on boterkoeke, as if nothing had happened. Well, I thought, now it had.

My confession, Katherine, is not that I shot Ackerman. Hunting incidents are common enough, are they not? They are two a penny in England during the season, and we accept they are part of the chase and the bloodletting; the cycle of country living. What I confess is that I felt nothing. No remorse. No regret. No asking forgiveness of God. Just a void, where answers should be.

I stood over him and watched him fade away. How long it took, I couldn't say, for the wound was deep and he fought it. I was quite happy to leave him there for the ants and the other jungle scavengers but then the others arrived. It could have been hours. Or minutes. I couldn't tell. Emmerich, good fellow that he was, insisted we take the body back to the village. Rather fittingly, I thought, we piled his body onto a makeshift stretcher just as we had done with the Mias, pulling the heap behind us.

And I thought it right and proper to call them my apes now, for Ackerman no longer had use of them. I also took his ledger. The others wanted no part of it. I offered them a percentage of the money, knowing the

British Museum would pay me handsomely. San and Uman refused, saying the Mias bodies carried evil spirits and the money would lead to despair. Mr Banta said I should at least give something to the mother in Vlissingen. He said he would tell her the news when he returned to Holland, and this would be sooner now than he had originally planned.

So there you have it. What more can I tell you, Katherine? Perhaps the forest played its part and deceived me. And as I write this, I can still hear Mr Demarest calling out in his devilish fever. His voice is not so unlike Ackerman's. But these are not the words spoken as Ackerman held on to his guts and the last vestiges of his life. Mr Demarest's words are what you might expect of a good man, who is dying and must make his peace with his God.

But Ackerman, his last strength failing, had pulled me down, held me tight, his fingers around my wrist, digging. When I look there now, I can still see the marks. He pulled me down, till my ear was at his mouth. He wanted me to hear him; he wanted me to hear his secret.

Your faithful servant,
Benjamin Broderig

Madame Martineau finished reading the letters and pressed the scroll to her lips. And kissed the golden parchment not once, but three times. A secret. And how she loved a secret, because secrets were eminently valuable. Perhaps not now. Perhaps this secret would have to wait a little, but still it was definitely worth knowing about. She smiled at her own brilliance and pushed the scroll into her muffler because it was cold in the alleyway where she was sheltering, and it was still snowing, although she didn't mind the weather and let the flakes flit upon her blue-black lashes.

CHAPTER
TEN

BISHOPSGATE STATION

At the entrance to Bishopsgate Station, Inspector Adams was grabbing whatever was being pressed upon him by a posse of policemen. It looked like paperwork to Hatton. Mountains of the stuff. The Professor had left most of his behind in the morgue, thinking Roumande was a capital fellow when it came to that sort of work. Hatton watched Adams as he shook off the Specials and joined himself and Mr Broderig near the ticket office. "Have you got the autopsy report for Lady Bessingham, Professor?" asked the Inspector.

Hatton rummaged in his surgical bag, but had to start walking, because Inspector Adams didn't wait for an answer and was in danger of losing him in a wave of hats, cases, and umbrellas. Fat ladies in huge flounces with trunks, and children of varying ages with governesses, were looking cross and agitated with their charges, as the crush of excitement pushed the men along the platform of the Great Eastern Line.

"Shouldn't we get our tickets first, Inspector?" Benjamin Broderig tried shouting above the tremendous roar of the engine, which was spluttering great billows of steam into the air.

"What?" cried the Inspector, still moving at great speed through the hurly-burly. "What did you say? Come on, gentlemen, or we'll be left behind."

"All aboard the ten-fifteen," shouted the guard as he puckered up his lips to blow the whistle. Adams waved a card in his face and the guard ushered all three men to the front of the train.

The Inspector sat down in First Class, facing Broderig and Hatton, his great legs stretched along the carriage floor. "You'd think I was leaving for China the fuss my superiors make. I shouldn't have to ask permission. I shouldn't have to explain myself. Now then, gentlemen, first things first." Adams dumped his huge pile of papers on the seat.

A minion was duly summoned, and on return to the carriage, settled down a large tray of sandwiches and tea in a polished silver pot.

Adams wiped the crumbs from his mouth with the back of his hand and, after checking that the carriage door was shut, said, "So, Lady Bessingham knew this Dr Finch, you say Mr Broderig? Do we know how well?"

Broderig shrugged his shoulders. He had a green ledger on his lap and seemed intent on studying it, but with a sigh shut it again and answered Adams. "As I told you, Inspector, they were in tacit discussions about the Nature of Man. Dr Finch is of a mind that God had made us savage, but Lady Bessingham felt he went too far. It is very indiscreet to discuss these matters, but . . ."

"Please, Mr Broderig. This is a murder inquiry."

"Indeed it is, Inspector. Very well." Broderig cleared his throat, putting the ledger back in his bag. "I have reason to believe that Dr Finch put Lady Bessingham in a compromising position. She would never admit such a faux pas, but she wrote to me when I was in Borneo. She was very upset. She believed Dr Finch's theories on Man were being stretched to suggest our appetites were essentially ungovernable. That God had created not a harmonious world, but a simmering sphere, perpetually spinning in chaos. That no matter what harm was caused or where it led us, our desires should be followed. Like many theologians, I surmised that Dr Finch had lost his faith in God, but not his rampant interest in women."

Adams smiled. "But how on earth did they meet? They seem worlds apart."

Broderig replied, "Finch is a great admirer of Charles Lyell, from what I've heard. I believe the pair of them met when Lady Bessingham held a soiree some years ago, in support of ideas contained within *The Principles of Geology*. Have you read it, Inspector?"

Adams laughed this time, and said of course not, but he'd read another quite like it. Broderig smiled, a little mockingly. "Not *Vestiges*, Inspector? I didn't think a man in your position would have time for such a tome. What did you think of it, sir?"

Adams took a rolled cigarette, lit it, and said, "As a Christian, I have concerns as to its suggestions on the origins of the universe, but on the whole, what thinking man could argue with the facts of all these recent discoveries? That the earth is made up of sediments and layers of rock, which have formed over time? But essentially the book is a jumble with all of its ramblings about the cosmos. It is a hodgepodge, really, and I couldn't understand its point."

"You are not alone, Inspector. It is a shoddy piece of work and far from scientific. You should read Charles Lyell. The man is a genius and a great supporter of other scientists, such as Mr Darwin. And you, Professor? Have you read it?"

Hatton bristled slightly at the idea, the book having gone out of fashion some years ago, despite the furore it caused at the time. "No, but I have a few fossils at my lodging rooms in Gower Street and it seems eminently right to me, as to any Man of Science, that they represent the magnitude of time. And that transmutation is an argument few of us can deny, whatever the Church would have us think." Hatton looked out the window, recalling the arguments he'd had. His student days at Edinburgh had been hard graft, broken up only occasionally when he lost his temper with someone, rarely over a woman, but more often, on a point of fact. His interest in forensics only just beginning to form, knowing that it would be a long haul before he could get to where he was going. But in the meantime, he would dedicate himself to seeing off the ignorant, the bigoted, or the simply unknowing.

The ripples of discontent science could cause in Society never failed to astonish Hatton, because to him it seemed obvious that Man should pursue Truth. No matter how many feathers it ruffled. *Vestiges* had Bible bashers frothing at the mouth, but frankly, it was only a continuation of other people's work. Erasmus, Darwin, Lamarck, and many other thinkers agreed that the world must have transformed over millions of years, that man's brain was not so unlike the apes when it was dissected. Hadn't notable surgeons already proven this in the cutting rooms of Edinburgh University? And yet, despite all the evidence, this work was seen as sacrilegious and disreputable by those whose positions might be upturned by any unsettlement of the status quo.

Adams spat a little of the tobacco on the floor. "So initially this was a meeting of minds, which quickly led to an uncomfortable spat? A beautiful widow with ideas in her head and a lascivious academic? Is that what you're saying, Mr Broderig?"

Broderig leant forward in his seat and said, "All I know is that he was removed from University College by force, and was very lucky to find himself another position at Sidney Sussex. They are extremely liberal at that college. But I believe he has been troubled by scandal on and off for years."

Hatton intervened, "And our victim, Mr Dodds. Any views on him? Could they have known each other? His bookshop is but a hop from University College."

"I cannot help you with that sorry case. Before you told me of the terrible murder, I had never heard of the man."

"Well, perhaps this Dr Finch will be able to illuminate us." Adams closed his notebook and seemed suddenly impatient. "I hope this isn't going to be a wasted trip. It seems I have to answer for every minute of my time these days. But let's leave that conversation till we get to Cambridge." Adams put his hand out to Hatton. "I had better look at the autopsy report now."

Hatton handed over the reports, both the one Adams had asked for and the one he hadn't. "Two reports for one death, Professor? You have been busy at St Bart's."

Hatton was embarrassed, but he'd promised his friend.

"The other is for the pauper girl, Inspector."

The Inspector raised an eyebrow. "Which girl? Last night's or another's? As I say, these girls turn up time and time again. It sounds harsh, Professor, but you of all people know that London is made that way."

Hatton took a sharp intake of breath. What was wrong with the man? But he said simply, "Monsieur Roumande specifically asked me to give you the report. The girl we found yesterday evening was different from the others, but we are convinced her death is somehow related. She led us to Dodds and there were clear pinpricks around her wrists. But she wasn't gay. She was a virgin, Inspector, her hymen still intact, and the previous ones were beaten and tortured. But Roumande believes whatever the cause of death, all these girls fall within the jurisdiction of The Yard, and he has written to you, I believe, on a number of occasions, because the body count goes back some years now, and yet we've heard little."

Adams glanced at the document. "Thank you, Professor. I am aware of your diener's letter writing. How could I not be? All answered, I believe, by myself or one of my colleagues. But what a marvel that

153

Frenchman is. Quite the capital fellow. Where on earth did you find him?" Hatton smiled at the Inspector's sarcasm, and took it for what it clearly was, the guilt of doing nothing. Adams continued, "I will look into these deaths, but it amuses me that an Englishman should be so steered by a foreigner."

"He's been at St Bart's for far longer than I, Inspector. He was promoted to be Chief Diener some time ago, and as you know, is widely admired. His work goes far beyond that of a simple mortuary assistant."

Broderig had been listening and chipped in, "So another girl was found yesterday, Inspector? You made no mention of it before. Is she worth so very little?" He shook his head, his disapproval palpable.

"The pauper girls are no concern of yours, Mr Broderig," said Adams sharply, lighting up another penny smoke.

"Of course." Broderig smiled. "But you're wrong about foreigners, Inspector. I am greatly admiring of them and have been fortunate enough to work with many during my travels, and nearly all have impressed me with their competence. I watched Monsieur Roumande at work in the morgue yesterday. His stitching was excellent and he took such care of the cadavers, especially the little girl — far beyond simply a mark of respect, if I may say."

"Ah yes, the stitching, as well as the writing." Adams dragged on his cigarette. "And you let him wield the dissection knife as well, Professor? Is that not just a little unusual?"

154

Hatton chose not to answer but instead looked out of the frosted window. The train was gathering speed, shuddering through the eastern parts of the city. His travels through these parts were rare, but Roumande and his team of body collectors were regular visitors and knew each turning alley, especially in the summer when the fevers hit, clasping a choking hand around the rookeries. But looking at this frozen city now, it glistened, a fairy-tale place.

The Chief Inspector, putting the pauper girl's report aside, continued, "But let's stick to the case in hand. Is there anything in here I don't know?"

They'd already discussed the ink and wax earlier, but Hatton had kept a little back. "I don't think I told you about the opiate test we carried out."

Adams nodded to him to continue. Broderig excused himself. He'd clearly had enough, and so Hatton waited for the young man to leave, not wanting to worsen the situation. Suffering the indignity of the cutting had been enough, and there was definitely more to his relationship with Lady Bessingham than Broderig was saying.

"Well?" said Adams.

"All vital organs were extracted, Inspector. We took a sample from her abdomen and a large piece of her lower intestine and surrounding stomach wall. The odd odour I detected in Chelsea was a mild opiate."

"You're sure, Professor?"

"Quite sure. Poisons, once digested, are notoriously difficult to identify, but I'm embarking on a method which is widely practised in Germany but not something I would want anyone else to know about." Hatton looked over his shoulder where he could see Broderig just beyond their carriage, walking up and down the aisle. "We made a little stew by boiling the stomach samples with water, straining it, and removing all bits of flesh. You've heard of the Metzger Mirror, of course?" The Inspector nodded. "Well, we used the basic principle of that test but have perfected it, trapping the vapour rising off the liquor in a test tube and then inserting a shard of cold metal at the opening. We scraped off the film and added two drops of sulphuric acid; by its colour it definitely wasn't arsenic. Lady Bessingham wasn't poisoned. She was probably using laudanum."

"Impressive stuff, Professor. I have bouts of insomnia myself, and take the odd drop when I need to. There's no shame in it." Adams took a pencil from his frock coat pocket and jotted down a note or two. "All very illuminating."

The train by now was hurtling along and London was a whisper, a memory. Adams sat back, patted his report and closed his eyes. Hatton watched the white world slip past as the train rolled and juddered.

"Is he asleep, Professor?" Hatton looked away from the frosty window to see Broderig come back in the carriage, and smiled at his companion, suggesting more tea.

"Allow me, Professor but not tea for it's almost noon. I'll get something a little stronger." He was quickly back with two glasses and a bottle, swinging his travel bag onto the luggage rack. "I think the Inspector has definitely nodded off." The new friends laughed as they looked at the older man snoring, whose burns lifted in a nicotine breeze.

"I don't blame him," said Hatton. "I'm exhausted myself. Your health, Mr Broderig."

"So, Professor. Have you told the Inspector everything? On both reports?"

"But still no news on the maid? Lady Bessingham always wrote such promising things about Flora James. She was quite taken with her. She told me that although the girl was young, she was clever and had the ability for self-improvement. I understood Flora often accompanied Katherine on visits to places of interest, as a friend and a confidante. I think Flora provided company while I was gone from her."

Hatton agreed, though in truth knowing little of women and their needs but he was sensitive to others and quickly changed the subject. Broderig stared into space but then seemed to recover himself, asking Hatton about the wider aspects of forensic work, and at once Hatton felt the weight of the investigation lift. He was delighted, because he'd never found such enthusiasm for the subject beyond his own medical circle.

This young man's mind was like his own. Eagle-eyed, seizing on every detail. They discussed the rapture of dissection, telling their own different stories. Hatton in relation to time, death, injury. Truth lit by microscope and lamp, tested, tagged, and concluded.

Hatton felt more at home as he said, "My work is a burgeoning science, which unfolds the truth about men." Hatton poured another glass and offered one to Broderig.

"We understand each other, Professor. Botany tells us similar truths. Truths about our world. In Borneo, I touched its very centre. Its overwhelming variety."

And Hatton felt it, too, as the young man's voice ebbed and flowed like a wave on a distant shore. He let this new world take him on a journey, the sound of each vowel and consonant triggering colours in his mind, leading to discovery.

And as Hatton listened, the land was getting flatter, but the two friends had gone elsewhere, to a place that soared into azure and rose up majestic, verdant and luminous. Monkeys chattered, birds fluttered, lizards dipped and basked. Hatton let it all devour him. This tropical storm. This tale of Borneo.

Sarawak
December 1st, 1855

Dear Katherine,

Months have passed, so forgive me for this neglectful silence, but I have not done much letter writing. I have been playing only chess but I have read your letters, for which I thank you. By now, you will have most of mine. I cannot say what you will make of them.

All was left behind in Empugan. Good as their word, the boatmen arrived to deliver us back. We drifted through the lilies and as the boatmen dipped their oars in the pools of amber water, with each push and stroke homewards, I felt the memory of the ape hunt slipping from me.

Mr Demarest did not survive, Katherine. The fever took him. This strong fellow was skin and bone when death came. I wish I could tell you that the end was sudden. We buried him next to Ackerman, but it didn't seem just.

Emmerich has kindly offered me the rice store for as long as I want it. I am exhausted from the trip, but I am happier here, in my little kingdom of sago plants and mudskippers, than in the forest. Emmerich comes to see me every evening, just as before. We never talk of Ackerman or what happened. He must be bones by now, his flesh mulched down into the ground, consumed by the earth.

I am not so well. It is a malaise. I find it hard to do anything much. Even letter writing, for my pen now moves over the paper like a broken finger, barely working.

Emmerich tells me all I need to know of life in Sarawak. News travelled quickly on the Dutchmen's deaths, but they were accepted. It seems it is not so uncommon here, just another death in the eastern tropics.

I still have the ledger with its names of various customers, which I need to follow up. Although I hated the man, it would be foolish, under the circumstances, to miss an opportunity. To square the circle, so to speak.

I miss San and often think how much he would love my gentle world here of lizards and butterflies. When they left me, I gave the boy a regular English bear hug and as a gift, my rifle. San gave me a glorious feather in return, with a line of spectacular eyes. The eyes of the Argus pheasant (Argusianus argus) to watch over me.

Today, I felt a little better. My strength is slowly returning, day by day, and I have decided to join Emmerich on a trip to meet another collector, who I am told currently resides in the Rajah, Mr James Brooke's mountain cabin. Emmerich met Mr Brooke in the town and mentioned my illness and our endless chess playing. It seems that the Rajah and a collector from Usk have been playing their own matches in the foothills of Mount Santubong, but are so well matched that they long to challenge another.

The collector in question is a great deal older and more established than me. I think I have mentioned him before? He has quite a pedigree, having travelled extensively in South America, more specifically the Rio Negro and the Amazon, and he has already had a number of essays and thoughts published in the Journal of the Linnean Society, Chambers's, and the Ibis. He even knows Mr Charles Darwin. Perhaps you have read of him, Katherine, or even demanded an audience? It would not surprise me! His name is Alfred Russel Wallace.

Emmerich is delighted to receive an offer of hospitality from Mr Brooke, which, to some extent, seals the Professor's reputation in Sarawak, which perhaps, until now, has been shaky. He tells me his excitement, however, is nothing to do with that.

"Lauter Unsinn. Utter nonsense, Mr Broderig!" he shouted at me, quite cross, and vowed emphatically he had no interest in "quasi-English royalty" and that it was merely that he had heard a rumour that there was an abundance of Vanda lowii near this country retreat.

I do not think we will be gone for too long. I have nets for moths and butterflies and no longer feel the need for a gun. I will use this time to build my knowledge in all things entomological. It will be good to be the student again. So, I have no more sketches for you this time, Katherine. Are these words enough? I fear they are paltry and boring. But I am sure that I will have tales to tell you from the Brooke riverside cottage, shall I not?

Until then,
Your servant
Benjamin Broderig

CHAPTER
ELEVEN

CAMBRIDGE

Hatton looked out of the window and saw the spires of Cambridge. Inspector Adams yawned and asked, "Have we arrived?"

Broderig answered, "We're here, Inspector. The sun will be setting in an hour." Then he jumped up, swaying a little, and threatened to topple, but steadied himself as the train pulled into the station.

"After you, please, gentlemen." The Inspector picked up his things.

"But haven't you forgotten something?" Broderig pointed at the little girl's autopsy report, which lay flattened against the seat.

"Ah, yes," the Inspector hurriedly picked it up, and pushed it firmly into his bag.

"Are you always so forgetful, Inspector?" Broderig smiled, sweetening the insult. "I never leave anything behind. My travel bag, for example. I never leave home without it!" Broderig hugged the bag to his chest, as if the crown jewels were in it. The Inspector scowled at the younger man and arched a bushy brow at him. "I rarely forget anything, if you must know. Not anything important."

"The girl's not important, then, Inspector?" Broderig winked at Hatton who shook his head like a disapproving schoolteacher, but if the truth was known, he was glad his new friend made a point of it.

"So, shall we get a carriage?" said Adams. "How far is it to the College?"

"It's a hop by coach, Inspector. Follow me, gentlemen." Broderig pushed through the hordes of other passengers.

"Sidney Sussex, as quick as you like," he said to the coach driver.

The three men jumped in and the carriage took off. Hatton peered out of the grimy window as they sped into the city, watching sycamore trees bending in a blustery wind.

After fifteen minutes, or less, the carriage hurtled to a stop.

"How much?" the Inspector asked the driver as they hopped out.

"A shilling, unless you gentlemen want to pay more."

Broderig laughed and found some change in his pocket. Hatton watched a shiny guinea pass from one hand to another.

"Do you always tip so heavily?" asked Hatton, genuinely curious.

Broderig smiled, strands of hair blowing across his handsome face. "I liked his coat," he beamed.

The huge main door to the College entrance was shut.

Broderig said, "Allow me," and twisted a blackened handle, which opened the door with ease. The men stepped into the lodge, which was brightly lit, almost welcoming.

The Inspector sprung forward and rang the bell sharply. An ancient porter appeared rubbing his eyes.

"Yes, sir? Can I help you, sir?" asked the old man, brushing down crumpled clothes.

"We're here to see Dr Finch," answered Adams, shaking clumps of snow from his coat.

"Is he expecting you, gentlemen?" The porter peered at the visitors more closely.

"Hurry yourself. We're from Scotland Yard on a matter of urgent police business," Adams shouted at the porter.

"Scotland Yard? Alright, alright. Just give me a moment — these old bones need wrapping up, for it's perishing outside." The porter found his coat. "This way, then."

The men made their way out of the porch and into Chapel Court. They crunched along the gravel, thick with snow, keeping to the path. Hatton shoved his hands in his pockets, because despite his gloves, they were freezing. The light was ebbing fast, as the porter banged on the door, with, "Dr Finch, open up please, sir."

Sidney Sussex wasn't the richest of Cambridge's colleges, and despite its ornate mullion windows and grand arched entrance, rooms in Chapel Court were on the scruffy side. The paint on the door was peeling. Hatton smiled to himself. It was as bad as the morgue. "Dr Finch, answer the door please, sir." The porter

164

hammered again. "I have some gentlemen here that wants to see you." But no answer came.

"Do you have any idea where Dr Finch might be if he's not in his rooms?" the Inspector asked.

"No, no, I haven't seen Dr Finch for a long time. And many would say good riddance to him. Why don't you gentlemen wait in the bar and I'll get the key. He might just be sleeping. He keeps odd hours, does that one."

The Inspector scrutinised the porter's face. "When was the last time you saw him?"

The porter rubbed his nose and coughed a little. "'Scuse me. I have a terrible cold. It's the weather. I can't recall exactly, but it must be several weeks or more. It don't get any easier, you know, when you get to my age, trying to remember who is where and what is what. Dr Finch comes and goes and does as he pleases."

The old man looked vexed for an instant and then brightened up saying, "I'm sure he's about. Quite often, if I recall, he's off collecting beetles and the like. He came to us as a theology don. But like so many of our Fellows these days, he's more interested in Nature than God."

Broderig clapped his hands together to warm them and said, "I'm in that line of business myself." The porter looked intently at Broderig, and Hatton watched them. He saw the dimming eyes of this porter, the white ring about them. Cataracts. His father had them. The porter was almost blind.

"Really, sir. Well, as I say, you gentlemen should wait in the bar. I'll be with you in a jiffy."

A glassy-eyed barman acknowledged their arrival in the bar with a solemn nod, and a "What'll it be?" before returning to his task, which consisted of rubbing dirty glasses with a dirty rag which he spat on, and then rubbing again.

Broderig got the round in. Three brandies for half a shilling. Adams drummed his fingers on the table, rattaty tat, rattaty tat.

"Ah, well, here I am as I said I would be," the porter stepped into the bar with a large bunch of keys. Inspector Adams stopped his drumming, and took his notebook out. "Before we go, rest your legs a little and tell me what you think on this fellow, Mr . . . I'm sorry, I don't know your name."

"Mr Henry Hedge, sir. My father's name, too, I'm proud to say. Porters from the other Colleges is less inclined to be forgiving of Dr Finch. They say to me, 'He's a right troublemaker.' But I says they're only jealous. Oh, he's very handsome-looking, Dr Finch, and appealing to the ladies . . ." The porter winked at them. "And he isn't so discriminating. He likes the lot of them. Loves variety, and when you are my age you can only dream what a man like that might get up to, the lucky devil."

"Indeed," said Adams, folding his arms.

"Is it a crime you're investigating?" The porter looked at Adams, his bad eyes glistening.

"Yes," Adams replied. "A very serious one."

166

"Well, well, and Dr Finch at the middle of it, eh? Can't say I'm surprised."

They crossed the quad and the porter picked through his great clump of keys till he found the right one. The door creaked open. "Wait a minute, gentlemen. I'll light a candle."

As their eyes adjusted to the gloom, an odd smell immediately hit them. The tallow's pale light illuminated the floor before them, which Hatton could see was strewn with books, old bits of bread, and fetid mutton unfinished on a greasy metal plate, but this was not the smell which greeted them. "I know this scent," said Hatton. It was odd, sharp, unpleasant.

A tut tut came from the porter, like a mother hen. "The way dons live today. It's a disgrace." Hatton ignored the porter and, peeling his gloves off, bent down and picked up some of the papers. He asked for another candle to be lit. The room began to form around them and in the midst of the debris lay a book, which caught Hatton's eye. Sumptuously gilded on Morocco-grained cloth; he ran his finger over it and read its title, then flicked forward a page to a simple dedication, but no name from the giver, only a date: October 1856. He laid it down again.

"This is a right monster mess," Adams's voice boomed around the darkened place as he crouched next to Hatton, amongst the piles of books. "What's all this, then?" Adams read the titles out. A ragged, well-worn *Ibis* and umpteen fingered copies of the *Cybele Britannica*, a myriad of theological tracts and sermons torn out of papers at random it seemed, and a

167

splattering of one shilling episodes from a new work by Mr Dickens. "*Bleak House*. Indeed. Well, I can't argue with that!"

And as the flame of the candles swelled, the men stood up and looked around them at the main room, which was a sad, pokey affair.

"He's in dire need of a wife," said Adams.

"The College would never allow it," answered the porter.

"We haven't checked the bedroom," said Broderig.

"After you," said Adams, gesturing to the second room.

The young man pushed the second door with a thrust, the strange stench now overwhelming.

"My Lord, what a thing is that? Smells like, well, I don't know what it smells like. Is it alcohol? It's a strange sort of gin. I don't think Dr Finch is much of a drinker. He likes other things." The porter stopped suddenly.

"Not any more," said Adams.

The corpse sat bolt upright in its chair. Its eyes, glass. Its skin, leather. Henry Hedge had seen squirrels done this way and ducklings dressed in bonnets. He and Mrs Hedges had laughed at the sight of the weasels in wedding dresses, and had called them "dear" and "fetching", until they caught sight of the kitten with two heads. Perhaps, whoever had done this thing to Finch had thought it a joke to dress the academic up in his Sunday best. But Finch was not perfectly finished and carefully wrought. This taxidermist had been in a hurry. The poor man's skin, despite liberal applications

168

of preservatives, had started to lift and curl around the edges, where face met hair. More loose flaps hung around his jowls, where the stuffing had been botched. And despite the neat parting of the hair, the polished nails, the handsome and distinctive nose, Finch was deformed and unnatural.

The men stood dumbstruck, but questioning. Where was the flesh? The blood and bones? The guts and the fluids? And worse. Worse than the act itself. What screaming terrors had this thing faced before the end? The elderly porter hit the floor. Inspector Adams broke the silence.

"Can it be possible for a man to be skinned, stretched, tanned, remoulded, and padded out in a matter of hours? Even without forensics, Professor, I think we can safely say this man died some time ago." And as he spoke, the Inspector seemed puzzled and surveyed the preserved academic as if looking at a rare, zoological exhibit. He craned forward, demanding a candle. He peered closer still, so that he almost touched it, and then stepped back to consider his next steps. "What is this smell, dammit?"

Hatton found his voice. "Vinegar mixed with spice for preserving cadavers. Unmistakable."

"Get a gas lamp from the other room, Mr Broderig, light it, bring it here, and check on the porter. Make yourself useful, please, sir."

Broderig, as meek as a lamb, did as he was bid and came back, his shocked face lit by the orangey glare of the burning oil. The lantern made things clearer.

Finch had been arranged as if in study. His left hand grasped a quill. There was a book in his other. Hatton peered closer at a leather-bound copy. *Vestiges*. The publication they had discussed on the train.

The creator of this thing had been thorough, if not exact. With Adams's permission, Hatton touched it and felt the human leather. He moved around and pressed his fingers into the form. There was no blood, no gristle or mucus. Nothing to suggest the terrible violence which must have preceded the crime.

"So, Professor. Best guess. When did he die?"

Hatton answered, shaking his head in disbelief, "It would have taken time to do this sort of work, Inspector. There can't be that many people in Cambridge who could do it."

"Yes," Adams said. "We shall need to round up anyone who dabbles in this art. We must start at once. Three bodies, now. Dammit." Adams lit a penny smoke, his agitation showing. "The local Specials will help us. The remains must be somewhere."

Hatton stood for a few more seconds, but staring at this form didn't help. They needed the rest of the body. The Inspector was right, so Hatton followed Adams into the other room, where the porter and Broderig were now flaked out together, the old man mumbling, the young man comforting.

"I want everything left untouched, Mr Hedge. No one is to enter this room. Do I make myself clear? Then I want everything you have on Finch. All the papers, all the documents. Anyone who knew him, worked with

170

him, talked to him, liked him, hated him. And Mr Broderig, a little more information from you, too, sir."

"You know I have told you all I can, Inspector."

"You have told us very little about the content of the letters you seemed so concerned about. What, sir, was the nature of your correspondence to Lady Bessingham?"

Broderig stared at the floor and then looked to Hatton, who looked to the ground, not knowing what else to do. "My letters were personal but essentially the details of my journey to Borneo, a few sketches, illustrations, some rough ideas. Nothing else. But I want them back, Inspector. They're not worth killing for. They had nothing to do with Dr Finch and are all that I have left of Lady Bessingham."

Adams stubbed his cigarette out. "Well, I'm very concerned about your safety. Each of these murders is linked by science and you, too, are a botanical. You need to mind yourself, Mr Broderig. May I ask if you carry any means of protection?"

"I have a small pistol which I keep in London. It's at Swan Walk, under my pillow. Are you suggesting I carry it, Inspector?"

Adams nodded. "And Mr Broderig, I also suggest you keep it in a locked drawer, or in a safe with the safety catch on. I can't tell you how many gentlemen I've known who have accidentally shot their own heads off keeping a gun under a pillow. It's easily done."

Adams helped the old man up, and then without waiting for anyone, marched out of the room. Hatton turned to his friend and said, "I'd better keep in his step, Mr Broderig. Are you sure you're alright?"

Broderig nodded. "It's poor Mr Hedge I'm worried about. I'll stay with him awhile."

Mr Hedge started to retch but Hatton could see he was in good hands. Broderig was stroking his hair, telling him, "No, I won't leave you and it's nothing to be ashamed of. I feel sick to the stomach myself."

Outside, the Inspector was frantically hailing a carriage.

"Hurry up, Professor. Get inside. No Mr Broderig, then? Not that we need him now. Three botanicals dead. What a damn mess." And he yelled at the driver, "Hurry up, for God's sake, man, or I'll drive the thing myself."

The local Cambridge police station was nothing like The Yard. For a start it was quiet.

"Never thought I'd see myself back here again. Bloody useless lot when I left. I see nothing much has changed. Oi! You! Yes, you, Officer Dimwit. Look lively, and get me whoever's in charge."

A desk was hurriedly found, a line of command decided. Hatton watched as Adams, a terrifying taskmaster, bellowed at the rural constabulary and they jumped, every last man and boy. Whistles blew, papers flew, telegrams were dispatched at will. Interviews and searches commenced at speed. Cigarettes were rolled quicker still, and as each corner of the city was turned over, one man cast his shadow. But as night became day and day became night . . . nothing.

172

"I need an extensive netting and wading of the Cam," the Inspector barked, but as the dull sun broke out fractured beams from a grey dawn, still nothing.

Dead cats, abandoned books, and bicycles were hauled up through the broken ice. The following morning passed and Hatton watched from the sidelines. By midday, still no body parts.

The meeting in the makeshift incident room told Professor Hatton little. And what they did know, Adams read like a riot act. "No talking at the back." He paused, letting a billow of smoke swirl about before addressing the now hushed room.

"Finch was almost friendless, having courted controversy once too often. He'd not been seen for weeks. He was apparently quiet but when he did speak up, was arrogant. We know he was well turned out in silk shirts from London, but lacked manners."

One brave soul asked, "Do we know about his family, Inspector?"

Adams looked at his notes. "All we know so far is that he came from a teaching post at University College, but was thrown out for something he said or wrote. Nothing's verified. No paper was circulated. And there's nothing immediate to link him to our other victims, Mr Dodds or Lady Bessingham, other than what we already know. So, anything else on Finch?" Adams looked around the room.

One Special spoke out, "Well, he never went to church. Some thought him an atheist. Others, a genius. Ladies liked him for his wan good looks, and for his intellectual daring, as well, until he wrote something or said something which upset people."

"Yes, but where is this thing? What the devil does it say?"

No one seemed to know. More detail followed, and Hatton sat at the back of the meeting room where he listened to how Finch played cricket in the summer, enjoyed beetle collecting, went to London whenever he could, but kept himself to himself. Finch's life in a nutshell.

One of the Specials spoke up again, trying to look useful. "We have three taxidermists in Cambridge and one in Ely. We've talked to nearly all of them. But have nothing to go on."

"But not spoken to everyone, then?" Adams stared back at the hapless policeman.

"Word is there's a skilled stuffer in the Fens. He's a breedling, Inspector. A waterman, otter skin hat, the lot. He's out on a punt by day slipping through the waters round Wickham way. It's hard to catch him, for he blends in with the rushes and doesn't relish the law. But our boys will track him, be sure of it." Adams caught Hatton's eye.

"But it makes no rhyme or reason to me for a bog-trotting breedling to bother with this sort of freak show, unless there was money in it. What's this slodger's name?"

"Locals call him Mucker. By all accounts he's a strange fellow, living off the marshes like a regular wader and selling his trade of skinning and stitching when the fishing season's on."

174

Hatton was intrigued and began to follow these strange words. It seemed breedling and slodger were one and the same — watermen. Men who still lived off the Fens in a traditional way. He knew a little of their history. How they'd been thrown off their islands and inlets when the drainage men came. Some had put down their nets to work the land, but others still lived in the remotest parts of the Cambridgeshire marshes. By all accounts, they were strange people, half savage, living in damp huts and muddy holes.

"Well," said Adams, "for God's sake, let's go there." Adams pushed his chair away and moved quickly to the door. "Come on, Professor. I'll need you for a start."

"What about Mr Broderig, Inspector? Should we check on him, or at least tell him what we're doing?" Hatton guessed where his friend might be and felt bad simply leaving him. But Adams was insistent, saying, "He'll be at The Eagle, perfectly happy. I'll send word for him to wait for us there. He's had enough shock for a lad of his age. A week or more, you reckon? To stuff a man like that?"

Hatton nodded, knowing where this was leading. A week or more. Finch had been the first.

CHAPTER
TWELVE

WICKHAM FEN

Snow was falling and Hatton feared the search would be hampered, although Adams had given orders to swell the search party to twenty more able men. Sources at the local tavern proved good and the men were soon led out to Wickham Fen, a mile or more from Ely. Word was, the Mucker had a hut somewhere along the banks, but to the untrained eye, it was well hidden. They took a lad with them who had said he knew trapping and could act as their guide. With a nod of encouragement from the tavern owner and a shilling from Adams, the child seemed happy to oblige.

"What's your name, child?" Adams asked him, as they set off.

The boy looked him square in the eye. Not frightened, as Hatton would have been at his age. He seemed fearless, despite the posse of men who stood with the Inspector like a pack.

"Bob Feltwell and I know Wickham. My family, when I had some, were breedlings. I know the Mucker, too. He takes the best pikes but he's getting creaky now, and I'm creeping up on him. Last summer I caught a nine-pounder. He stuffed it for me, for a mean price, the old miser. But it was worth it, for I sold it and ate like a king." The boy sniffed and rubbed his face as he talked. Hatton felt sorry for this strange child. Countless children who roamed the streets in London were far worse off than he, yet somehow his poverty touched the Professor. The boy's hand-me-down clothes had been gathered from who knows where, and they were fit for a man of twenty, hanging off his tiny frame.

"Well, young Bob. You find this Mucker for us and you'll be supping like a king with a bevy of stove-piped Specials before sun goes down," Hatton said to the child, smiling.

The child, head down and trudging along the frozen banks of the waterways, replied, "Maybe. Though I'm not intending to sit with no Specials. They are not inclined to favour boys like me. I hide from the law, but if the money's right, well, I'm here, aren't I? I'll find him alright. He thinks he's the king of trackers, does Mucker, but I'm creeping up on him."

"Does he live alone, boy?" asked Adams.

"He had a daughter once, same age as me, but she disappeared. They think she was drowned in the marshes. It happens when the floods come. No one ever found her body, nor nothing to say she'd ever been alive. It was all the talk for a while round these parts. But it's not so unusual for children to die here."

And the boy trudged on along the icy boardwalks till they reached a flat gully of water, and then he skitted away, up a bank of snow. Adams stopped in his tracks and, twisting round, cautioned the men to fall silent.

The silence felt like hours. Had the boy given up? Adams seemed content to look at his boots, hands behind his back, gently rocking back and forth. Only the bite of the wind through thickets of scrub and spindly hawthorns broke the eerie silence. Wickham Fen was a desolate place, empty and sullen.

Then, suddenly, the caw of a crow and a low whistle. The boy appeared down the slope covered in frosted twigs and grasses. He had tracked the old man. Hatton was sure of it.

The boy mumbled something to Adams who in turn beckoned to the Professor.

"It appears we have the breedling in his little winter's nest. Mr Feltwell here has tracked him, helped by a little smoke which is rising from his hut. The men can stay here till I give the call, for this Mucker fellow is afraid of the law, and will be off like a frightened rabbit if we don't step softly. Professor Hatton, you seem to me to have an uncommonly light touch and an enquiring nature, so I suggest you come with me."

Up and down banks of snow, the two men followed the child, until they reached a huge, expansive lake, edged by a tangle of rushes, frosted and hanging bent in the cold. The lake looked treacherous. The boy lay on his belly and gestured at the ice. Then slipping along, he pushed his body skidding across it. There was little choice and they followed. But as he glided, Hatton heard the sound of cracking, and was sure he felt the water and the lake dragging him down, but no, the boy was right. The ice held solid. Hatton's hands were tingling, but the sight of the curling smoke ahead made him forget his lack of comfort. The child had not failed them.

The old man's hut was a tumble dwelling made of muck and bits of old wood. No windows, just a hole in the roof for the smoke to escape, and for a door, a mouldy, mildewed cutting of spruce wood. Outside the hut was a collection of tools and frozen fish heads. Bits of old leather hung over branches in the surrounding trees. With no window to look through, Adams knocked on the door.

"Who goes there?" asked a rough voice from inside.

"It's Bob Feltwell, Mucker. I've men here that will give you money."

Adams glowered at the boy, but the child paid no heed and pulled the wood flap back on its hinge.

Inside the hut it was dark, airless, womb-like. In the centre, a small fire was lit, heating an ancient black cooking pot on a big metal chain. Something was bubbling away, something rotten. Just a hint of tanning in the air. Hatton had seen the fish leather outside, left hanging over the sedge, like forlorn oily flags.

And curled up tight, in a ball, was the breedling. At first, he was hard to make out. His feet were swaddled in reed, his body tangled up in a torn cape of strange leather, slimy and badly done. As Hatton's eyes adjusted in the dingy light, the Mucker's face formed. No beard but rough, caked stubble full of twigs, dirt, and grass. His eyes, fishlike.

"What d'ya want? Speak now," the voice was scratching. Then, without even moving, he spat on the floor.

"What do'ya want with old Mucker? Speak, why don't you?" The breedling slowly sat up and looked at the door. Adams sensed the escape and held back, using his full height to block the only exit. The Mucker fell back on his bed.

The boy spoke up, "These men want information. They will pay a handsome price. There's a man gone missing. I told them you are the best of trackers and that maybe you can help them."

"Help them? I had someone once. She went missing. None helped me, though I begged them. Men like you came, said they'd do something, but they did nothing. Missing, you say?"

"Yes, Mucker. I told them about your daughter. But look at the state of yourself. You could do with a pouch of baccy, couldn't you?" The child was clever.

"Money, eh? There's money says I know nothing."

The Inspector took a step forward. "The boy's right, there's money if you help us. And if you don't, well, let's just say I've heard there's been a fair lot of fish being poached on Mr Wade's land and there's plenty of fish skins hanging out to dry on those hawthorns. They look like trout to me; not the sort of fish you'd get here in Wickham." Adams lit a cigarette and billowed out the smoke as he spoke.

"You the boss, eh? The jailer? I'm not afeared of your threats. You have nothing on me. I keeps myself to myself and those skins are pikes. Just look at their size. There's no trout rustling in December. You think I'm a fool, don't you? Well, I'll tell you Mr Jailor Man, I'm ancient, I'll grant you that, but I'm not afeared of your type. You wants old Mucker's help, well, I'll give it but not with these threats. Money is the speaker here. As I bet it is with you. I know your sort, sir." The "sir" was said with a snarl, and though this breedling was cornered, Hatton could sense even Adams was wary.

"Well, given that we understand each other so well, what can you tell us and how much will it cost? Mind you, any jiggery pokery and we'll pay you nothing."

The boy laughed to hear Adams's retort. And the breedling scratched his damp, matted head. Lice, Hatton didn't wonder. He was probably crawling with them.

"There was a strange gathering of birds up yonder on Barnet's Mound, maybe a month ago. Like there was food to be had. I did think it strange at the time, for its winter and not feasting time for crows. They had gathered up there like it was autumn on sowing ground. Hovering, cawing, and flocking about in a round. Maybe you'd best look up there."

"Can you take us?" asked Adams.

"Take the boy. You know the mound, boy, don't you? I've been out all night tracking badgers."

The urchin nodded yes. But Adams remained tight-lipped and continued, threatening, "Badgers? A likely tale. What if I told you that a man has been murdered? That this man has been flayed and skinned. That some devil has stuffed him like one of your pikes. What would you say to that, stodger? Would you know anyone who could do that to an innocent man, rise in the morning, and go about his work not flinching or praying for God's mercy?"

The breedling stirred in his bed. "God's mercy? What's that? I know no mercy in my life. There's no God's mercy for my kith and kin. It's just the rich that's served. Stuffed, you say? That would be a job. To tan and stuff a man. I've heard that there are those that will do anything. But I just do fish. Nothing fancy. My tools are over there. You can check if you like. Try the rich taxidermists in Cambridge — they're the artists. How was he done? Fancy like or plain? Was he in a cabinet or sat down for tea? That's what they do, those charlatan stuffers. They dress owls up as schoolmasters and rabbits as maids. I see nature for what it is. I stuff little things. Not a man." His voice faltered as he shrunk back.

"Just look on the mound. I know nothing more. You'll leave me the money, won't you?" Adams looked in his purse and pulled out a shilling. Even he seemed moved by this pitiful creature.

"If this money's for nought, I'll be back old man." Adams stubbed his cigarette out on the floor.

Back across the ice, and up the bank, Adams blew his whistle and in a minute the Specials arrived. "Let the boy lead, come on."

"This is it," said Feltwell. "This is the mound."

It was hardly a mound, but a smallish rise, barely six feet long and five feet wide. But it stood out against the unrelentingly flat horizon, which stretched for mile upon dreary mile. There were no crows fluttering or otherwise, only a solitary bird cawing plaintively across the Fens from a frozen ash tree. Adams shrugged.

"Well, it's as good a place as any, I suppose, and it's not unlike a grave."

He gave the command, "Right boys, start digging."

And it wasn't long before, bit by bit, Dr Finch came up. Some chunks, raw and meaty, frozen like lamb. Other bits wrapped in flax. The local boys worked hard and brought up the pieces with iron-like bellies, though some of the Specials had to stop and billow up their breakfasts. Adams all the time stood grimly puffing on his cigarettes. "Well, Professor, peat is the perfect preserver. Whoever buried him here needs some geology lessons if they thought he was gone."

"Over here! Quick!"

A short man with a shovel in his hand stood over a hole. Hatton took a step back, although he'd seen a hundred like this, taking students through their rudimentary lessons. They often spent time on the head at St Bart's, which the dieners skinned neatly, leaving the brain exposed so the student dissectors could pick, bit by bit, to the core.

And yet in that moment, as Hatton recovered briefly from his own shock at this morbid discovery, he wondered why it was that the head should cause him to flinch more than a muscle? Or a thigh? Or even a heart? Perhaps, Hatton thought, this is where a man's soul lies? All thinking, feelings, ideas. All love, desire, passion. Everything that makes Man human. But Finch had been made featureless. Just a bloody ball of flesh and skull, now.

"Go back to Ely with the Feltwell boy and tell him to shut his mouth about this sight. Pay him more if we need to. There'll be a hundred gawpers here if we don't move quickly. I need wire and boards to fence this lot off." Adams seemed unfazed. "Professor Hatton, I'm going back to see our breedling friend. A guinea says he knows more."

Hatton watched the men shovelling deep into the ground. He shivered as the men worked, digging and crunching their blades through the peaty snow. The wind whipped up with flurries of snow. Was this God's work? Was it fate? Ant-like, the men continued, black shadows in the failing light, the sun dipping palest yellow. And the snow fell.

At The Eagle, Broderig was playing chess by himself. But on their entrance, he stood up, putting his hand out to greet them saying, "Can I buy you both a drink, gentlemen?"

"We'll have two pints, Mr Broderig," replied the Inspector. "And chasers to follow. It's been a long day."

"You found him, then?"

Hatton nodded. "The meat and the organs have been preserved. They will easily survive the train journey back to London. I have asked Inspector Adams to put Finch, in his entirety, on the first train tomorrow. We're going to be busy at St Bart's."

Broderig pulled out a chair for Hatton and said, "My understanding is limited, but I could make myself useful at the morgue. It's better than doing nothing."

Hatton was touched by a genuine offer. But he shook his head. "No, but thank you, Mr Broderig. We'll cope, but it will be time-consuming, exacting work. Finch's

184

body parts have been severed into many pieces but each chunk may offer us a clue. But I think he was the first and I believe the others, Lady Bessingham, Mr Dodds, followed on. The timing of the deaths, I would suggest, spaced out over the last ten days or so. Maybe longer. So extreme violence precipitated by something which connects them. But as to what? I cannot say. Any ideas, gentlemen?"

But Broderig just stared at his hands while Adams knocked back an ale, followed by the chaser, followed by three more, called for in quick succession. His voice slurring, he said, "It's all a question of motive. Who would want these botanicals dead? Who has something to gain by this? I had a message from London. Our missing maid had been to the British Museum, it seems. A footman remembered, after an intimate chat with one of my Specials. But who she was meeting there, he couldn't or wouldn't say. An academic was all he would offer. So that hardly narrows it down. But at least it's a lead. Anyway, gentlemen." The Inspector put his glass down, wiped his mouth with the back of his hand, and said, "Early start tomorrow. And I'm badly in need of some shut-eye, so goodnight, then."

Leaving Hatton thinking he ought to do the same. But something about Broderig's face made him hesitate. "Are you quite well, Mr Broderig?"

"What can one say, Professor? I'm troubled, as you must be. Perhaps you have seen such violence before?"

Hatton stared at his empty glass. "I've seen many things. But today on the Fen, it sickened me. Of course, as a pathologist, I am expected to be inured to these sights. To get my notebook out. To make comments. To delve and decipher. But today, I felt I lost my way a little. There was a boy who helped us. He took a shine to me, if you could call it that. And though he was nothing to me, I felt . . . oh, I don't know. Like Inspector Adams said, it's been a long day."

"He felt like your child? Is that what you mean, Professor?"

Hatton ran his hands through his hair and yes, he thought, the boy felt a little like his own child for a second, and he wondered where the boy was now. And although there was barely a taste of the whisky left, he picked up the tumbler and pressed it to his lips, to sip the very last drop. The bar was closed. Last orders had already been called.

"I understand," said Broderig. "There was a boy I met in Borneo, and if I ever marry, I should like a lad like that. A strong boy, who can look after himself. I gave the boy my gun before I left. I am no lover of weapons, but in the jungle they're only tools, I suppose." Hatton watched the young man's face in the gloom cloud a little. "I need the letters back, Professor. There are details in them which might be misconstrued, taken out of context, cause trouble."

Hatton shifted on his seat. "Cause trouble for whom?"

"Something happened, Professor. I cannot say what. I told Katherine, and she forgave me. It's all over and done with now and I'm only twenty-five. I have my whole life ahead of me."

186

Hatton smiled wearily, not wanting to press Broderig on something which was clearly a private matter. When it came to women, he'd had his fair share of youthful misdemeanours, which were best left in the past. And so he stood up and left Broderig idly shifting chess pieces and went to his bed, which was perfectly comfortable; a little garret room, not unlike the room he had as a child in Hampshire.

Hatton sat on an arched-back chair, which had been positioned by the window, and heard a dog bark and some drunk fellows laughing outside, but they quickly moved away and it was soon silent.

Hatton moved to his bed, removed his shoes, and lay down. He didn't want to think about the case any more. He wanted to think about other things. His own future, for example. To map it out in his head. To contemplate this day, and the next and the next after that, and where this journey called life might take him. He was dog-tired and although he tried to stay awake, the day had taken its toll.

CHAPTER
THIRTEEN

THE BOROUGH

Yesterday, Ashby recalled that the Duke of Monreith had seemed preoccupied, all the time looking out of the window, looking for someone or something, his baritone voice replaced by a husky murmur, "What did you say, Ashby? Speak up." There were no visits to the docks, no checking up on business, even the speech-writing had stopped.

Then, left alone in the office, Ashby had wandered over to a shelf to fetch some ink and, as he turned around, caught sight of the Duke through the mullion window far below on the glistening pavers of Westminster, talking to what looked like two Specials. They wore no uniform, but Ashby was long enough in The Borough to know a policeman when he saw one. They talked to the Duke for a while, shook hands, and then went on their way. The Duke's giveaway thud back up the stone stairs was recognisable a few minutes later.

"Have the newspapers arrived yet?"

Ashby quickly located *The Times* from a heap of other journals. The Duke snatched it, went to his armchair, and flicked through cover to cover, then threw it on the floor. "Word on the street is that a terrible crime's been committed. Have you heard anything?"

Ashby said nothing but continued with his work. The Duke seemed to stumble a little. He got up, paced the room, and wrung his hands. "A cold-blooded murder in Millford Lane. Mr Dodds, the Purveyor of Fine Books. And I went there only the other day. Apparently he was pinned like a moth to the floor of his shop. Do you remember the place, Ashby?"

Ashby said, "Yes, sir. You dropped me on The Strand, I recall."

"It was your fault, Ashby."

"I'm sorry, sir?"

"I said it was your fault. I wanted the Hooker paper. But you failed to secure it, so I had to go there myself. Do you remember?"

Ashby's head hurt. Yes, he remembered, but he was muddled.

"Well, any questions along those lines, from anybody snooping around, you keep your mouth shut, d'ya hear? Fucking botanicals. Another one dead, they said. What of it? I never went there. Understood?"

Then, for some reason, the Duke of Monreith mellowed and did something he'd never done before. He lay a trembling hand on the old man's shoulders. "But sometimes things have a way of turning out well, do they not? But I was never at the bookshop, Mr Ashby, understood?"

Ashby shook his head at the Duke's words. "*I was never there, understood?*" But other voices were calling him today. He staggered from his bed, opened his secretaire, and took the letters out again, untying the bright blue ribbon. A rank smell rose in the air from the flesh-coloured paper, the "M" taunting him. He didn't want to read the words, but the pleading was explicit, the voices begging.

It was still dark outside, but the other tenants downstairs were long up, and Ashby heard clearly the whack of a child, the shout of "You little wretch," and a howl. The trouble with the poor, thought Ashby, was that they had too many children. They could look after one or two, but they had eight, nine, ten. There were just so damn many of them. Still, there were ways to curb this sprawling population.

Like vermin they were, the Duke had said, at one of his many private gatherings some months gone now. Bred like rabbits, he'd said. And they were eaters, children. Big eaters. And the more you had, the bigger the eating became. And where did that lead? What was the use of them?

"Hear, hear," said one of the guests.

"Malthus should be required reading for all leaders of men," said another.

"The poor must be controlled. Or they will burst the seams right open."

"And we'll go the way of the French," said the Duke. "And it will be bloody, gentlemen. Heads will roll. It will be anarchy. I for one think the segregation of the genders below stairs is an excellent idea. And children, like women, must be kept occupied."

Ashby shuddered at the memory and he was still reeling from the vice-like clutches of that blackmailing whore. He looked at his arm in the grey light of dawn, which hung limply from his nightshirt. It was a hard word, whore. But that was what she was. Her fingers had marked him black and blue. He dressed himself slowly and looked at the painting of the old house where his mother had once worked, herself just a child. It hung above his treasured secretaire.

The ruby ring was gone, and if this didn't stop, the furniture would be next. And then what? There was only one place where a poor old man with no furniture went, and he knew his days were numbered with the Duke. Why, it was as clear as day that he would be discarded soon. His little treasures gone. His bits of china, his French lace, and, most treasured of all, the collection which he showed to no one. Just a peek, he thought.

Not that he would get much for them. He only ever preserved the little creatures. The beetles glistened in their frames and little boxes, polished black onyx. Others green and petrol brilliant, caught, bolt-metal hard, as he had found them. His cataloguing and classification scrolled in delightful calligraphy, just as if he was a real Man of Science. *Cryptocephalus coryli, Clytus arietis.*

This skill required precision and, of course, a certain interest in anatomy, for good taxidermy suggested life. Ashby used a little knife for his hobby, the knife that peeled his oranges, and when he looked at his beetles, it made him wistful for a time long past. When he'd been younger, sauntering along the banks of the Thames to far-flung places with country names like Barnes and Twickenham. Each village, a Norman church and a river bend, barge men and fishing folk, dairy maids and meadows. And as summer came, swallows soared overhead, their whistling cries melodic in his ears as he headed west, leaping over stiles and crossing fields on his epic English journey, miles away from London. He smiled lovingly at the little creatures, and then with a sigh, shut them up again in the drawer's gloomy dark.

His mind was made up. He would pawn nothing else, for surely a man in Monreith's position with so much to lose would listen. A leader? A parliamentarian? One of the richest men in England? Surely the Duke would see reason.

So Ashby took his coat, left his lodging rooms, and eventually found himself at Monreith House, Number 1, Monreith Square.

It stood, resplendent, a monument to trade, stuffed to the brim with colonial treasures. Once or twice he'd caught a glimpse of the gilded clocks, candlesticks dripping with cherubs, and around every corner, Grecian goddesses, their bronze limbs voluptuous and dark.

Ashby hesitated. Should he go straight in? It was the Sabbath. He paused, then walked to the corner of the road and caught sight of a throng of happy children, who were laughing and throwing snowballs at one another. One lad had his sister on a sledge and was pulling her along, her apple cheeks bright red and her head thrown back begging, "Faster, faster!" Ashby smiled, touched by it all. By the freedom of the snow which had fallen fresh in the night. Perhaps he should just go home, he thought.

But then he saw Monreith, accompanied by a bevy of liveried servants, ready to set off somewhere. And though Ashby's eyes were dimming, he could see there was someone else already in the carriage. A red-furred bonnet and a svelte-like figure, which greeted the Duke and put tapering arms around him. It was Madame Martineau.

So Ashby decided to follow them and hailed his own coach. "Where to, old man?" asked the driver.

Ashby put his finger to his lips. "Follow that barouche, but hang back a bit."

"Whatever you say, sir."

The barouche set off. It headed to The Strand. The hansom followed. The barouche slowed and took a left where part of the road was cordoned off and outside the bookshop was a sign which said *Metropolitan Police / Keep Out*. The barouche sped up, passing the bookseller's on Millford Lane, not stopping, but heading due south.

Vauxhall Pleasure Gardens had seen better days before the turnstiles dropped the price and let the riff-raff in. Ashby had never been here in its halcyon days, but had heard that the entire Battle of Waterloo had been played out, by a cast of thousands. Men, officers all, resplendent in glinting uniforms, had charged as if to their deaths. Ladies dressed in furs had screamed and fainted at the crack of the guns and the gallop of the horses. But those days were long gone. The champagne dried up. The fireworks spent and fizzled. The throngs of happy couples, rich and cultured, vanished.

The gardens now offered a different sort of entertainment. For amongst the rubbish, the old bottles of spent beer and scattered whelk shells, moved shadows. Ashby paid the driver, skulked in, but hung back from the couple up ahead. Shadows stepped out and spoke to him.

"Got a nice one here, old man. Ain't she lovely? She's yours. Go on . . . you know you want to."

"Penny for your thoughts, ducky. You remind me of my father. It's Amy. You remember. Cold, ain't it? A shilling says I'll make you warm."

Blocking out the voices, Ashby followed the Duke and the swish of Madame Martineau. It was cold in the gardens but he was shielded by the fog, made invisible. He waited for what? He wasn't sure.

The Duke and dressmaker were still in Ashby's sight but only just, and at that moment, thick clouds shuddered across the sky. Ashby shivered as the two figures stayed ahead of him, motionless. Madam Martineau brought a gloved hand out and gave the Duke something. Monreith took it quickly. A scroll of letters, golden parchment tied with rattan. Hand met hand as the pair become a form, transmuted by fog and soft pelting snow. Movement, payment, and whispering as Monreith pushed the weathered scroll deep inside his pocket.

Ashby waited. He watched the pair move back towards the turnstile. They seem distracted. They

194

seemed to be looking for something. And then he saw all that he feared.

Because another shadow had moved towards the Duke, and as Ashby's eyes adjusted, it morphed into a filthy old hag who seemed to know this pair. Madame Martineau was welcoming, nodding, agreeing, and the old woman was leading a little thing dressed like a ballet-girl. Curly locks, a satin frock, a tad ragged. She had a hoop. She must have been freezing. Ashby strained to hear what was being said but held back, tucked tight within the grasp of a sycamore. But the words muffled in Ashby's ears, mixing with the scrawls he'd seen on those flesh-coloured sheets, embossed with an *M* and tied with a bright-blue ribbon now buried in his secretaire. The words were humps and mounds. The words were lips and tongues.

And then he heard her, bell-clear, the old lady's voice was rasping, "Is she not a nice little girl? Would you like to see her dancing?" And Ashby watched the Duke touch the girl and Ashby shrunk, enveloped by the shrouding pall, but he knew the truth. No more fooling himself. The Duke would not stop. Ashby, horror-struck, retreated back to the turnstile.

Hours later, the Duke of Monreith sat in his vast rooms in Belgravia, lit by a flicker of candles. He knew the name, Broderig. Not this Benjamin Broderig fellow, but his father who was a so-called Liberal — a betrayer to his own class. Monreith had faced Sir William many times across The House on issues of trade, religion, and governance. And this presented a problem which he'd need to think about.

He knew where the Broderigs lived, of course. Swan Walk, positioned directly opposite Chelsea Physics Gardens, surrounded, like him, by privilege. But unlike him, not untouchable, he thought. Monreith pondered on that as he moved away from the window and back to his seat, where he undid the rattan and took the scroll of letters out, for a moment admiring the golden parchment and the weather-beaten words, his silk-stockinged feet up on an ornate desk.

Santubong

December 10th, 1855

Dear Katherine,

What a tonic this place is and what a relief to be lifted, as I have been, from my stupor. These gentlemen have ideas and are thinkers and I can hardly believe my good fortune, but they seem happy to chat endlessly with me about everything I most enjoy and long to question. I cannot say we all agree with each other, but if we did, where would be the fun in it?

Emmerich is in his element. The orchids here are magnificent and our German professor is up and out before breakfast, coming back hours later, his breeches covered in mud, his hat askew, but his face beaming, a new and rare bud in his hand.

I, too, have my little excursions. The cottage of Mr Brooke is surrounded by fruit trees. Bright green buprestis abound, many of which I have spiked already and boxed. And as you would expect in his own lush gardens, something very special — the velvety Ornithoptera brookiana, named by Mr Wallace after the Rajah himself. What a creature. This butterfly looks like a bird, for it is large enough. Only yesterday, I went out for a short walk with Mr Wallace, and we caught one, not less than seven inches from wing to glorious wing. Wallace caught it in a trice. He's quite the expert; with great care, he picked the fluttering insect out of the net in untarnished perfection. Its head is scarlet like one of your finest rubies and its wings are soot black.

Mr Brooke generally leaves his guests to do as they please. He holds his views on all things scientific and religious with gusto, but is still inclined to listen carefully to others, and let them have a view. He is a Christian of a sort, I believe, though it is rumoured that he keeps a Muslim wife. If he does, what of it? He is a fine gentleman and has no doubt as to the way of things and how the world should run and is a great believer in conversation, free speech, liberty — and so, by God, am I!

As I suspected, he's a very fine chess player and can argue a point of theology quite lucidly whilst calling "Checkmate!" and quite confounding his competitor. I have learnt to listen. And what conversations are these. They speak freely here on every subject, Katherine. Politics, morality, religion. Nothing is spared. Not even the question of Creation.

But Emmerich takes little interest. He is the Master of Tiny Things, but on questioning the bigger picture, the place of life which we all inhabit, he seems happily oblivious. I say happily, because although it's exciting to ask questions about the Nature of things and Man's place in the world, it is also a burden. And for me, this burden became almost unbearable in Empugan.

But Borneo is not like London, where our intellectual questioning is contained. Here it is different. In the forest, the mind constantly asks the question, "And to what purpose?" Life stripped to nothing, laid bare to an emptiness which has left in me only doubt. I have found no absolute answers here. But I do know this. We move about like ants. We follow a pattern. We start and finish. We are at once bursting with life like the forest, but then, when it ends, we are hopelessly hollow.

This is where my mind runs to, if I let it. And always back to Ackerman. He is less than a pupa now. All spent and come to nothing. I still hear his voice, Katherine, in my head. And his whispers stay with me and taunt me. Where is God? Who are we?

But it is good to be here with Mr Wallace because unlike this novice, he has been in Indo-China for two years now and his work has only just started. He has plans to travel east as far as Macassar, the Aru Islands, and New Guinea, where he is not only bent on collecting extraordinary specimens that I could only dream about, but where, I gather, he will be testing some scientific theories on transmutation, which is an interest we all share.

I could listen to Mr Wallace forever. He is not The Intellectual, but perfectly practical in his outlook; his ideas are grounded in statistics and fact. He is a very utilitarian collector and for that I admire him all the more. He is quiet and steady and looks rather like a local parish priest with his huge beard, gangly frame, and spectacles. I have my doubts, however, that Wallace is a God-fearing man. Dare I confess that Mr Wallace and I are of the same mind on the subject of religion? But if I share my concerns about God, Katherine, am I putting you in danger? I fear I am, and yet, I know you welcome such conjecture.

He is resting here, in Brooke's cottage, and preparing for his great trip east having already catalogued thousands of new species. I have seen some of his drawings and classifications. They are extremely impressive and he keeps them in a series of green leather-bound books. He is very careful as to their whereabouts and at any given hour in the day checks them with acute agitation, as if they might disappear at any moment. He never talks about it, but I have it on good authority that he lost everything once in a shipwreck, costing him thousands. Now that is loss. Incalculable loss, and I can only admire the tenacity of a man who didn't give up, but who gritted his teeth and, like a true collector, went on to gather up treasures again.

Although he is bookishly silent sometimes, and ponderous, clearly he sees more than just the science and the cataloguing. He sees the world around him and all of us in it. And he has passion. A considered, quiet passion which burns.

Last night, for example, we sat together admiring the stars. There are so many foreign constellations — Aquarius, Aquila, and Capricornia. We picked them out to test each other, and I fared better at this game than at chess. It was just the two of us. Both English collectors, a million miles from home.

At first, he talked of nothing but specimens. Their numbers, their characteristics, their locations. Plants, birds, insects, invertebrates, mammals, shells, even interesting rock formations, minerals, and stones.

I listened intently as he shifted his talking to more than numbers and creatures. I had heard his arguments before, when Brooke would slap him down and call him a heretic. But I had not really heard them at all. Until now.

He sat back in one of Brooke's old swinging chairs which the Rajah had brought here from India. Covered comfortably in a pile of cushions, he had the best seat of the two of us and slowly lolled back and forth with it creaking as he puffed on a slim cigarette. He offered me one. It was Javanese tobacco, the very best.

He said that Brooke's cottage was to him, after so long travelling, sheer luxury. To play chess, to swim, to have everything done for him, allowed him time and leisure. I had to agree with him and I said so. My own time in Borneo had been short by comparison, but I, too, felt the need to recover. And this little spot was perfect for quiet contemplation. He nodded at me and said that he had been able to make notes here, which, when he had time, he would craft into a paper and send to England, to the Entomological Society and his agent, a Mr Samuel Stevens.

Of course, I pushed him on the notes and their meaning. He said he was happy to tell me and that he welcomed another's view and opinion. It seems that since he has been in Borneo, Wallace has been gathering evidence. That such a huge variety of species found in such specific locations, found nowhere else on this earth, could only mean one thing. That species could not be immutable. I agreed with him. I had read Lamarck, I told him. He looked troubled, and stressed that what he thought was beyond that.

He suggested that species had altered, over many, many years, like Lyell's rocks forming in layer on layer. Evolving and shifting, changing and moving, adapting to their particular world. Brooke, when Wallace had suggested this (and yes, I had heard him), had only bellowed, "So, we are all the orang-utan's brothers, Alfred? Is that what you are saying? You'd better have the evidence, or half of England will skin you alive." I laughed almost out of politeness to my overbearing host, but Mr Wallace was stony.

So I sat down that night on a spindly rattan chair and I listened. For some reason, as he talked, it seems ridiculous now, but my eyes grew hot. Quite unprompted and strange. And I felt held to my chair, frozen. The black velvet sky hung low and leaden. The night was Godlike, heavenly, omnipotent. I think it was The Truth that held me rooted there, Katherine. His words like a beam of light. He had answered Brooke at the time. And he answered me now. It was such a simple answer, almost lost in a whisper. "No," he had said then at the chess game, and to me now repeated, alone, "Not brothers, but cousins." Cousins. Like you and I, Katherine. Everything about Borneo, that night and before, shouted out loudly. And its noise was deafening. Whirring cicadas, the low melancholic echo of tree frogs, a breeze through the stirring leaves lifting and fluttering, the hiss of a moth wing burning.

All of it, Katherine. All of it, bound up together, related and connected. Birds with fish. Fossils with flowers. Think on it. Share it. Of all people, Katherine, you can do this. Your influence is greater than you think.

I know Wallace is right. He is gathering evidence which will rock the world. And his thinking has not stopped at these connections and transmutations of life. He believes that at the core of this adaption is a force of nature. And that force is the pain and struggle to survive. It is only the best and the most perfected of the species which moves on to the next stage. The weak are left behind. That, in short, Nature is brutal. Not just.

And after this time in Borneo, I must agree. But then, what are we left with? The ebb of a tide, our so-called faith, withdrawing. A swirling vortex of nothing. A world without God.

He has given me some essays to look upon, not quite complete. Some half-finished notes, some hurried illustrations. Some penned ideas, which even in their unfinished form entice me. He is the master of absorption and has read so much that we have shared, but Wallace shines a light on these works which I had not, until now, understood. William Lawrence, Thomas Malthus. But he is so unconnected, Katherine. He is shy and he is awkward, a man obsessed with his work and not caring for, or even knowing, Society, but I think here we could help him.

Wallace is not a man to keep ideas or his passion back. His excitement for Nature is almost like religion. He confessed to me that when he finds a rare, undiscovered specimen, his excitement is so overwhelming that he feels he is close to death.

And it will not surprise you to hear that for the last day or two, Mr Wallace and I have given up on chess, for there's another game in play, which if we could win it, would be a prize worth having. But this game's not static like figures on a chessboard, but is ever-changing, swirling in the sky and moving in the depths of the forest. It's dipping in the water and basking on the rocks. Each wondrous creature I observe seems so utterly perfect, so suited to its designated place, and there's such an infinite variety that I have to ask myself, can all of this be God's work? Were all these creatures made in the blink of an eye?

I have so much to send you. Your house will be overflowing with the most marvellous specimens. But you will have your own opinion on all of this, Katherine. Of that, I have no doubt. But Katherine, when I beg you to share this knowledge, I also beg you to wait, wait till I return because these thoughts are too embryonic and I will need to think on it. Wait for my return from Borneo so that we can work on this together. I know how impulsive you can be. Let's take our time because there are many who will not take kindly to such thoughts. We know who they are. They sit in The House and they rant from pulpits. But there will be many others who will welcome us. We will have your soirees and your parties, fear not! But you must wait until I'm back in London and I have my wits about me as to how best to proceed with these ideas. You will be at the centre of the vortex, Katherine. I promise you. You will be the eye of the storm.

Yours etc.
Benjamin Broderig

CHAPTER
FOURTEEN

BISHOPSGATE STATION

Inspector Adams's hope for an incognito arrival was dashed at Bishopsgate Station. There was no mistaking the crowd of men who waited at the platform, notebooks to hand, and, in another place, standing to attention, Specials, including one holding out what appeared to be a note.

"How many hacks are there, do you think? I see five, six, seven, and more coming. They've smelt blood alright, but whose is it?"

Hatton's answer was drowned out by a boy shouting from the platform, "Read all about it! Read all about it! Society beauty butchered in her bed! Read all about it!"

"Well it's out, then. It'll be me they're after. I'll meet you at St Bart's, Professor, when I've given these boys a little morsel to keep them quiet. No word about this other body, though."

And with that, the Inspector pushed the door of the carriage open and fell into the waiting mob, which practically swallowed him in a swirl of hats, great coats, and hollering. Hatton meanwhile followed Finch's cadaver, or what was left of it, the victim's body having been put in an ice-packed trunk and labelled, "This Way Up" and "Handle with Care. St Bartholomew's

Hospital, Smithfield." Broderig, who was walking beside him, swung his bag over his shoulder, saying, "And don't forget that I meant what I said, Professor. That you must call on me any time in Chelsea, if I can be of any further assistance." The two friends smiled, shook hands, and then Broderig set off at a brisk pace in the direction of the waiting carriages.

Meanwhile, Adams was still in the huddle of journalists saying, "Move back, gentlemen, and give me some air. For God's sake, back, I say, the lot of you or you'll get nothing from me today."

"Inspector Adams? The *Morning Chronicle*. Can you say anything about the Lady Bessingham murder? We hear she was bludgeoned to death with a fossil?" The reporter, who had bad breath and a squint, continued, "And a bookseller in Millford Lane, we've heard was pinned like a moth and had his heart cut out. Is there any connection between these two deaths, Inspector?" Adams looked at the one good eye, happy to oblige.

"It's true that Lady Bessingham was found dead. She was murdered in her home three nights ago. But on the details of her death, I'm afraid I couldn't possibly divulge the murder weapon. It might hinder our enquiries. And as for Mr Dodds, it's far too early to say."

"Inspector Adams" — it was a fellow from *The Standard*. "We understand a maid in Lady Bessingham's service is missing. Word is she's a suspect. Are you going to arrest her? We know you Scotland Yarders are great ones for chasing maids."

206

The Inspector indulged the chortling, saying he was strictly a family man. Hatton watched from the sideline, intrigued. The Inspector was good at this. Orchestrating the press. He even looked like he was enjoying himself.

"We're very keen to find the whereabouts of Miss Flora James as soon as possible. She is, I should say was, lady's maid to Lady Bessingham. It appears she was last seen at the British Museum. I believe her to be a crucial witness and we are not sure why she took flight, but I have my suspicions." Adams let the pause speak for itself. The hacks stopped scribbling and looked up, waiting for the great London detective to speak. "But I cannot divulge them, as that might hinder police enquiries."

A great shaking of heads and nodding from other quarters.

"Inspector Adams. Do you have a picture of the maid that we could put in our paper?"

"I have already asked an illustrator to put a likeness together. Now, gentlemen, I think you have enough for today. I have no further comments, I'm afraid."

Adams turned to have his picture sketched to go with the story. He straightened his tie and lit a cigarette, just so, something of a trademark since his celebrity. The sketch finished, Adams was just about to speak to the Special who held a note towards him, when a voice piped up.

"Inspector Adams? Correspondent for the *Illustrated London News*. Word's out, apparently there's another body. Found in an alley, a hop from Fleet Street this morning."

Adams was taken aback. He stumbled. "I'm not aware of anything. No comment."

"Not so fast, Inspector. Some say you have a pathologist constantly by your side. A Professor Hatton? Can you tell us more about the nature of his work? Rumour has it that you are dabbling in something called forensics. For the sake of our readers, Inspector, to reassure them you are doing your job. Can you tell us what this forensics is when it's at home? Is it helping you or slowing you down?"

"No comment. No comment on any of that." The Inspector pushed through the throng and headed over to his waiting officers. He furrowed his brow, took the note from the Special, and bent his head in conversation with his men. Then waved frantically to Professor Hatton to come over and join him.

"Bloody hacks." Hatton watched Adams wrestle with a Swan, then drop the lit match from his hand. "Jesus, now I've bloody well burnt myself. And where the hell has Mr Broderig gone?"

Hatton looked around him. "I just said goodbye to him. He's gone home, I think, but what was that about another body, Inspector?" Hatton stopped and watched the trunk being pushed towards a waiting wagon by two burly constables. Adams shook his head. "No, they don't know about Dr Finch yet. This is a different one, it seems. I'd better get over to Fleet Street, as the press are already on to it."

"And I see The Yard greeted you with one of their infamous telegrams, Inspector. Have they found the maid?" Hatton attempted a smile, but Adams seemed puzzled at this question.

"No? Why do you ask?" Hatton shrugged, and felt himself redden, but he had every reason to ask, damn it.

"Well, I am the acting pathologist on this case, and Medical Jurisprudence specifically demands a clear information flow between St Bart's and . . ."

"Good God, man. Enough, I say. I don't want to answer any more questions from anyone." Adams was already away, his walk turning into a run. A carriage door was promptly opened. Hatton, crimson-faced at such rudeness, got in ahead of Adams, but not before the Inspector grabbed a waiting constable, his eyes still on the pack of hacks behind them. "Why the devil didn't you telegram me, you numskull? About the body in the alley? I left clear instructions before I left. Any developments, I said. And I'd say another body qualified. Leaving me like this, ready for a public hanging. Get Professor Hatton's morgue assistant to meet us at Fleet Street. And make it damn well snappy." The constable looked lost. Adams said, exasperated, "He's the Johnny Foreigner. The letter-writing one. You'll know where to find him."

The schoolboy constable blushed and nodded. He'd been the one flapping the note at the platform. Hatton added, trying to be helpful, "The Inspector means Monsieur Albert Roumande. Black hair, brown eyes. He's very distinguished-looking and everyone knows him at the hospital. You'll find him in the mortuary room at St Bart's. Tell him Professor Hatton has asked for him."

"Yes, and now shut the fucking door, Constable Numskull," Adams spat out, as he did the task himself, leaving the constable reeling behind them.

"Half my men can't follow the simplest task." He rammed his cane on the top of the hansom and took his tobacco tin out. "Are you sure you don't want one, Professor?" Hatton shook his head, dumbfounded at the Inspector's behaviour. He waited for an apology but none came.

Hatton crossed his arms, knowing he was not without faults, but at least he kept his composure. The Inspector must have read his thoughts because he suddenly leant forward. "Do you sometimes feel everything is spinning out of your control, Professor?" Hatton shrugged. This was close to the bone. All the time, all the time he *felt* it, but he never let it show. "I think you are a man who has his life buttoned down." The Inspector lit his penny smoke. "My life is a different story. My job is difficult, treacherous even. I feel as if I'm sometimes a fly caught in a trap. And this fame. It doesn't help." Adams gazed out of the window, then looked back at Hatton, his eyes searching for something. "I have seen you at your work. You are very precise. Is it so in all aspects of your life or are you more human than I give you credit for, Professor? The Greeks were right, you know, we all have one."

"I'm not sure what you are saying, Inspector. We all have what?"

"An Achilles' heel, Professor. You never talk of your home life. You're a man dedicated to your work, not that there's anything wrong with that, but do you have a secret? You see, in my experience all men have one. A secret or an obsession. What's yours, I wonder?" The Inspector laughed a tight laugh from the back of his throat and patted his tobacco tin. "They can be innocent, of course, like this little drug, for example. Are you sure you don't want one, Professor?"

Adolphus Hatton was sure he did not. "Whatever the claims, I'm convinced tobacco is bad for the health. Why, look at you, Inspector." Hatton took hold of the Inspector's free hand, turning it this way and that. "As a medical man, I should warn you that your pulse is too quick and your hands are shaking."

The Inspector pulled his hand back, laughed again, but more nervously this time, saying, "Are you calling my bluff, Professor?" Hatton's face clouded in thought as he looked at the man before him.

Fleet Street was not a part of London that Hatton felt any great affinity for. In his opinion, it was a sorry collection of tawdry pubs and unenchanting bookshops, but as they approached, he could already see a crowd had gathered on a corner. Hatton braced himself for the inevitable onslaught.

Roumande arrived ten minutes later, and glued to his side, the schoolboy constable. The Chief Inspector barely acknowledged them, having pushed his way through to where the body lay sprawled. Crouching down to the corpse, his eyes firmly on his notebook,

Adams said, "He's met a pretty end this one. Good stuff this, strong as a noose. And here, Professor, this will interest you, there's a load of little holes about his flabby neck like he's been punctured, and some devilish tailor has pulled the thread through." Adams bent further over the body. "Stitched up, you might say . . . good and proper."

Hatton leant down and touched the swollen wrists where the linen thread had cut through. Tiny bite marks and sharp scratches could be seen around the dead man's fingers. Rats, though they had not had a real go yet. Rats, if they really want to, can devour a man, but there was plenty of other rubbish for the creatures to feed upon. Just a yard away was a mound of stinking trotters chucked out from some nearby eatery.

"Time of death?" spat Adams.

Hatton shook his head. "Roughly, bearing in mind the weather and the look of the corpse, maybe a couple of nights ago. I'll need to do an autopsy to be absolutely certain."

Adams was delving in the fat man's pocket. "One Olinthus Babbage. He's conveniently put his name on the front of his notebook. What say you to the stitching, Monsieur Roumande? You're a Frenchman and live in Spitalfields, don't you? You can tell us perhaps a little more about this silk thread? It looks very similar to the stuff you use at St Bart's."

Roumande and Hatton bent down to look closer at the skin on the neck, which had been flattened around the slit, then folded in a seam.

"It's not silk, Inspector Adams," answered-Roumande, keen to help. "It's linen. This thread is used for bookbinding. Weavers don't use this, but there are plenty of binders round here. I would say these markings on his neck have been made by a sturdy needle. By the way, Olinthus Babbage is known to me."

Adams straightened up. "Really?"

"Well, only his byline. He writes for the *Westminster Review*. I subscribe regularly. We both do." Hatton gave a curt nod in agreement. "Yes, we both read it, along with *The Lancet*. I should add, we do not agree with its radical politics, Inspector. The *Review* runs articles on forensics from time to time, but it's philosophical in its outlook, rather than informative."

"Ah, yes. Well, that appeals to the French. So what else can you gentlemen tell me about the body?"

Hatton nodded for his friend to go ahead, and Roumande answered Adams as if describing the weather. Hatton listened but his eyes were intent on the cadaver. The man had been garrotted. His trachea and larynx compressed until the pressure around his neck had stopped the airflow to his brain. He had been asphyxiated in seconds, cut at the throat and then, for some strange reason, stitched up again. "Maids can stitch," said Roumande. "Any news on that missing maid, Inspector? Although I think I must be mad to ask you, because no girl could do this. This work was done by a man. Large, good with his hands."

Adams nodded. "Yes, a man. Large enough to topple this lump over, yet quick and nimble. I think you're right on that count, monsieur."

Garrotted, compressed, and asphyxiated. His throat slit. Then left in the blood-covered snow like so much rubbish. Hatton suddenly felt light-headed, so he let Roumande keep talking and stumbled away from the pair. The other two kept on with their discussion of time, place, evidence, weapon. "*Bruises round the neck . . . blue tongue hanging out . . . the strength of ten men needed to hold this weight down.*" Hatton found a place to sit down, the icy cobbles numbing him.

"Adolphus, are you alright, friend?" It was Roumande back at his side again. "Constable, get this man some salts. He's going to faint."

But Hatton didn't. "I'm perfectly well, Albert. I just need a drink."

Roumande laid his hand gently upon Hatton's shoulder. "I think we all do, Professor."

The ancient tavern jutted out onto Fleet Street, its once whitewashed walls now a dirty yellow. Inspector Adams sat down, took his coat off, put his hat down, and took his notebook out. He turned to Roumande.

"So, you're quite the expert on stitching."

Roumande gave the Inspector a weak smile. "My wife takes a little sewing in at home. She taught me all I know and helped me to develop a more delicate line for working the cadavers. But I've never seen a fellow stitched like that."

Adams nodded to himself and called out, "Now then, where's that bartender? I'm gasping for a pint. Monsieur Roumande? What'll it be? A glass of cassis? Isn't that what you French fellows drink? Purple stuff which looks like a lady's cordial. And you, Professor, you'll join me in an ale?"

Hatton nodded quickly as his eyes flitted to Roumande, feeling the insult.

"So," continued Adams, "let's look at this notebook, shall we? Perhaps there are names in here. Perhaps he knew our other victims." Adams ran his finger down the scribbles on the page. "Well, there's little doubt. A treasure trove, you might say. Here's just a few. Shall I read them out?"

Hatton sat forward. "Never mind the names, look at the headline, 'Essay on the Immutability of Species'. He was writing about science, Inspector."

"Well, he never got to start, never mind finish. How very irritating, but look here. The initials "L.B." Perhaps a coincidence, but I don't think so. And the word 'source' written as well." Adams carried on flicking through. "Various eateries and bordellos mentioned with times and dates. We'll check up on those, but no mention of any Dr Finch or Mr Dodds. And here's a name I don't know, a Dr John Canning, and next to it the word 'verification'. Any ideas, please, gentlemen?"

Hatton spoke. "He's an academic at the British Museum. Why, only the other day Mr Broderig mentioned him. I believe he is something called an anthropologist. It's a very new science. Mr Broderig spoke highly of him and even had some of his books. Lady Bessingham's tattoo is very similar to a native people from Borneo, I believe."

"Indeed." Adams raised a brow. He called over one of his Specials who had been slouching at the bar, "Get over to the British Museum, again."

"We've interviewed everyone there already, sir," said the policeman.

Adams stood up, gave the policeman a thwack around the back of his head, and said, "Well do it again, and this time ask specifically for Dr John Canning. And if he's not available, seek him out. Find out where he lives, where he goes, if he takes sugar in his tea — and make it snappy."

Adams sat back down again, shaking his head, and looked at Roumande.

"So, monsieur. How well did you know Mr Babbage?"

Roumande shrugged. "It is as I told you, Inspector. He was a general commentator and invariably got it wrong. I'm no admirer of these broad-brush writers. Like the Professor, I'm a man of fact and detail."

"I can see that, monsieur. I watched you with the knife the other day at the morgue. Turning it into an art, I might say. But I digress. Here's our ales, but still nothing for you, sir. Maybe not on the job, eh, Professor? A knife-wielding mortuary assistant, drunk before noon?" Adams laughed, but Hatton braced himself, knowing what was coming.

"*Merde. Quel trou du cul! Excusez-moi, Professeur, je sors prendre un café.*" Roumande spoke French rarely. "So you know, Inspector. I find English ale to be vile like some Englishmen's manners. I need some air."

216

The Inspector gave Hatton a wink but the Professor shrunk from it. It would be best to let sleeping dogs lie. He sat stony-faced with the Inspector, sipping his drink, and through the mottled window, Hatton could see Roumande chatting to a coffee grinder. Roumande seemed animated; they were sharing a joke together.

"Let me introduce you to Mr Gad, Professor, He's the landlord here."

The man, who was now standing in front of them, laden down with plates of steaming food, bowed obsequiously. "Inspector Adams. It's an honour, sir. I follow all of your cases in the papers. An honour, sir, an honour indeed."

"Yes, yes," Adams said impatiently. "Let's have the food, then. I for one am hungry. Sit yourself down please, Mr Gad, because I want to ask you about one of your customers."

"God rest his soul, is it poor Mr Babbage that brings you here? What a business to slit a throat like that and so near to The Old Cheshire Cheese. And poor Mr Dodds as well, just a hop from here."

"Well, I suspect, Mr Gad, that's why you're so busy. A little notoriety never does a tavern any harm, eh?"

Mr Gad forced a laugh. "You're jesting, of course, Inspector."

Adams lit a cigarette and blew the smoke in the landlord's face. "I never jest about murder."

The landlord nodded, his face now suitably solemn.

"So, Mr Gad," continued Adams, "what do you know of Babbage? And also Mr Dodds, for that matter?"

Gad scratched his badly pitted skin. "Mr Babbage was a radical when it suited him, a columnist for the *Westminster Review*. He was a regular here. Mr Dodds came in now and then, although you'd hardly know it. He was the very opposite to Mr Babbage. Quiet as a mouse, kept himself to himself. Would order half a pint and make it last all night. He was the sort of customer I had no wish to encourage. Not that I'd wish him dead."

"Go on, Mr Gad. I'm listening."

Adams asked if he'd seen anything suspicious in the last few nights, anything out of the ordinary. The tavern owner replied that he had noted Mr Babbage, God rest his soul, dining with a youngish man only the night before last, in fact. "Boiled potatoes and chops, or was it beef? Making notes Mr Babbage was, nodding and laughing with the man, and when they'd finished their food, shaking hands. I was distracted a little as there was, now I recall, someone unusual sitting in the corner. She kept her eyes from me, but such lashes. An unusual flower, I'd say, of the foreign variety."

The tavern owner continued, "Anyway, the men were locked in conversation. Mr Babbage was a regular customer, but I had never seen the other one before. But he looked out of sorts, Inspector. And shifty. Shifty, yes, that's the word."

Mr Gad continued, hoiking the odd bit of spit up as he talked, "Gorgeous she was. Tiny waist." He sent a spray of spittle before him. "Dressed in black, red rabbit fur. Quite the little lady. An actress perhaps." Gad winked. Adams laughed. "And little boots. I noticed that. Her ankles were slim." Mr Gad winked again, this time at Hatton.

Adams unfolded a piece of paper from his left-hand pocket. "Anything like this, Mr Gad?" Hatton looked, too, and saw the likeness of a maid, clear-faced and pretty. Gad laughed. "No, nothing like that. She's very plain, ain't she? No, this one was," and he smiled and drew a shape in the fetid air of the tavern. Out, in, and out again.

Roumande came back in, rubbing his hands together.

"How was your coffee?" asked Adams, looking up from his notebook.

"The coffee was excellent. French and of the finest quality, according to that costermonger, and he's been running that stand for nigh on a decade."

"Really?" Adams smirked. "How interesting."

"Well, he's heard of you, Inspector, and he remembers when you used to work around The Strand. Says it was your patch for a while, along with St James' Park, when they were clearing up the molly boys. Do you recall him, Inspector? Says you were in charge of vice."

"Recall a coffee grinder?" Adams drew on his cigarette. "I hardly think so. It's well known I ran vice for a number of years, earning my stripes. And the molly boy thing was a while ago. We did an excellent job, and what of it?"

"Nothing," said Roumande. "Nothing at all, but yes, he does remember you. Says you also do quite a bit of private work for toffs around Belgravia and Mayfair."

Adams shrugged, and knocked a glug back.

"It's no secret. We all do. Do you know how much The Yard pays a policeman? Even a senior one?"

Roumande smiled, but Hatton felt uncomfortable. "If you are finished on Mr Babbage, perhaps then, Inspector, we can discuss the girls?"

"Girls? Which girls do you mean, monsieur? I have my mind on one only, and her name is Flora James. I've got the whole damn Force looking for her, as we speak."

"Are you being deliberately vague, Inspector? Not the maid. The other girls. The one I did the autopsy for and the little angel sleeping in the box, which led us directly to the bookseller. Do you know how many I've seen like that? I make it four now, in the last three years. All of them, save the last, tortured, slashed, and dumped in an alley. But the last was different. She was a virgin, Inspector. Do you know what I think?"

Adams sighed. "What do you think, monsieur?"

"That the killer of these children is either getting more daring or less fussy. It's not just gay girls he's after any more. But didn't you look at the autopsy report on the train? Adolphus gave it to you, didn't you, Professor?"

Inspector Adams, even in the half light of the tavern, grew pale. "Professor Hatton, please spare me from the wrath of this man. How many times, monsieur? We got the endless letters you sent us, but we have no time to answer them all. You simply send too many, and I know you speak against The Yard when you can. You think we're stupid, don't you? You're a foreigner and have little understanding of an Englishman's reputation, or The Yard's, but if you damned well suggest I'm not doing my job, I'll . . ."

Hatton quickly interjected, "But perhaps you should look again, Inspector, for Roumande thinks all these girls are connected. You didn't look at the report, Inspector, did you?" Hatton felt something. Was it panic or relief? He couldn't tell, but he was glad he'd finally said something which felt like the truth.

Adams stood up. "What do you take me for? To suggest I care more about these botanicals than children is an outrage. I have a job to do, leads to follow, and when I get through my mountain of paperwork, a home to go to. Today is the Sabbath, if you hadn't noticed. I've nothing left to do here. Mr Gad, good day to you, sir."

Hatton watched Adams leave. The Inspector left the door open so the snow whooshed into the tavern, and he turned back fleetingly, his face a vapour. "Unlike you two, it seems, I have to report back to my superiors. Get the autopsy for Dr Finch ready, Professor. This is the last time I'll ask you nicely. If you can't cope, I can always send the cadavers to St Mary's. Would you prefer that?"

Hatton, exasperated, stood up and followed him, picking up the hack's notebook, which had been left on the table. Outside the air was freezing. "Inspector, please. If we have overstepped the mark, I apologise. Let's not part on these terms. Of course we can cope. We will do the exacting work we always do. Monsieur Roumande is a capital fellow and he loves children, sir.

He has five of his own including two girls, and that's his concern. He meant no harm and did not wish to insult you."

"Do you think I am so high and mighty I can take no criticism? Quite frankly, I'm used to it. But as it happens, if you genuinely want to make my life easier, then please tell your friend I could do with him at the station. I didn't mean to offend him, either. I think it might be useful to show him what I have on these girls. Could you spare your excellent fellow for an hour or so? To put his mind at rest? I can show him all the case notes pertaining to these girls when we get to The Yard and then perhaps he'll be satisfied."

Hatton nodded, relieved, and was about to speak again but Roumande had already joined them out on the icy pavers, and spoke for himself, the cold making his face glow. Roumande smiled, his front teeth chipped and stained, his hair unruly in the whipping wind, and said he would be happy to go with the Inspector, if it helped. Hatton looked at his watch, turned to Roumande who was waiting to get into the carriage. "But Albert, then an end to this? There are three full autopsies for us tonight and I cannot do them alone."

Hatton headed back to The Old Cheshire Cheese, where Mr Gad was standing by the bar. There were no other customers, save a couple of old men playing chequers, who didn't look up from their game. Hatton asked for porter. Mr Gad gestured over at a rough-faced barmaid to fetch it and said, "Strange sort

222

of fellow though, ain't he?" Here we go, thought Hatton, more unwanted comments on Monsieur Roumande, but instead the barman continued, "That Inspector Adams. Odd for a policeman. Not the usual type. He's too tall, and if you ask me, he smells funny." Hatton couldn't help laughing, and said, "Well, Mr Gad, I cannot say I've noticed an odd whiff about him."

"No? Well, you're perhaps not as observant as I, because he wears cologne. Like a rich man. Not that I smell too many of those round here, but occasionally I walk past them on The Strand when they arrive in their carriages. They come here for the musicals and the theatre, their women smelling of lily of the valley, and the men smelling of something different. Cologne, I'm telling you. Overpowering stuff."

And Hatton knew Mr Gad was right, and that he had noticed the scent but given little thought to it. Odours were part of his forensic work, but he applied the question of their source only when dealing with the dead, not the living. And there was no fault in it, because far from being a man unconcerned with outward appearance, Professor Hatton was not above a little toilette, himself. He knew it became a gentleman, or a man striving in that direction. His sister had many times made mention that it was beholden upon him to make a little more effort than a quick shave and a rub-down with carbolic.

"Darling brother. Outward appearances matter. Here, let me do that for you." And she had leant forward to brush a little scurf off his collar. "You're a handsome man, Adolphus, but you make so little of it, hidden away in that morgue of yours. Have a fitting with a tailor, brother, for this suit is shabby and your shoes are scuffed."

"But Lucy, I have no need for anything fancy. I do little other than work."

She had turned him to face her. A face which was open and sunny. "Exactly, Adolphus. And if mother was alive, she would speak very plainly. Very plainly indeed, as I shall. You're turning into a recluse, my darling boy. And you cannot marry a cadaver."

Lucy. He smiled to think on her now. Her oldest boy would be twelve come March, and her youngest baby was walking already. They kept in touch through letters, but where she wrote ten, he sent only one in return. One in twelve months, he remembered with appropriate shame.

Was this his secret?

A man so intent on success that he would sacrifice everything to achieve it. Hatton put his drink down and headed out of the door, but instead of going back immediately to the morgue, decided to walk a little. He still hadn't looked at the crime scene for Mr Dodds. He quickened his pace and carried on, further up The Strand towards Millford Lane, to be overtaken by what he thought must be two Specials, running in the other direction. They wore no uniform, but he was long enough in a policeman's company to know a peeler when he saw one. He wondered what calamity was calling them to race like that?

And then he saw up ahead, more men with a huge pump heading for Millford Lane, and at the top of the road, a little huddle of people gawping as great plumes of black smoke billowed into the air. "Stand back!" shouted one of the fire officers. The flames were wrapping around the building. The cadaver had been moved to St Bart's by now, but the ledger book, the details of customers, the minutiae of Mr Dodd's life, were ablaze. The smoke hurt his eyes, but Hatton still stepped forward.

"Stand back, I say!" repeated the fire officer.

"Is anybody in there?"

"Are you the owner?"

Hatton shook his head.

"The shop went up like a timber box. Now, sir, I've asked you nicely. There's nothing to gain by standing there with your mouth agape. Move up to the end of the street."

Hatton did as he was told. The building was an inferno. He was sure that Adams would be informed immediately, and they could visit here together later when the fire was quelled. The pumps were going like the clappers but there just might be some scrap that would survive, though he suspected not. There was nothing to be gained here. He was better off at the morgue.

Back in the morgue, hours had passed. No word had come about the fire, which, yet again, was against procedure. The scene of the crime, devastated. Crucial evidence lost. Hatton shook his head and put his scalpel down, feeling this was no coincidence. Someone had something to hide, but what was it? He remembered the locked room at the bookshop and the Inspector's eagerness to get him off the premises. He shook the feeling off. Those men he'd seen running? Were they Adams's men? Or someone else's? And where the devil was Roumande? He was never late. In fact, he was impossibly early.

Hatton looked at his pocket watch, thinking to himself, how long could it take to look at some case notes? Then suddenly, of course, it occurred to him that Roumande had probably already left the station and gone to a local tavern. Perhaps he'd learnt something and wanted to think. Hatton smiled to himself, tucking his pocket watch away. But these cadavers wouldn't cut themselves and so Hatton headed through the North Wing and was just about to leave the building when he saw a policeman and his Hospital Director, Mr Buchanan, shaking his head, and then a glance in his direction. What was this? More trouble, thought Hatton. God forbid, not another murder. There was no more room in his day. Three corpses tonight for dissection, and not another thing would they get from him. Damn the lot of them. He needed Roumande back right this minute or he'd never get home this evening.

Hatton walked towards the porch, swinging his cane theatrically as he glided past his Director, sending a clear message that he, yes he, was someone of importance with places to go and things to do.

"Excuse me, Professor Hatton."

There was something odd here, because Mr Buchanan only spoke to the pathologist when he was suggesting another budget cut. But this voice was grave, concerned even.

Hatton turned around.

"Will this take long? I'm in a bit of a hurry, as you can see. Monsieur Roumande has taken it upon himself to go off on some jaunt. So, if you don't mind, sir, I'll wish you a very pleasant evening."

"Adolphus, we need to speak."

Adolphus? When did he ever call him that? Was it Lucy? God, no. Not his sister. Had something happened to her or one of her children? The Professor's blood ran cold. His Achilles' heel. Wasn't that what Adams had said? And now Hatton would learn his lesson the hard way. It would be his fault for neglecting his sister and thinking only of himself. The faces looking back at him were drained and anxious. But it was not Lucy.

"It's Monsieur Roumande, Adolphus," said the Hospital Director. "I'm afraid he's been arrested."

CHAPTER
FIFTEEN

THE ISLE OF DOGS

The rustle of her dress was barely audible above the loud din of the printing machine as Madam Martineau swished past her huddle of dedicated print workers, giving a nod in their direction, because they were artisans and she admired them. Compositors, engravers, and lithographers — the new aristocracy. "And they are rising, fast," she thought. But by God, like her, they earned their money. Forty hours at a stretch or more, these men would stay at the printing press if the job required it. And she knew what drove these men. It drove her, too.

Because the demands of the ladies she stitched for bore down on her. A little lower. A little higher. A little tighter. Another button, another flounce, the bustle perter, the silk softer. She provided what her customers required, however irksome, with the sweetest of smiles on her face and a deferential dip of her bonnet. But all the while, her head pounded. The powders usually worked, but a day was fast approaching when she would not be this servile stitching, scurrying, waist-nipped person. What nonsense was required of her? What vacuous conversation?

She sometimes despaired of her sex and all this whim-wham of the fashion world. But still she hoped that all of this frippery was leading her somewhere, because she'd heard the radicals in Hyde Park promising her that change was coming. That the old order would fall away and that even here in England, revolution was possible.

Madame Martineau looked at her money. She understood her purpose. They called it sedition but she knew she was a purveyor of the truth and that words were power.

The first room Madame Martineau stepped into was dedicated to printing production. Not bound up and hand stitched like one of her dresses, because this was not a bookbinders for the burgeoning middle classes. There was no leather here. No gilt or moire grain. This was education for the masses, and Madame Martineau's investment in this little venture had been more than significant. And to raise this money had cost her everything. On a purely practical level, she'd had to embrace a new sideline or two, but if snooping about a bit paid the rent, what of it? Yet all this risk was a heavy investment. She ran her palm down her throat as she looked at their latest scoop. "What's this?" she asked one of the printers.

"It's the story you got us about the lord who lives with pigs. The cattle sit on his sofas, do you remember, miss?"

She smiled and looked at the picture. It was a perfect likeness, the old goat. What was his name? Lord something or other? "Did you get the reference in about his beau?"

The printer laughed, turning the page for her. The illustration was perfect. The lord bent over; the dog looking surprised.

She ran her fingers along the page a little further.

"His bill on curbing wage increases for rope makers is coming up next week in parliament. Make sure you release it then. Oh, and . . ."

"Yes, miss?"

"Ensure a copy gets into The House. Did you mention his syphilis?"

"Yes, miss. It's the dénouement, so to speak."

"Well done, and your French, by the way, *c'est tres excellent, monsieur.*"

The printer blushed and pulled his forelock. All of this her quiet revolution. Her step-by-step sedition.

She put the leaflet with a pile of others, took her powders, and, taking her little hand mirror out of her velvet bag, applied a smudge of rouge. A tad tired, perhaps. Was that her first grey hair?

"*Vive la Republique,*" she whispered, but the face looking back was empty.

She sighed. Just one more job, and then all would be completed. A hundred pounds to finish it off, Monreith had said, and that a man called Benjamin Broderig was now their biggest threat.

"He is the author of the letters. And what he knows could soon be common currency and topple us all. Need I remind you what a commotion this would cause if his letters are made public? How the nature of his material might be misconstrued? That my name and the House of Monreith might be dragged into scandal, madam? So here's a hundred to finish it off, once and for all."

Money was nothing to him, but to her? She took the offer of another hundred pounds willingly, because how many hearts could she capture for that price? How many minds could she turn?

Madame Martineau poured herself a whisky. A hundred to finish it off? She bet the men the Duke hired got more than that. Why, only this morning, she had seen two plain-clothed coppers, leaving the Duke's residence, despatched on some errand or other, and they looked in a hurry.

And it must have been more than a year ago now, when she hid down an alleyway, unnoticed, and watched another man coming out of Monreith House, a wad of lucre in his hand. At first the man seemed afraid and kept looking behind him. He lit a newfangled thing, a Crimean cigarette. And she remembered him specifically, because Madame Martineau had an eye for a tall fellow. He had long legs and was distinguished in a gabardine coat. He'd swaggered off towards St James' Park stuffing the loot into his pocket. One in a long line of private protectors, she didn't wonder. The police were all like that. And she'd said so to one of her tawny girls that very same day, who had been whimpering and dragged fresh from the docks. "And don't worry about the Specials. They're not like their names suggest. They're no better than the rest of us."

CHAPTER
SIXTEEN

SCOTLAND YARD
WHITEHALL

Scotland Yard was busy but Hatton elbowed his way through the throng, demanding, "I need to see Inspector Adams, immediately."

The Special behind the reception desk was chewing a pencil. "You can find Inspector Adams up the stairs on the second floor in the detective's room, but mind, you can't just go barging in there. You need an appointment first. Take a seat and we'll call you when we're ready."

Hatton had no time for this so he pushed past the Special who was already yelling, "Oi! You in the derby. I just said you can't go up there!"

The detectives' room was piled high with files and papers and thick with smoke. No sight of Adams, but there was one desk which caught Hatton's eye. At the back of the room was a desk with an ashtray overflowing with half-smoked cigarettes, a bottle of Machars whisky, and a tin of tobacco. Hatton looked at the lid. A Crimean soldier on the front.

Hatton turned to a man sitting close by. "Is this Inspector Adams's desk?"

"And you are, sir?"

"I'm the Medical Jurisprudence adviser on the Lady Bessingham case. Inspector Adams has just made an arrest, I understand." The word "arrest" stuck in his throat. What the devil had happened here?

"They've gone for a pint. Great news, ain't it? Banged up a French murderer. Always the bloody foreigners, ain't it? Hanging's too good for 'em. If I could get my hands around his swarthy neck why I'd . . ."

Hatton yanked the vile policeman by the scruff of his neck. "You'd like to what? Hang him yourself? Is that it? Without a trial, or a scrap of evidence? Yes, I bet you would." Hatton left the officer slumped gasping for breath and, at a pace, headed out of The Yard.

Outside on the pavement the gas lamps were lit, a tangerine glow, so that the whole stretch of Whitehall was now ablaze as carriages hurtled past him. Hatton made a dash for it and up ahead could see The Northumberland Hotel, knowing this was exactly the sort of place Inspector Adams would frequent with its dazzling cut-crystal windows and elaborate inscriptions inviting him in to drink "The Only Real Brandy in London". Hatton stepped in and found Adams standing by the bar with a glass of cognac in his hand. He was surrounded by his usual flunkies.

"You took your time, Professor. I thought you would have been here an hour ago." Hatton staggered back from this audacity, but he'd seen this before. The arrogance of a man with too much admiration thrust upon him.

"Where is he?" Hatton gritted his teeth.

"Your French fellow? Monsieur Roumande? Listen, friend . . ."

"I'm no friend of yours, sir, believe me." Hatton's words tumbled from his mouth.

Inspector Adams didn't meet Hatton's eye as he said, "He's suspected of at least two crimes, Hatton. Why you only have to look at the man to see the violence in him."

"Violence? What are you talking about, Inspector?" Hatton was lost. He knew Roumande, and he was the best of men.

"He's French and, like the Irish, they're full of it. Violence, Professor. My officers are no strangers to Spitalfields. It's a den of dissenters, atheists, and drinkers who fly into such a passion when they're angry. Everything points to him. His very way of being. His manner and his character. His swarthiness plus, of course, the linen thread, the stitching, and his knowledge of anatomy. Need I say more?" Inspector Adams put his brandy glass down.

"Are you mad, Inspector? What are you talking about? Roumande has no motive. He has no knowledge of these people. He is wholly innocent of the crimes you charge him of. You don't have a scrap of evidence."

"Come, Professor. There's a free table at the back. I've got something to show you."

Hatton was disarmed by this sudden change of tack, but Adams held all the cards so Hatton had no choice but to listen to him. Adams carried on talking about motive as he rummaged in his pocket, and Hatton at

234

once recognised the note given to Adams on their arrival at Bishopsgate Station.

"More than just a scrap of evidence, I'd call it. By all means, Professor, read it out loud."

Hatton was flummoxed but he recognised the hand and his heart sank.

Dear Lady Bessingham . . . a leading institution . . . appealing for your Ladyship's heartfelt interest . . . surgical instruments required for the pursuit of excellence in the field of forensics . . . all donations gratefully received . . . signed, on behalf of Professor Hatton of St Bart's . . . Albert Roumande (Chief Diener).

Hatton's hands were shaking as he muttered, "But this means nothing, Inspector. Roumande has sent a thousand like this to anyone with money in this city. Lady Bessingham was a well-known patron of Science. Does he even remember signing this? Have you asked him?"

"It was amongst her general correspondence, dated six months ago. He recalled it but when asked simply shrugged in that annoyingly Gallic way of his and said, 'Quoi?' and then clammed up. Silence is just another show of guilt, in my opinion. He killed her because she wouldn't advance the money. I had one of my men check with your Director at the hospital. Despite the begging, she gave St Bart's nothing."

"Are you seriously suggesting that Roumande would murder for that? It's ridiculous. And Babbage? Dr Finch? Mr Dodds? And what about the little girl leading us to the bookseller? How does that fit in? Are you pinning all of this on my friend, as well, Inspector?"

"I'm not sure I welcome this tone, Professor. The link is tenuous, granted. But we'll get there."

"There's no connection and you know it. And while I'm about it, have you followed those other leads? Dr Canning? Flora James? The only connection we have, Inspector, are Broderig's letters, which are missing. There's a trail, Inspector, and yet you seem happy to ignore it. Someone has these letters and is willing to kill for them, or kill anyone who has seen them. Broderig will be next."

"You need to calm yourself, Professor. You are at sixes and sevens."

"Very well, then. Tell me I imagined it when I saw the bookshop on Millford Lane ablaze this afternoon. All evidence lost, Inspector? Coincidence? I am happy to swear I saw what I thought were two plainclothers fleeing from the place. Not unlike the fellows who you were with at the bar. On your orders, were they?"

"If you carry on like this, Professor, I'll have you arrested."

Hatton could see it wasn't working. He took a seat, sat down, his head in his hands as he said, "Have you spoken to his wife yet, Inspector? Roumande will have an alibi and I can vouch for his character. Please, Inspector, was it something he said to you?"

Adams leant forward and lit his cigarette. "I know my job, although it seems to me you think you have some sort of elevated understanding of police work. I'm still waiting for your final conclusions on the autopsies, and yet here you are, picking holes in my arrest and making all sorts of accusations." Hatton went to speak, but Adams held his hand up. "Not that I have to justify myself, but so you know, we did indeed trace one Dr Canning to a place in Gordon Square, but by the time we arrived, it was empty. We did, however, find an invitation to Lady Bessingham's funeral, which he must have dropped on the floor. If Dr Canning is not some lunatic killer, I shall have a chat with him tomorrow, assuming he is on his way there. As for the bookshop? Accidents happen, Professor. But I have nothing else concrete to go on, and I am under considerable pressure to draw this situation to an end. Four people are dead. The little girls are another thing, altogether."

"But you will draw nothing to an end, Inspector, by arresting an innocent man." Hatton looked at his adversary. "I'll raise the bail, Inspector." But this man wouldn't be moved. Hatton only had to look at him to know it.

And as Hatton watched the Inspector's face through a haze of smothered blue, he knew that this was a smokescreen. God knows, it was what everybody said about The Yard. Hatton looked at the cut of Adams's suit. What had Mr Gad said? That Adams smelt like a rich man. Money was always at the bottom of things. Adams was hiding something or protecting someone.

"You dress very well, Inspector, if I may say so. And no stinting on little pleasures. I saw the single malt on your desk. Whatever your claim to the contrary, The Yard must pay you very well."

Adams toyed with his glass, as he said, "I think I've heard enough from you, Hatton. It's not easy to accept you've been wrong about a man, but if you think you have any future with police work, you had better get used to it."

"Get used to it? Put up with it? Do as I'm told? Is that what you mean, Adams? Is that what you do? I'll leave you to your brandy, Inspector. I hope it chokes you."

"Thank you for seeing me like this, Mr Broderig. I didn't know who else to turn to."

"This is the most ridiculous thing I've ever heard. There's no evidence, then? Nothing to link your friend to any of these crimes?"

"No. Adams simply wants someone in a cell and he's picked up the first man to come to mind. He muttered things about letters and linen thread." Hatton took another slug. "But I can't help thinking he's covering something up. Do you know anything about him? Beyond what we read in the papers?"

"I know only that he also does a little private work and he has a lodging house in Whitehall. I suspect he keeps a tart there. But I don't criticise him for that. It's his relief from the pressures of the city. Here's mine." Broderig topped his glass up. "Can I get you another, Professor?"

Hatton shook his head but it was good to have someone to talk to, knowing this young man's mind was broader than most. Broderig had travelled, seen the

238

world, and he was prepared to think beyond the usual, as the Professor must.

"Do you know, I still haven't got my letters returned and I know they were in the house at Nightingale Walk. It's very strange that they should disappear. They were very distinctive and written on parchment. And as I think I mentioned to you on the train to Cambridge, there's some delicate information contained within. You see, I met an extraordinary man in Borneo. His name is Alfred Russel Wallace."

"Yes, you've already mentioned him, but what of it?"

Broderig shifted on his chair a little before answering. "Well, the reason I mention it is I rather stupidly jotted down a few ideas of his and sent them to Lady Bessingham. I regret sharing them now, but since my letters have vanished I can't help thinking, after what you've said tonight, that the Inspector knows more than he's letting on. Perhaps he has secured them for someone, or means to sell them himself."

"They are of value, then?" Hatton asked, intrigued.

"To some they are. To others they could spell trouble, but as I say, they were only jots and scribbles. Some embryonic ideas, nothing more, but perhaps it was enough. These ideas bring everything we know into question. Not just how the world was made, but how the world should be governed. I asked Katherine to keep them so we could discuss them properly on my return. Well, I returned a month ago but have been busy with my other work and Katherine was a very impetuous woman. I think she may have spoken to someone or done something with them that she shouldn't have done." As if remembering something, Broderig pushed his chair away from his desk, moving across the room to a display cabinet, and opening it up, said, "I have something here to show you, Professor. I brought one or two specimens home with me. The rest will be here any day now. Do you remember I told you about the ship I travelled on called *The Advancement*?"

"The one that was circumnavigating Indo-China?"

"I see you paid attention, Professor. Well, apparently there were problems with the crew and they were forced to abandon the mission on the coast of Borneo. Inside the hold are one or two crates of mine and they will shortly arrive in England. They include a creature called the Mias. Have you heard of it, perhaps?"

Hatton was fascinated, saying, "Yes, you mentioned the Mias on our journey to Cambridge."

"Well, I didn't tell you everything. I held a baby once. It died you see, and the grief I felt, the anger, was a little overwhelming, but it has abated now after all that has passed." Broderig opened a small, lacquered box. "Look, Professor. They're very small but perfectly preserved."

Hatton was intrigued. "Ants?" he asked, because Hatton wasn't totally sure.

"Exactly. Giant forest ants. *Camponotus gigas*. They look ferocious, but are harmless enough. And such a singular sense of purpose, it's wondrous. Many times in the jungle, I lay on the ground and marvelled at their blind faith, their sense of absolute conviction. We would put bits of bark in their way, stones, handfuls of mud,

240

but nothing would stop them. On and on they would go till they got the job done. But come, this is no time for ants. You have work to do. Why don't you go back to wherever you left the Inspector? See where he goes. If he has a secret, as you say, and this arrest is some kind of elaborate cover, follow him and who knows what you'll discover."

Broderig was right. Hatton shook the young man firmly by the hand, thanked him for his time, and before leaving said, "Be careful, Mr Broderig. Four are dead. Have you located that pistol yet?"

Broderig patted his top right-hand pocket. "Don't worry, Professor. I have taken heed of the Inspector. I can take care of myself."

Hatton waited outside The Northumberland Hotel. It was closing time and after a few shouts, the Specials tumbled out followed by Inspector Adams, who took a different direction to his men, heading towards St James' Park at a brisk pace. Was he heading for his lodging house, then?

Hatton watched the Inspector turn left into Whitehall Road. Adams carried on, his black beaver on, his face shielded against the snow. Hatton followed as the Inspector turned right, left again, and then up a winding street with a sign, "Grenadier Row". Hatton was half expecting the detective to look round at any minute and announce, "You fool, Hatton, do you really think you could follow me?" but Adams didn't.

Towards the end of the street there was a hotel, The Horse Guards Arms. Hatton watched him go in. Who was he meeting here? Hatton waited in the shadows and beat his hands together, very gently, so as not to make a sound, but the cold was creeping into his bones and flakes were gathering on his lashes. He wiped them away, for a moment blinded, and then saw something.

Two men, arm in arm, leaning on each other, but not through drink. Hatton looked away. Why was the Inspector here? Was he meeting someone?

Hatton heard bells chiming, telling him it was midnight, as he moved towards the tavern. It was dark, dimly lit, but he could still make out Inspector Adams sitting in a bay window talking to someone and they sat close to each other, furtive and whispering. But who was this man? An informer or a witness? Through another window, Hatton could see a few soldiers, a throng of other men and a very dapper looking landlord, standing at the bar. There was the tinkling of light piano music and a hubbub of male voices in the air, as Hatton crept forward, pressing himself close to a wall, where he spied Adams huddled over a brandy, still talking, still whispering. And then, Hatton saw all he needed to. Adams was brushing the other man's hand with his lips, caressing him, and he wasn't a man at all. He was a youth, highly rouged, smiling and fluttering his eyelashes, like a woman. Hatton staggered back. Roumande was in a cell somewhere. There was no going back on anything. Hatton knew the sentence for this perversion, but here was Adams, secretive yes, but still able to be seen, in the front window of a hotel with a molly boy. Surely he knew the terrible risk he was taking?

242

Hatton waited back in the shadows. For how long he wasn't sure, but when the Inspector stepped out of the hotel again, he was alone. Hatton watched as Adams looked over his shoulder before taking a swig from a small silver hip flask. Adams passed him, head down, and was muttering something which sounded like "God forgive me" or "God protect me."

Adams stopped suddenly and lit a penny smoke, which wasn't easy in such filthy weather. Adams was shrouded in a veil of smoke as Hatton stepped out of the shadows and touched the Inspector's shoulder very lightly. So pale, Adams was a ghost, and his voice, when he spoke, faltered. There were no bombastics now. He simply said, "How long have you been following me, Professor?"

"Long enough," Hatton answered. "I know everything."

Benjamin Broderig shut the box. It was late but his mind was spinning, like the earth on its axis. He thought of Katherine, who would be buried tomorrow. Perhaps she could see him even now. Her breath in the air; her words, a whisper in the night.

But this was London. There were no rocks, no flowers, no water spirits. The sky was sullied. It was unclean, despite the feathering snow. Broderig thought about his journey here and the places he still wanted to go. He walked over to his desk and found the map of the Aru Islands, and with a quill plotted out the route he might take and thought about how if he went there, he would have no one to write to and no one to share it with as he had when Katherine Bessingham was still alive.

Sarawak
December 22nd, 1855

Dear Katherine,

I think I have changed. Not just that I am a little bearded now, and less like the boy you once knew, but that I have changed in my outlook. I think this is more profound a change than the physical, don't you think? And of course, with bated breath, I am in some anticipation to hear your reaction to Mr Wallace's ideas.

But I am still surprised that he shared his thoughts so freely. Perhaps here in Borneo, away as we are from England, a man can really think about the way of things. There is no fear here. No Society. Yes, of course, there is fear of a snake bite, perhaps even a fear of reputation. But we are freer here. Less formed.

Mr Wallace will return to Singapore before he plans his next adventure. He said he only waits on money. I had hoped that he might see something in me, and ask me to join him, but sadly, he did not. He is clearly a man who is happiest when he is working alone. Perhaps this is what makes him so good at this trade. I can see now that I was just passing his time for him, playing chess, talking of theories whilst he readied himself for the next expedition.

The day we left Brooke's cottage, Emmerich packed up and got ready in the greatest of moods. I beard him chatting on the veranda. His "ummings arrhings". And his hilariously Germanic, "Jawohls" at each of Mr Wallace's questions. So polite and deferential.

I am slightly at a loss to be back now in Sarawak and wish Mr Wallace was here. Don't get me wrong. Good old Emmerich will always be my friend, no matter how far I travel. But it is close upon me, I can feel it. The time for leaving again. The rainy season is just around the corner when collecting will become impossible. The forest will be beaten down with pounding rain and Wallace will escape it by heading east. Emmerich, on the other hand, enjoys the rainy season and the immobility of it all. And the more I think on this, the more convinced I am that he will never leave. In Sarawak, he needs little to live on. He has his house. His trade in orchids. But I have none of these things now the Mias are spoken for and my Dutch friends are gone and little San, who I think of often, far away with my gun in his hand.

I have even started to gather up my belongings and pack away some instruments no longer needed in boxes marked "Handle with Care".

I heard a church bell ringing this evening. There is a Calvinist chapel in Sarawak. It must have been the way the breeze was blowing that let the low, plaintive rings reach my ears. So out of place in this world and yet when I heard it, I felt homesick. I wandered down to my moonlit beach in the vain hope that I might see a ship I knew, but there was nothing on the horizon. No chugging steamer, no glorious junk, no surveyor's ship. Just flat black ocean; sea and sky melding together into a void. I sat down on the beach and then noticed it was moving.

First flurries of sand flying into the air. Then tiny creatures: turtles. Not one or ten, Katherine. To my astonishment, there must have been a thousand or more, moving across the sand to the sea. Where were they going? Would they all get there? Something was calling them. I picked up a little hatchling. It was a leatherback (Dermochelys coriacea) and it struggled in my hands. I was not God, but I felt, just then, at that moment, that if I wanted to, I could be. It made me shudder. So instead, rather than killing the little creature as "The Collector" should have done, I set it down. Released, it scuttled forward, kicking up the sand with its tiny flippers. I watched it go. The gentle waves lapped up onto the beach and as the sea pulled its might out again, I saw my little turtle rise up, then disappear.

When the spectacle was over and the beach was left with only two or three stragglers, I wandered back. And like the turtles, I knew it was my time to set off in a new direction. To have faith, if not in God, then in destiny. To stop looking out hopelessly at horizons, but to pack up my cases and go home.

The rest of my thoughts, my ideas, my journals I will keep with me, for you must be growing tired of my rambling letters, Katherine, and so I promise you this is the last. Journeys home are not the same as journeys leaving. The next words you shall hear from me shall be face to face, together at Ashbourne. And thinking of that, of home and familiar company, yes, it's true to say,

I feel almost myself again. In fact, quite content with the world and well.

Yours etc.

Benjamin Broderig looked out of the window and his hot breath steamed up a panel, so that he could easily draw his own initials on the glass. He breathed on the letters purposefully again, so the initials evaporated. Then somewhere in the house, he heard a voice. Perhaps his father was up? But the voice sounded rough and inelegant, so more likely a servant. He folded up his map again and placed it by the bookcase and as he did so, heard a soft creak of wood, and the fall of footsteps. Broderig looked at the door, braced himself, and took his pocket pistol out. Inspector Adams had been right about one thing, he knew he was in danger. But there was nobody there, and so he put the pocket pistol back, deciding a snap of cold air was needed. Just an echo in his head, he thought to himself.

The topiary garden was heaped with snow, the gate left swinging open. Broderig started towards the city, hugging the wharfside as he went. Every now and then stopping and looking out at the vast expanse of flattened water, veiled in a shroud of low-hanging mist. Broderig kept going until he reached the shadows of Parliament. He had some shillings in his pocket. He passed a church, but the place he needed was just across the street. The tavern looked long closed up. But Benjamin Broderig rapped on the door, and a panel slid open and an eye presented itself, unblinking and bloodshot. "W'dya want?" said a voice from within. Harsh and unwelcoming.

"Porter," the young man replied. The door opened.

CHAPTER
SEVENTEEN

SCOTLAND YARD

"Get the keys, and release him. Don't argue with me, Constable. I give the orders round here."

Hatton stood at Inspector Adams's side, waiting for the key to turn, and there he was, sitting in a corner and looking at his fingernails, as if nothing had happened.

"Albert. I am so glad to see you. Inspector Adams here will be the first one to say it. You're a free man, innocent of all charges. Come, friend, your wife is fretting. But I've sent a message to say you'll be on your way as soon as possible."

Hatton covered his joy in a rambling account of procedures to follow. Roumande looked up at his friend and smiled, another stickler for detail.

"Released, you say? How long have I been here? Anyway, I've been thinking about the number of instruments we are lacking in the morgue, and I'm sure I could get them sent over from Belgium at half the cost."

Roumande? Would you credit him? Any other man would be counting the hours till they knew the time would come when they would surely swing from a gibbet. But not this man.

"Have I ever told you what a fine fellow you are? And how we could not, would not, cope without you at St Bart's? But promise, Albert. No more letters, I beg of you."

Roumande thumped Hatton hard on the back. "Come, Adolphus, we have work to do. Send another message and tell my wife I'm well, and I'll return home when we've finished the autopsies."

The two men left The Yard and headed back to St Bart's. They hung their coats on the meat hooks and set to work, starting with Finch. It was hard to give the bloody lumps a Christian name but the leather form didn't seem to deserve it, either. It was propped up, Sunday best, in a corner. Its dusty appearance was the same as before. Hatton looked again at it and the book it still held. *Vestiges*. Why that particular book, he thought to himself? Was the killer making fun of Finch? It was ten years out of date and already the world of science had moved inevitably forward. It was a book only read now by the masses. Why not something more suitably erudite by Mr Darwin or Charles Lyell?

Roumande, hand to his mouth, was caught in a momentary thought and then said, straight to the point, "It's a sorry job, badly done. Why a halfwit or a child could make less of a mess of it. Look at the bulges, and as for the stitching, I wouldn't let them hem my trousers, Adolphus. It's hardly a masterpiece."

The two of them laughed, their gallows humour a condition of the morgue.

Roumande addressed the Professor in a more serious tone, "If you permit me to say so, we never actually managed to inspect all his organs as thoroughly as we might have done. Perhaps we should start with the meat, before we conclude anything final about the form?"

Slowly, they unwrapped the body parts which had been preserved in excellent condition, having absorbed a great deal of the Fen's peaty soil. Finch's brain put to one side, still wrapped in calico, Hatton moved to the heart.

"The large tweezers, if you please."

Roumande handed them over.

"And pass me the three-incher, Albert, if you would be so kind." Hatton was still looking for something, but what, he didn't know.

The heart was a good one. An upside down, pear-shaped pumping machine. Hatton weighed it. Eleven ounces exactly.

But there was something else, and he traced the point of his knife along it. It was not large. But it was there. A small lump of scar tissue and a thin slash of a wound.

"Do you see what I see, Albert?"

"Yes. Cut it out, Professor, and put it under the microscope."

Carefully, Hatton took his smallest blade and made a sharp incision into the left ventricle wall. "This knife isn't working, Albert. I need the circulating biopsy tool."

With a simple pressing down of his hand and a sharp twist, the instrument they had improvised themselves lifted a perfectly cylindrical sample of the tissue.

251

Hatton walked over to his microscope and peered down the viewing rods.

And he was right. Twisting the little wheels, the tissue's cell formation spoke only to those who could read it. Success. Forensic evidence. A sharp blade had been pushed through Finch with considerable force. There was a clear disruption to the tissue cells. Deep bruising and abrasions which had not, due to the brown discolouration from the peat, shown themselves to the naked eye initially, but more than that. A shard of silver.

"Tweezers, Albert."

The tweezers grew large and cumbersome under the lens, but Hatton plucked the shard out and held it up to the light.

"It's a sliver of steel. Which means our killer must have used tremendous force for the metal to break off like this." Hatton was beginning to understand what might have happened. The weapon had been pushed through Finch's heart; the cut deep and at an angle. That Dr Finch had been facing his murderer when he died was clear. So, had they known each other? Had they been friends? Lovers?

"Can I see it, Adolphus?"

Hatton stepped aside. "I think I know this type of tip end, Adolphus." Roumande held the tiny shard of metal up into the light using the tweezers. "It's not from a dissection knife. This might be a wild guess, but I think this is for hunting or fishing."

Roumande was right, and Hatton knew it. The shard of metal had a tiny point which was razor thin, and the beginnings of a crescent-shaped dip, a groove in the metal.

"I think we can surmise that Finch was stabbed through the heart with a fishing knife by someone he knew, as you suggest, Albert. He was overpowered. His body parts were then cut up and carted to the Fens. How and by whom, I cannot tell. But I have my suspicions. The mess was cleared up, the parts deposited, and then whoever was the culprit came back and rebuilt him again. Quite an undertaking and not for anyone fearful." Hatton didn't mention the Mucker, but he thought it.

The next body was Mr Dodds. There was little else to discover beyond their original conclusions. He'd been garrotted, strangled by a rope, and his heart cut out. "His heart again, Albert? He was dead already when whoever played surgeon decided to put it on a plate."

Roumande prodded the heart with a scalpel. Pickled enough to hold its shape, but as for its colour? It had turned from claret jelly to something leathery. They sliced it open. But there was no telltale metal. "No ink on his fingers." Hatton turned the digits, examining them closely. "Nothing to link him to Lady Bessingham, or Finch for that matter. But to pin him to the ground like that? To make a display of him?"

Roumande shrugged. "Property of D.W.R. Dodds, the book said, leading us from a sleeping angel to this sorry form. The pins around his genitals and flaps of skin, as one might display a moth, but perhaps they are relating to something else? Pinpricks, Professor. Like the pauper girls."

Hatton's head hurt. Yes, these crimes seemed linked, but who Mr Dodds was, beyond a seller of scientific periodicals, he didn't know. Nothing seemed to be forthcoming on this particular victim. Adams had shown he had something to hide, and that he could be easily blackmailed. Hatton was sure the Inspector was in the pay of someone, but the man seemed intent on helping him now. Perhaps the best strategy where Adams was concerned was to let sleeping dogs lie. To feed him information, to keep him close but to know the Inspector was not to be trusted. What had Adams said about this type of police work? Hatton nodded to himself, knowing he would follow the same strategy. He would proceed with stealth.

"The heart, Albert? The organ which pumps the brain with oxygen. The organ that makes us live, that's barely bigger than a fist, which contracts and expands and is made up of chambers and cavities."

Roumande laughed. "Ever the anatomist, Professor. Your sister Lucy's right, Adolphus. And Madame Roumande agrees with her. Did I tell you that they regularly correspond with each other, enquiring as to your health, your living arrangements, your lack of a sweetheart? The heart has another purpose. What are the two main reasons for murder, in your opinion?"

Hatton smiled, knowing the answer to this question. "Money. Or the lack of it. And love, Albert. Passion."

"Exactly, Adolphus. A thwarted affair. Jealousy. Lust. Lady Bessingham had many male admirers. Perhaps a

254

lover kills her first in a seething rage, and sets out to finish the others." Hatton shook his head, thinking of Benjamin Broderig and his friendship with Lady Bessingham, what little he knew of it. "Finch was first, Albert. Lady Bessingham was next, followed by Dodds, and then Mr Babbage." And he thought, as well, that it was not possible for Broderig to be involved. Broderig admired Lady Bessingham, perhaps even loved her, but there was nothing to suggest he could hurt her. When Broderig spoke of Lady Bessingham, it was with real grief, real loss. He was not her murderer. Hatton was sure of it and so shook his head again, and turned his attention to Babbage.

The final body was massive and splayed over the sides of the post-mortem slab. At first, they found nothing not already surmised in the alleyway. Cause of death: asphyxiation. Throat: slit after strangulation. Signs of an awl and a bone folder. Distinguishing marks: cut area restitched using linen thread. "Let's unpick the stitches," suggested Roumande and as they did, they noticed something. They were waxy. But not with the thin layer of coating normally found on bookbinder's thread. This wax was thick, globular, and blue.

"It's exactly the same, Albert. The same as the wax we lifted from Lady Bessingham's finger."

Hatton went over to the little shaving mirror. They were making a little forensic progress, but not enough. Two bodies were linked by the same blue wax: Lady Bessingham and Mr Babbage. But the other two bodies — Dr Finch and Mr Dodds? Absolutely nothing.

Hatton looked at himself. The hawkface looking back gave no clues. He was dog tired, his mind a blank, and it would be light soon. He needed to think.

So Hatton left Roumande, heading back to Gower Street along the icy streets, his mind numbed by the air. No gas lamps were lit at this hour. No shadows, just a black, patternless, formless world. Hatton tried to force some sense of logic, to find that place in his mind where the truth would unfold, but it was pointless. The dark and the cold nullified reason, but he was almost home.

The hansom back to Isleworth was bumpy. His throat felt dry, so Adams pulled the small silver flask from his pocket and slugged back a glug. He breathed slowly, and then gently knocked on the door of his house. With no yapping dog to wake his family, nothing stirred. He knocked a little harder and through the window saw her come to him, sleepy and lit up by a single tallow. She opened the door and he put his finger to his lips. Her nightclothes were crumpled and the scent of warm bedclothes rose off her skin. "George," she whispered, "whatever time is this? Come out of the cold before you catch something." He rubbed his face with his bear-like hands and stepped across the threshold, pulling her into him. "Sshh, don't wake the children," she said.

CHAPTER
EIGHTEEN

ASHBOURNE

Flora James had tied a makeshift strip of black cloth around her bonnet. It was all she could find in the time allotted because the journey to Surrey had been swift. They had fled London like criminals, but two days was all it took before they became aware of the next murder. A chance sighting of the *Illustrated London News* suggesting the body of a journalist had been found, a hop from The Old Cheshire Cheese. It was Olinthus Babbage. It had to be. No mention of the parchment letters, but a page on, the picture of a maid. It was an excellent likeness, as if looking in a mirror.

"The letters are gone, Flora. Perhaps to be destroyed, for ever. But at least we're safe."

Safe enough, in a little boathouse by an icy river a few miles from Dr Canning's birthplace, but only safe if they hid, and remained like fugitives. Pacing the room, speaking in whispers, peeping through the cracks to make sure no one was coming, and asking themselves, how it had come to this? The police were bound to be looking for them. Asking questions. They knew it wouldn't be long before dogs and whistles surrounded them. So on the morning of the funeral, together, they

257

made their way to Ashbourne, prepared to face whatever would await them.

Ashbourne was not large enough to be called a village, and apart from the Georgian stonework mansion which sat in a bowl of lawn, there was just a single line of dismal workmen's cottages, ending at a small Norman church. The churchyard had been dug down for burials so many times that the tombstones were supine, as though the stones themselves were dead. The new graves were few, but they were prominent. An angel, hands clasped together in prayer, weeping silent tears for the child that lay within. "Herein lies Esther Rose, our only daughter." The baby's grave had been hemmed in by spiky railings, and in the middle of the plot, a mottled glass vase had been placed with a single, wilting flower.

And when the earth was thrown over the ebony coffin, beside the infant sepulchre, nobody wept, save a young woman dressed quite disgracefully in a battered bonnet and fawn dress leaning on a bookish-looking man, who steered her away from the church and up towards the house.

Inspector Adams peered at the girl over his notebook. "So, Miss James. You've finally decided to show yourself. You've been giving my officers quite the runaround, but I suspected you might come here. May I enquire as to the name of this gentleman?"

"My name is John Canning, Inspector. Curator at the British Museum for anthropology, and a grateful beneficiary of Lady Bessingham. I understand you have been looking for us."

"Indeed," Adams said, as he sucked on his pencil, desperate for a cigarette, and looked at Hatton, both men now sitting in Lady Bessingham's drawing room, the funeral over. The Professor hadn't slept a wink last night and before first light had caught a train here, knowing this was where Inspector Adams would be found.

The drawing room was draughty despite a roaring fire, and oddly plain for a country residence. A walnut desk, a chaise longue, some potted plants, and a few unknown artists on the wall. But even in the depths of winter, long sash windows showed the garden to its advantage. Hatton, however, wasn't interested in the scenery. He took the girl in, who sat opposite him. So this was Flora James, thought Hatton. On the face of the furore which had surrounded her, she was a little disappointing. She was a girl, nothing more. Her face, one notch up from ordinary, but like his sister Lucy's, it was honest and open. And when she spoke, her voice was bell clear.

"On the day before she died, I left Ashbourne early and went directly to Nightingale Walk. I was given strict instructions. Where the letters would be and to whom I should deliver them. Dr Canning was a name I'd heard mention of before. Lady Bessingham had even visited him once, a number of years ago, and I had waited for her on a little bench outside his room, next to a display of hummingbirds."

Adams nodded. "Carry on . . ."

"Dr Canning enjoyed the patronage of my mistress. But it was his expertise in anthropology and the natural sciences which I believe was the purpose of his involvement. Madam wanted him to view the letters and then to distribute them to an appropriate journalist. Madam was a great lover of controversy. It was her belief that the letters, and the ideas contained within, would add to a debate, she'd said. I believe the author had recently returned from abroad and wanted to discuss them further. But my mistress did as she pleased. And so I was sent on an errand."

Hatton interjected, "But then why not come forward and tell us so? You committed no crime."

The girl's resolve crumbled and Dr Canning spoke, "We learnt of Lady Bessingham's murder and we hid. A mistake it seems, in retrospect, because now another is dead. It was Olinthus Babbage found murdered, near Fleet Street, wasn't it?"

Adams didn't look up from his scribbling, and so Hatton continued on behalf of them both, "And there's nothing else at all that you can think of? You see, you and Dr Canning are the only witnesses to not just one but two serious crimes, and I'm afraid we don't think the killing is finished. You were probably the last people to see Olinthus Babbage alive."

Dr Canning raised an eyebrow and addressed Hatton. "Are you a policeman, sir?"

Adams put his notebook down. "Forgive me, gentlemen. I am country bred and my manners are lacking. This is Professor Adolphus Hatton of St Bart's. He's our Medical Jurisprudence adviser and is helping me on the case. Answer his questions, sir, the same as you would mine."

"Inspector Adams," Flora replied, her face pale. "Believe me, Dr Canning was all for staying in London, but I persuaded him otherwise." Canning laid his hand on the frightened girl's shoulder. "The letters had a theory in them and she was a great supporter of Dr Canning's work, but their friendship was of a formal nature, whereas I . . ." The young woman began to cry. Adams didn't nudge her or bully her and did anything but accuse her. It seemed he had decided that Flora James was no suspect after all.

"I am very sorry for your loss, Miss James. But knowing precisely what was in those letters may help us catch the murderer. Can you think of anyone your mistress was out of sorts with? Was there anyone she withheld patronage from or slighted?"

Flora shook her head and looked towards an opening door. Hatton followed her gaze as Benjamin Broderig entered the room and pulled up a chair by the window.

Dr Canning failed to acknowledge this new arrival but instead bent down and took a book from a bag. Hatton read its spine. It was a book he had in his own lodgings at Gower Street. It was *The Principles of Geology* by Charles Lyell.

Dr Canning cleared his throat as if readying himself for something. "Lady Bessingham gave me this book and it categorically shows that our earth was not created in the blink of an eye, but evolved over thousands of years. Who knows exactly how many, but one day, we shall know the answer. And this work has led us to a fundamental question few dare ask. But not Lady Bessingham."

Still making notes, Adams asked, "And the question, Dr Canning?"

Canning smiled. "If rocks are not immutable, then what about the creatures of the world? We have so much variety, perhaps we ourselves have formed, layer on layer, like the rocks. And this is what drove Lady Bessingham's life. A thirst for knowledge and a lust for questioning. And she was not alone. Our numbers are swelling. We who feel the weight of ignorance bearing down on us. It stifles us, gentlemen. We are the true voice of liberty and so, too, was Lady Bessingham. She was a freethinker. A dissenter. A creative force."

Adams nodded. "Of course. And so Lady Bessingham was intent on publishing letters which would upturn the apple cart? Is that what you are saying, Dr Canning?" Adams spoke, not looking up at the academic but making his endless notes, looking for a prompt.

Hatton took his cue. "Lady Bessingham set out deliberately to rock the boat. To print a theory which she knew would destabilise everything. That's why she chose the *Westminster Review*. She wanted a political furore. But why didn't she just send them to Babbage herself? Why all this subterfuge?"

Canning shook his head as if the answer was obvious, and said, "Because she was a woman, Professor. A clever woman, but still a woman, and she needed the affirmation of men. And who better than myself and Mr Babbage? But the letters were dangerous, Professor.

There are many who would not gain by such thinking. There are those who speak against Science, damning us to hell at the pulpit and decrying our names in Parliament. Well, let them. Ignorance will bury them. Olinthus Babbage was a good friend to the enlightened. The *Westminster Review* is one of the few forums open to these ideas. That's why we gave him the letters, Professor. I presume as a Man of Science, you are sympathetic to the cause."

The cause? At least four people were dead, possibly more, yet this man spoke of the cause as if it was all that mattered. But before Hatton could say so, another voice spoke.

"But Dr Canning, forgive me in pointing out the obvious, but they were not really your letters to give. Nor Lady Bessingham's, and on return from Borneo I suggested she wait. I no longer wanted them circulated. I wanted to think it through a little." It was Broderig, a half smile of query on his lips. "They were private letters, poorly written in haste from the depths of a forest. They were not fully formed and certainly not for public consumption. Some of my thoughts to Lady Bessingham were of a personal nature. And though I should not speak ill of the dead, they were not Katherine's to further distribute, although at first, I had stupidly encouraged her. They were my letters, weren't they, Flora?"

Flora reddened at the accusation and Broderig shook his head at her. "They were my letters, but not my ideas. You passed on Mr Wallace's thoughts on species, didn't you, Flora? And Dr Canning, you read them and perhaps elaborated with your knowledge of the native man, acting as a rubber stamp of authority. Lady Bessingham knew she couldn't just pass them into the world without a real Man of Science's support, and you, sir, are a member of the Linnean Society. It all makes perfect sense to me now. Poor Mr Babbage must have been salivating at the very thought of it. How very clever of her. It was her final triumph."

Inspector Adams turned around and faced Broderig. "Mr Broderig, if these letters are as you two gentlemen describe, then I would like to understand what ideas really passed between you and Lady Bessingham, before another tragedy unfolds. I want names, sir. I want detail. Speak now, very plainly, because it seems to me you are being deliberately abstruse. Do these letters deny God? Are they heretical? Are they seditious? Are they perhaps even criminal?"

"As I said to you, Inspector, the letters were private and now, it seems, stolen. You are the policeman, after all. Why don't you find them? It seems to me you leave a lot of stones unturned."

"Be careful, for you are treading on thin ice," said Adams as he stood up and glowered at the young man and Hatton watched them for a moment. They were not exactly arguing, more a war of attrition.

"Perhaps you should make more notes. Take a leaf out of the world of the scientist, and catalogue your thoughts, Inspector, because justice requires it. I have watched your work with interest and tried to help where I can. Take the little girls, for example. In my work, we must look at the detail first, but then how the detail relates to everything else. How the death of the smallest creature can signify something bigger. How everything is connected, everything is a pattern."

"You have lost me, Mr Broderig. I am not like your London botanicals. I am a simple man," quipped Adams.

Broderig laughed. "I'd say you were very complicated, Inspector. But what I think of you doesn't really matter. All I know is that you are not very thorough. Perhaps it is your age? My father is similar."

Adams, unperturbed or perhaps just bored by the juvenile insult, looked away from Broderig and directly back at Dr Canning. "Do you have names, Dr Canning? Anyone you could specifically point to who might want to destroy these letters or bury them?"

Canning shook his head. "Not to the point of killing someone, if that's what you mean, but when I return to London this evening, I'll talk to some of my colleagues. I'll send a note to Scotland Yard if I learn anything useful. You never know, I might find something to help."

Adams thanked the academic, and turned back to the girl. "So, Miss James. Can you think of anyone who might have had access to your mistress's room in Chelsea? Anyone at all? Somebody she knew?"

"There is one person, sir. We were at sixes and sevens and some of my duties had fallen to Violet, the scullery maid, but she is such a meek creature."

Adams gestured at his little tin. Miss James nodded to go ahead. "Miss James." He rolled it up and lit the penny smoke. "Would you be good enough to accompany myself and Professor Hatton upstairs? Perhaps seeing the last place you spoke to your mistress alive might jog another thought."

Flora smiled weakly in submission and was helped up by her attentive companion. Hatton glanced across at Broderig, who had his back to them now. He was looking out of the window towards an iced-up pond and the way he stood, so upright, so stiff, his hands so resolutely clasped behind his back, Hatton knew the young man was deep in thought. Hatton often enough struck the same pose himself in the morgue.

But he knew he needed to keep Adams close. And he'd noted that the Inspector, for some reason, had said nothing yet about Dodds or Finch. And if Adams didn't mention them soon, he knew he would have to.

The private rooms upstairs were bare of ornament. Lady Bessingham's quills were still laid out on a polished desk, as if she had left them and gone to speak to a servant, or perhaps receive a visitor. Flora ran her hand lovingly along the polished mahogany saying, "She wrote her letters here. I brought her paper and sealing wax, anything she needed. Lady Bessingham was quite old-fashioned when it came to correspondence."

"Lady Bessingham used sealing wax? May we see it please, Miss James?" Hatton caught Adams's eye, but let the maid continue.

"She used the indigo wax for all her letters and pressed them shut with this." Flora held a little brass sealing stamp in her hands.

266

"Would you be so kind, Miss James?" The inspector reached into his pocket and gave the maid a box of matches. Obediently, she complied, lighting a taper and melting a pool of deep-blue wax. She dipped the stamp in the pool and then pressed it down onto a blotting pad.

"It was something Lady Bessingham had only recently adopted. In fact, it's a copy of something she saw once which caught her fancy. She often caught damsel flies in the summer when they landed on the pond here at Ashbourne. It's frozen up at this time of the year, but in the summer it abounds with dragonflies and her favourite, these delicate creatures."

Hatton's mind was racing. She used blue wax for sealing her letters. Blue wax. It was there on Babbage's neck. It was smudged on her hand. But nothing on Finch or the body of Mr Dodds. No connection there at all.

The Inspector had fallen quiet. He seemed distracted. Hatton knew that he was married with children and called himself a Christian. Hatton inwardly shuddered at the lingering image of this man, caught in the dimmed lamplight of a hotel, his lips brushing the hand of a molly boy. Hatton again spoke up for him. "Can you remember, Flora, where Lady Bessingham got the idea of the seal from? You said it was something she had seen which gave her the idea. Caught her fancy?"

"It was a daily visit, sir. For years she has used the same dressmaker — her parcels were always sealed this way. She delivered them herself, and often stayed late to talk. She was very charming and interested in madam's work. Madam loved the damsel fly which sealed the wrapping for the dresses. It was this image we had copied. The dressmaker's name is Madame Martineau."

It was as if Adams had suddenly woken up. "Madame Martineau, you say?"

Flora nodded. "Every lady of fashion and taste uses her, Inspector. Madame Martineau's cut is not to be beaten for its delicacy. She is a very elegant mantuamaker and owns her own workshop along the river in The Borough. I've never been there, although I believe Violet knows the place."

Adams seemed flustered. "We should go there at once." He turned to Hatton. "Do you remember what I said about Babbage? That he was stitched up good and proper. And although I did not say so at the time, a woman is capable of such violence. God knows, I've seen it before. But if she took the letters, then this Madame Martineau must be very well informed. Or was working for another and knew what to look for. Was she alone with Lady Bessingham often, Flora?"

Flora nodded.

"And where did Lady Bessingham keep Mr Broderig's letters?"

"They were kept underneath the brushing tray in the dressing room in Chelsea, which Madame Martineau used from time to time. In order to present new dresses at their best, Inspector. Even with the brown paper packaging, it's very grimy on the streets of London. I suppose she might have seen the letters. They were very "distinctive, written on golden parchment tied with a string of rattan."

"But surely this dressmaker wasn't allowed just to wander into the house and snoop about at will. Who dealt with her appointments, if you were busy elsewhere? Think now, Flora, this is very important."

"Well, as I say, many of my duties had fallen to Violet. And Cook thought it might stretch the girl a bit." She turned beseechingly to Hatton. "To give Violet a little more confidence. Do you think the dressmaker has some importance here, Professor?"

Adams cut across them both. "I think we should speak to Violet immediately. Professor Hatton, would you do the honours and stay with Miss James? I'll fetch her myself. We don't want any more maids taking flight."

The Inspector left the room and Flora looked at Professor Hatton, a question in her eyes. "He won't hurt her, will he?"

Hatton shook his head and came a little closer. "Miss James, may I call you Flora?" Flora nodded. "I understand that Lady Bessingham knew another academic, Dr Ignatius Finch?"

"Oh yes, Dr Finch. He had attended one of her parties, but after some short correspondence they had little to do with each other. They fell out sometime ago, I think it was something Dr Finch wrote or said. Something very shocking. I remember my mistress saying that he was a hateful man, and she wanted nothing more to do with him. Why, does he know something about my mistress's death?"

"Dr Finch is dead, Miss James. So there's nothing else you can think of which might link Dr Finch to your mistress, then?" Hatton held Flora's gaze, but she shook her head.

"No. I'm sure of it. Dead you say? I didn't know him but God rest his soul."

"One more question. Lady Bessingham was an avid reader, wasn't she?"

Flora looked back at Hatton. "She spent hours reading, Professor."

"Every tiny detail that you tell us now could save a life."

"Lady Bessingham was most particular. Her entire private library was regularly updated by a Fine Purveyor."

Hatton's heart was in his mouth and he instinctively crouched at the foot of her chair. "And the company's name, Flora? This is very important."

Flora looked astonished and awkward at this forwardness, and pulled herself bodily away from this man, who had a look of death upon his face. "Please, Professor. You do not need to kneel at my feet! It's no great secret. Lady Bessingham got all her books from the Linnean Society. Lord Bessingham had been a member before he died, and my mistress still enjoyed a standing order. All the journals came to her directly, once a month, every month, in her dead husband's name. She would use no other and was most particular about it."

★　★　★

"Take a seat, Violet."

The scullery maid stepped in, accompanied by Inspector Adams, Mr Broderig, and Dr Canning. Hatton didn't approve of such heavy-handedness where women were concerned, and this creature was the meekest little thing. The words "boo" and "goose" instantly came to mind. She looked at the gathering wide-eyed, and Adams gestured her to take a seat. She made a little curtsy, but didn't sit down. Instead she simply stood near Flora, or rather hovered.

"Sit down, Violet, please. I insist," said the Inspector.

"Have I done something wrong, sir?"

"Well, I think you have lied, a little. When I asked you before if anyone had come to the house, you said no. But that wasn't true, was it?"

Violet sniffed and rubbed her hands together a little. "I've told you already. I didn't see nothing. Why do you press me so?"

"No lady called Madame Martineau, then? It wouldn't be very hard to prove that she came that night. She did, didn't she? And you let her in, perhaps around the back. Why would you do that, Violet, and then lie?"

Was he guessing? Hatton was about to intercede on the maid's behalf, but before he could take a step, she was up and running for the door, but Adams was quick, blocking her path.

"Tell the truth, damn you, child. No more lying."

"Cook, help me," she pleaded, shouting to be heard downstairs. "For pity's sake, please, sir. I didn't lie. I've never heard of that lady. No, sir. Please, let me pass."

271

But Adams wouldn't, and held up his hand as if to thump the girl, and she cowered and then threw herself to the floor and started to crawl towards Hatton, saying, "You're a gentleman. Tell the copper, I don't know nothing. Help me, sir." And she was quickly at his feet, sprawled prostrate and sobbing. Pleading, over and over again, "Please, sir. I didn't do nothing, so help me God, I'm innocent. Cook says so. Says I'm an innocent lamb. I am, sir. Please, please . . ." and slowly she pulled herself up. The others melded into nothing. The room was spinning and she had her face pressed against his lap. "Please, sir, I'll do anything." And he felt her bite, and her hands wrestling, and she was sobbing, her hands working quickly. "Anything, anything, sir," Violet's tear-stained face, saliva dripping down her chin. "Please, sir. Anything you like. I saw it in your eyes, sir, and I know what you want. Just don't send me back to her." And Hatton wrenched her up, noticing a myriad of scars and pricks all over her spindly arms.

"Stop it . . ." Flora was screaming. "Stop it, Violet. Stop it. Please for pity's sake. Violet, leave the gentleman. Cook, come quickly . . ." Hatton was pushing her away, peeling off her hands, struggling.

"Anything, sir, please don't send me back to her . . ."

"She's asleep. I've given her something. She's my lamb. Leave her be."

Flora had gone to help prepare some broth. Adams was in the hallway writing notes, whilst Hatton looked down at himself, embarrassed and ashamed. Broderig

272

loitered by a chair, shaking his head but contributing nothing because what was there to say? Hatton knew it would be better if he asked the questions. To cover it up with the usual of time, place, and weapon. Only these were not the questions. He put his face in his hands and tried to recover himself. "Ask something, damn you," he muttered under his breath. He stuttered out the obvious. The cook answered, "Yes, sir. I found her three years ago in Mayfair. We had a position for a scullery maid at the time. I took her in. Lady Bessingham left all of that to me. She had no reference, but I could tell she was a good girl. She reached out to me. She had strong wrists. Good for rolling pastry."

"Can I see those wrists, Cook?" Hatton asked.

The cook turned her back on Hatton. "No, sir. You cannot."

Hatton pleaded with her, "Mayfair, you say? It could be very important, couldn't it, Inspector? Is there something you're not telling us?" Hatton moved towards the edge of the bed, where the girl lay, half asleep.

Broderig stepped further into the room, saying more abruptly, "Speak now very plainly and tell the truth, woman. Answer the Professor and be specific. He asked where in Mayfair, exactly? And tell us more on her wrists. They'll be no more secrets here."

The cook recoiled from Mr Broderig, her voice becoming a whisper. "She was slumped against the railings in Monreith Square, sir. I was visiting my sister who has a position in one of the town houses. But why do you ask about her wrists?"

Adams didn't look up from his notes but the cook wanted no part of it, whatever this Mr Broderig demanded, so she pulled the bedclothes up, then ushered them out, closing the door behind her.

"So, Inspector Adams," Broderig said, where they all stood now in the hallway. "Did you hear what she said? Monreith Square, where the rich and powerful live. But no one's above the law. Here's your chance, Inspector."

Hatton nodded. "And I saw her wrists clearly, Inspector. Cuts and slashes from long ago. And as for that crooked little back of hers? From a beating, I shouldn't wonder. She's afraid and she's definitely hiding something. It's as Mr Broderig suggests. Something happened to her in Monreith Square."

Adams shook his head and said, "There's nothing more to be got from Violet. And I've no more time to waste here." He shut his notebook. "I need a carriage to London and to find this mantuamaker. Professor Hatton, are you ready?" Hatton nodded, picking up his surgical bag, but Broderig pushed ahead of the Inspector, blocking his path, saying, "But Cook said Monreith Square. And the girl's wrists were slashed, Inspector. So after you've found this mantuamaker, you'll head straight there, of course?"

Adams shook his head in disbelief at Broderig's effrontery. "Good grief but are we all detectives now? Perhaps, instead of driving myself to an early grave, I should take early retirement?"

"I'm only concerned for the girl," said Broderig.

"Well my concern is for these dead botanicals, as yours should be. The girls must wait. I need to find this

274

dressmaker before she murders another. So, if you would excuse me, Mr Broderig . . ."

Hatton watched as Adams pushed past the younger man, who stepped back and almost fell against the wall, running his hands through his hair before saying, "Of course, you're right. It's most impertinent of me. You know your job. I'm sorry for my outburst. It's quite unlike me. It's all this death, Inspector."

Hatton sympathised. He felt this anger, too, but at thirty-three he had learnt to contain it.

Broderig continued, more calmly, "Do you know, I think I'll join you, gentlemen. I need to get back to the city, myself. My specimens are due in tomorrow. Is that alright, Inspector?"

Adams shrugged. "If you want," was all he said. "My work on this case is practically finished. We'll pick her up, this Madame What's Her Face. She's clearly on the make, working for someone. I'll squeeze it out of her. Not sure how she did it though, especially the men, because it would take nerves of steel to kill like that, but she'll hang for it nevertheless, and then I can draw a line under this sorry affair."

"Draw a line under it?" Broderig sighed.

"Yes, Mr Broderig. She'll hang and the press will have what they want. The Commissioner will leave me alone and there will be peace in the world." He smiled, and lit another penny smoke. "Case closed. Gentlemen, our carriage awaits . . ."

London loomed upon the horizon. Hatton kept quiet on the journey back, still reeling from what the girl had done, and also thinking about what it meant. Her wrists were like the other girls. And this Madame Martineau was a seamstress. But the angel was different. She had died by drowning and been dragged from the river, placed in a box which led them to Dodds. He rubbed his eyes. Or was the girl a miasma, a ghost? Nothing made sense any more, but even in his tiredness everything seemed connected. Violet had worked for Madame Martineau. That's why she let her into the house.

Hatton preferred to let the others do the talking. Adams puffed away, answering Broderig's questions. They talked a little of who he worked for, apart from The Yard, and Adams was not unforthcoming. "We all do it," he said, matter-of-fact. "It's no secret, and my superiors even have a list of my clients. Why, I even did a bit of work for your own father, Mr Broderig, not so long ago when he had an unpopular bill going through. London's a dangerous city. This isn't Sarawak!"

"And do you think the rich are a special case then, Inspector? When it comes to the law? Would you, for example, investigate someone you've worked for? I suppose what I'm asking is where do you draw the line between justice and order?"

Adams laughed and shook his head at the young man's naivety and youthful passion.

"The rich are a special case. The rich need security, Mr Broderig."

Hatton listened as the conversation continued. How Broderig thought that The Yard was more concerned with the rich than the poor. And that in his view, it was only the weak that suffered and that without vigilance they would be crushed by the wicked. Beaten, tortured, and then dumped in alleyways like the little girls, who were completely innocent, he said. And Hatton listened as Adams answered Mr Broderig that it was in the nature of girls from the streets to behave like Violet. And that they weren't so innocent. That they survived by what they offered, and adapted to the streets. "Evolve if you like," said Adams, and that he was not unsympathetic to their predicament, just pragmatic.

CHAPTER
NINETEEN

THE BOROUGH

The scaffolding that shot up the sides of the sweatshop looked unwieldy, as if it would crack across the joints at any minute.

"Mind out there, gentlemen, look out below!" A heap of debris came crashing down. Hatton looked up in horror, immobilised by fear, but as the deadly load hurtled towards the ground, an arm pulled him into the building's porch way and out of danger.

"Damn labourers. They don't care what they're doing. Nearly crushed us to death." Adams was angry but Hatton was simply relieved to have been pushed aside, once again into a corner, but this time the corner was one he welcomed with open arms. Hatton thanked him for it.

"Step in, Hatton. And light a match here. I can barely see my feet. How can anyone work in this half-light?"

They'd dropped Broderig near Whitehall, and were now in a tight little corridor. Hatton put his hands on either side of the walls to steady himself and stepped cautiously forward. He could no longer hear the workmen, who must still be above them, wheeling their precarious loads across rickety planks, but he could hear something — a whirring noise ahead of them — and see something, too — a thin shard of light.

"Strike another light, Professor. I think this is the place."

The first room was stuffed to bursting with fabrics and the air littered with fairy dust which settled on Hatton's hands, and for a moment he was transfixed by its beauty. "Sequins," said the Inspector. "Cost a pretty penny these fripperies do. But terrible for the lungs of those who cut and thread this stuff."

Ahead of the fabric room, the girls were silent and barely seemed to notice the entry of the two men. One girl with jet-black hair was at a machine, which worked at ten times the speed of her neighbours. The others stitched by hand.

"Good afternoon, ladies." Adams doffed his hat, the proper gentleman. "Is Madame Martineau here?"

An auburn-haired girl answered in a piping little voice. "Madame's not 'ere. You gentlemen after her, then?" A girlish snigger. "She only left a while ago."

"And your name is?"

"My name, sir?" the girl shot Adams such a look of artfulness, she suddenly aged from a child of twelve to a knowing woman. "My name is, hmmmm, what shall I be today then, girls?" The girls around her giggled nervously.

"Come, don't play with us. Your name child, if you please?"

"My name is Daisy so's you ask? What's it to you?" she winked at her friends and then picked up a pair of scissors to guard herself.

"Well now, Daisy. You won't be needing any scissors, so put them down. I don't want to alarm any of you girls but I'm a policeman, that's right, a regular bobby peeler." Adams doffed his hat again. "And if you mess with me, you'll be charged with obstructing the law. Do you know what that means? It means trouble, girls, with a capital *T*. Now then, I think I have made myself plain. Do you, Daisy, or any of the others, know where your mistress has gone? I need to speak to her urgently."

But rather than laying the scissors down as she'd been asked, Daisy held them out like a knife.

"Says who? Madame Martineau wouldn't appreciate no snitching. We've got strict orders to finish six gowns by daybreak tomorrow and it's heavy work. Why, Elsie 'ere" — Daisy put her arm round her freckled neighbour — "has a whole mourning outfit of silks to sort out, and if we don't finishes when Madame wants us to, we'll cop it. So's you best not be bothering us with your questions, whoever you are."

Inspector Adams didn't respond as Hatton expected him to, with a quick grab and a de-arming of her scissors. Instead, he laughed, genuinely amused by her effrontery. "Dear, oh dear. What a performance, Daisy. You're in the wrong business, my girl. I'll let your pa know he's got a regular Penny Gaff star. Now then, jesting apart, I'll say it again. Put the damn scissors down, shut your trap, and listen to me. Madame Martineau is in serious trouble. I'm investigating the murder of one of Madame's customers, and if I get one more word of gutter-snipe backchat, I'll have you down

The Yard so quick your teeth will chatter. So, where's your mistress gone?"

Daisy looked like she was about to bolt, but another caught her arm and patted it. "Sit down, Daisy, for gawd sake. Daisy don't mean no 'arm and she ain't got no pa. None of us do. She's just a little perturbed what with being shut up in 'ere all the time, ain't you, Daisy? I know where Madame's gone, Inspector. Once the orders are in and she's counted all her money and the like, she heads over to the Isle of Dogs. She runs another venture there. Printing and the like, though I can't read. But Madame can. She's a right clever one. We don't know any more. But if we don't get the dresses done, we'll more than cop it." One of the girls at the other table started to cry.

"Oh for gawd sake, Kitty. Shut up with your bloody sniffling. Give her a hanky, Margaret."

Hatton look around at the girls. There were perhaps nine or ten of them. Stick thin and raggedy. But in many ways, they were the lucky ones. Lucky to be in work, learning a skill which might one day lead them out of The Borough if they kept their heads down and didn't cross their mistress.

"So, the Isle of Dogs then, Professor?" Adams pressed Hatton.

But Hatton was distracted by one of the girls. The tawny one named Kitty at the sewing machine. An Irish name, but she was far from it.

"Come here, please, Kitty. I want to show the Inspector something. Don't be shy. I'm a doctor. Look, I even have a doctor's bag. Bet you haven't seen

281

anything as wonderful as that? Look at the brass buckle. Doesn't it shine? Come now, child, I just want to look at your arms for a second. I'll get you a buckle for you just like it, if you let me look."

Kitty was terrified. "Go on, Kitty, roll up your sleeves," said the bold one. "He won't harm you none. Show him your arms. It's the machine. We are always having accidents with it, ain't we?" The dark girl stepped forward, the other still speaking. "They're only curious. And it's a right lovely buckle, ain't it? And these are proper gentlemen, Kitty, not like Madame Martineau's sort."

The girl sniffed and held out her spindly arms. "Thank you, Kitty. Thank you, my dear."

Kitty pulled her arms back as quickly as she had shot them out, and gave a great final sniff before sitting down again at her work.

Hatton's eyes filled with a visible disgust at the sight of the needle pricks and the deep cuts where she'd been slashed by something sharp. They left the workshop girls to their stitching, Hatton hastily promising Kitty he'd return with a shiny buckle. "My word," he promised.

In the carriage, Adams was wrestling with his many pockets, agitated.

"I've bloody well lost something or one of those girls is a little thief." He began to shower the seat with bits from his coat. Scraps of string, a handful of coppers, cigarette papers, and several boxes of Swans.

282

"Is this what you are searching for, Inspector?" Hatton handed over a tin of tobacco, which he'd seen Adams place down on one of the trestle tables. The Inspector gave Hatton a look of such gratitude, it made the Professor laugh a little, though reluctantly, for he had not forgiven the Inspector. Far from it.

"I must confess that I cannot think without a puff or two. It helps my mind focus and you would know the importance of that from your own demanding work. Would you care for a cigarette?"

Hatton declined. To him, this drug was bitter and disgusting. "You're quite the purist, aren't you, Professor? No bad habits at all, eh?" The Inspector looked at the Professor for a second but Hatton said nothing. "You don't know what you're missing," Adams said as he lit one up. "Nothing like them in the world." Very slim and tapering, it hung from his mouth and he sucked it up into his lungs.

"Oh, that reminds me, Inspector." Hatton reached inside his coat and brought the notebook out. "I've been meaning to give this to you. You left it in The Old Cheshire Cheese. It was Olinthus Babbage's. Might it still be useful?"

Adams nodded and popped it in his waistcoat. "Thank you, Professor. Perhaps Broderig is right? That I am getting forgetful. There's some names still need following up and I might show this notebook to Dr Canning. He seems to know a great deal about the value of these missing letters. Perhaps if I show him this, it might jog something? Who might want them?

Who might like to buy them? But for now we must focus on finding this woman."

Hatton concurred for he, too, had been impressed by Dr Canning. He looked out of the window. The sun was dipping from the sky as the coach began to slow. The Isle of Dogs. Adams fumbled in his pocket again. "It's standard issue, Professor. Do you know how to use it?"

Hatton looked at the pistol. "Yes, I think so. Aim and fire?" Hatton asked, slightly perplexed.

"Aim and fire, Professor. Exactly. So, here we are then. This is where the girl said. One up from the Machars Trading Company. Salmon Street."

The printing rooms at the dockside were empty. The door was ajar. There was nothing to say anyone worked here at all, except for a pile of pamphlets and leaflets which were stacked up in the corner by one of the walls. Adams opened one of the leaflets, laughed, and handed it to Hatton, who looked at a cartoon of an old man having his balls licked by a surprised looking collie.

"Making that bitch's day, isn't he? Lord Carruthers. Did a bit of work for him, a while back. Bit libelish to spread such scurrilous rumours, though? Says he has six months left and has syphilis. Don't they all? Well, seems our Madame Martineau has ideas above her station, and this alone is enough to hang her."

Hatton looked askance. "For cartoons, Inspector?"

"It's seditious, Professor. Designed to destabilise order. Practically treason, you could argue. And believe

284

me, there's plenty who would. Come on, let's not dilly-dally. There's nothing here to help us. But where she's gone, who knows? I need to get my men stationed at both her places so the minute she shows her face, we'll have her. And I'd better see if there's been any progress on the other leads."

Adams continued, "So you reckon old Finch was stabbed by a fishing knife?" Hatton nodded, having already brought the Inspector up to speed. "Which means we'll have to go back to Wickham Fen, Professor. Not that we'd find him. But what's the connection between Finch and Madame Martineau, I wonder?"

"The Mucker said his daughter had gone missing," offered Hatton. "Perhaps she came to London and ended up in The Borough. Perhaps Finch got her with child and found her work with Madame Martineau. You heard the porter suggest he had a way with girls. And bought silk shirts from London. It's not uncommon, but she was only twelve . . ."

"Twelve is old enough. Put it in your report, Hatton, and I'll deal with it later. But nothing to link the Mucker, forensically speaking, with the other corpses?"

No, Hatton said. Nothing forensic at all. "So will you go to Monreith Square now, Inspector? As Mr Broderig suggested?"

Adams was non-committal with, "As I explained to him, I can't just waltz into any old house and start throwing my weight about. I have no name, as such. No actual address. No tangible link. And frankly, it's more than my job's worth. I'm looking for another person, entirely. And I won't rest until I have my hands on that woman. Once she's dealt with, the rest is just tidying up. So, a lift to St Bart's then, Professor?"

Hatton shook his head. "No, Inspector. I'll walk from here. The air will do me good."

Scotland Yard's main incident room was quiet, although a few detectives were still about. One or two greeted Inspector Adams as he hung his gabardine coat up. He couldn't go on like this, but he knew that he would, despite the dangers. Would Hatton do anything? Would he say anything?

Adams looked at the pile of papers on his desk, to see an envelope marked *Urgent, For The Attention of Inspector Adams*. He quickly opened it up, intrigued, and read the details written. At last. This case had done him enough damage. It would only be a matter of time before the Commissioner was on his back again, and despite his show of bravado in the carriage about how the case was almost closed, Adams knew full well he had to tie up all the pieces. And the note promised him this and more, but it also came with a warning. *Tell no one. And come alone.* The note was signed, *Yours faithfully, Dr Canning.* So, thought Adams, he must have come back to London and spoken to one of his colleagues, just as he promised he would.

"Well, I might as well get on with it." Adams stubbed the penny smoke out and, stepping out into the cold night's air, looked towards St James' Park. And it occurred to Adams that Hatton seemed really chummy with that Broderig fellow. What if he blabbed? And

286

there was Roumande, too. He shook his head, and remembered that molly boy comment at The Old Cheshire Cheese. How could he have been so stupid? He felt inside his coat and pulling out his hip flask, took a sip, thinking it was his word against theirs, if it came to it. There was no evidence against him. There was nothing.

He hailed a carriage thinking he'd give it up. The boy, the hotels, all of it. He'd damn well end it. Adams looked out of the window. He could see where they were. Great Russell Street. His legs were heavy but he got out and paid the driver. Gave him a tip. Why not? He looked at the colossus, which rose majestic, and above it, a flicker of stars in the night sky of London. The sky bore down on him. Just one more push and life could be good again. And he didn't have to stay in this city. He could get a position in Bristol, Leeds, anywhere else would do, but Adams knew he wasn't going anywhere. Life had already consumed him.

Adams looked ahead at the British Museum, its angular form a blank silhouette. He looked down the paving slabs which blinked, pinprick specs of silver, sequined ice warning him not to slip.

There was still a single light on inside, a porter keeping the night vigil and watching over the vast collection of treasures which lay encased within. Adams had taken his children here once on a rare day off, and with a smile, remembered the antiquities and natural curiosities, the elaborate headdresses from South Sea Islands and Paleolithic flint.

Adams flashed his card and asked for Dr Canning.

"Well, if he says he's here, he is. He keeps funny hours, that one. Can't say I've seen him tonight, but you never know," said the porter. "You look like a man who can find their own way. Up the stairs, then on a bit, then third door on the left. You can't miss it."

Adams passed under arches, up the central stairs, and along a long stretch of corridor to see a small light flickering at the end of the hall. Perhaps this was the place? Adams looked about him and a display caught his eye. A huge glass cabinet imprisoning a myriad of tiny birds, and their wings outstretched as if they were flying. They had needles for beaks and their wings fanned out like butterflies dipping in flower blossoms, drinking and pollinating. But the petals couldn't compete in beauty with the velvet tourmalines, copper heads, and emerald plumages of the little birds.

A glimpse was enough. He sighed, and felt a little less troubled. And now directly in front of him was Dr Canning's door. Dr Canning had promised he'd be here, and had said in the note that what he had to tell Inspector Adams would explain everything. Who the killer was. How all the murders were connected. The Inspector cleared his throat, and tapped on the door.

CHAPTER
TWENTY

MAYFAIR

Where the devil was Ashby? The Duke of Monreith had had a hectic day or two, not helped by the sudden absence of his clerk and several important discussions with several important people. Representatives from the Oxford Movement, revisions to the Factory Acts, and all matters concerning the government of his sprawling empire, which stretched from Belgravia to the farthest corners of the world. And then there was the matter of that bloody bookseller. Still, the fire had been a good one, ensuring no trace of the Duke's name anywhere. Any ledgers, any mention of customers and suppliers was now like its owner — ashes and dust.

The Duke of Monreith unrolled the parchment scroll again, poured himself a glass of Machars whisky, thinking blink and you'd miss it, but not Madame Martineau, who had an excellent eye for detail. One reference only, and not the Duke's name, but the name of his company. And that braggart Ackerman drinking his malt, and talking of secrets till his last sorry breath. He knew he shouldn't have sent the whisky, but a deal was a deal and he'd honoured it. Along with an endless supply of money. Did anyone else who saw these letters make sense of it all, he wondered? His little whore certainly had. She'd put two and two together. Well, although he'd argued against it many times in The House, it was one good reason for educating women. He laughed to himself a little uneasily, and then continued flicking through the rest of the parchment letters. So much nonsense about flora and fauna, and some boring old bugger called Alfred Russel Wallace, who played chess. Fucking botanicals. He was sick to death of them.

But the words which haunted him were not in Latin, relating to genus and species. They were hidden, dangerous, and made mention of children. Subtle hints, scraps of conversation, names here and there, poison which could ruin him. No different from being linked to that pornography merchant, Dodds. The Duke knew he would have to find another supplier, but there were plenty in Hollywell Street, where he presumed Dr Finch used to go to find examples to back up his arguments. To demonstrate clearly, Man was Beast. Monreith had read his various private essays on transmutation, and the general argument that Man was animal in his instincts. Yes, of course, Dr Finch was right. Man had needs, desires, impulses. Who could argue with that, because trade and the empire were built on such principles. And that at the age of ten, or even younger, those little madams were women. Why, hadn't they said so themselves, in the notes supplied by Madame Martineau? She sometimes sent him a few when the girls weren't free or were not to his liking. He always insisted on his own private paper and for the girls to write their words directly across his monogram;

across the *M* so the very curl of the font, the gold of the crest, like a mouth, swallowed them.

The Duke tucked these private affairs away in his desk, kept hidden. Such delicious words, they tormented him with how much they desired him. How they wanted to be touched and caressed. And had not God ordained it so? God must have done because Dr Finch, the great theology don, had said so. But at the thought of God, Monreith cowered, looking over his shoulder.

For pity's sake, didn't he, and those like him, help the poor? Put food in their belly? And wasn't it part of the order of things? He took the girls in, sheltered them. He damn well nurtured them, just like Ophelie Martineau, and look how clever she'd turned out to be. Though she was getting rather greedy. Still, she had one last job to do, and then perhaps he would be finished with her.

The Duke looked at the scrolls of parchment for a second, and then tossing them into the fire, one by one, watched the letters crackle then glow. Snow feathered against the window, whilst the blackened smoke curled and the words of Ackerman and his specimens were silenced forever.

Poor old Ashby. Every step up the icy flight of London stone was painful. It was so bitterly cold, but buried deep in his pocket were voices begging not to be ravished, but for mercy.

And this old wretch of a man, like the loyal old dog he was, had done everything in his power to suppress it.

Even pawned his dead mother's ruby ring. Not a wedding ring. She'd been a servant girl up in some great house in Scotland, till they threw her out making all sorts of lewd accusations. She had raised him as best as she could. She wasn't old when she passed away and Ashby had to fend for himself. But he had worked hard and even got a place at Ragged School where the schoolmaster, though he claimed to be a man of God, was quick with the rod. Ashby had learnt to listen intently, did as he was told, and never questioned any of it, knowing his station in life. Until this.

Of course, he wasn't a fool. He'd lived in The Borough and wasn't blind to the world. He saw the prostitutes and knew what they were. They often reared into him as he picked his way home. The desperate ones would shove a screaming baby in his face begging him to save the brat and offering him, "Anything you want, anyways you want, just say the word." Why didn't the poor help themselves and stop having so many children?

And this is where these children ended up. Their voices buried in his pocket, and bought with a pawned ruby ring. Most likely, that blackmailing whore would pluck it from some jewellery shop for a third of its value. Perhaps she'd written some of these letters herself, thought Ashby. He couldn't tell, but there was no denying the filth therein. And he knew the Duke's handwriting and the monogrammed paper with the *M* for Monreith.

Madame Martineau had stepped out of a corner clutching them as he went about his business and whispered in his ear that if he didn't cough up and protect his master, it would lead to calamity. And Ashby knew what calamity meant for him. The workhouse again. So he had given her the money and asked the Lord for mercy. But blackmailing never stops. Was it so mad to come here and try to reason with the Duke?

Ashby banged on the door. It made a terrible thud and this time a great cacophony of barking came. A livery servant opened the door. One dog yapped at Ashby and sniffed his leg. Another, the smallest, bared her teeth. The servant took the dogs away and ushered them into another place, along the hallway.

He would reason with the Duke. He wouldn't creep away this time, as he had in Vauxhall Gardens.

"Come at once," said another servant. He was polished, like the bronzes, and shiny, like the mirrors which hung from every bend and turn of the place. Ashby followed the servant up the great flight and into a marble-floored room. A fire was roaring in the grate. The Duke had his back turned and appeared to be watching the snow fall, white lace outside the enormous windows. And Ashby saw an old man, not so unlike himself. Same bent back, balding head, and widow's hump. The Duke heard his step and spun around.

"Where have you been for the last two days? Have you been ill, dammit? Why didn't you send word? It is you, isn't it, Ashby? You look different, somehow. Have you come with news about my speech? I received nothing but plaudits for the last one." Monreith sounded tired, the bark gone.

"No, sir. I've come about something delicate." Ashby's words came sure and steady like the snow outside and he had never been so bold before.

"Something delicate, you say. Is it money, you hound? I pay you enough. I've a good mind to sack you for the time you've missed."

"No, sir. Although it has involved some of my money, what little I have. I was given some letters by a woman. A woman who says she knows you and lives not far from me, in The Borough." Ashby hung his head. He'd taken the letters out of his pocket and they now hung limp in his hand, flesh-coloured, smelling of the workhouse and still tied in a bright-blue ribbon.

The Duke of Monreith felt a shudder run down his spine.

"What have you got there, Ashby?"

"Enough to tell me what I wish I didn't know."

"You read them then, you dog?"

"Yes, I read them, but I wish I had never seen the foul and unnatural words. They took me on a journey and I followed you, sir. To Vauxhall Gardens."

"I see." Blood drained from the Duke's face. "And now you have come to blackmail me, Ashby, is that it?"

Ashby felt the pain ebb away. For the first time, in this dim half light, he saw the real man.

"I have come to ask you to stop. You still have time to beg God for forgiveness, to see a priest, to turn over a new leaf. The woman has us by the scruff of our necks and if she wants to she can wring them. By God, I know she can. Look, I still have her marks upon my arm."

294

The Duke snarled, "You don't know anything. Now give me those letters. If my name's on them, they're fakes. I'll burn them in the grate. They're nothing to do with me, Ashby."

"You forget that I've been a scribe for more than thirty years. I've learnt to sort out what's true and what's false. I think we both know they're real. They're written on your very own notepaper. Some of the letters are signed by you and others appear to be from children. Are there more, like this? Because if there are others, she will trap you."

The Duke shook his head and said, "These girls are not children. They're whores. Whores that like to fuck for money. They are traded on the market, Ashby. A market of commodities. They eat because of me. They drink because of me. I have given them money, pieces of jewellery, and love. Yes, love. Don't look at me like that. I'll thrash you within an inch of your life, now get out! Get out of my house!"

The Duke had taken a poker from the fire and was wheeling it around him. "Get out! Get out of my house . . ." He kept repeating it, louder and louder, till Ashby thought his ears would split.

The liveried servants were now at the door.

"Get him out of here."

Ashby shook the servants off. "I can see my own way out," he said.

The Duke let the poker fall further to his side, the sweat now running in rivers from his face. "Yes. See yourself out."

Monreith collapsed at his desk, wrenched opened a drawer, hurriedly wrote another note which he thrust at a servant. It had been a while since they'd called on this man's service. Since they'd gone straight to the top. The servant knew the name and nodded. Inspector Adams of Scotland Yard. The famous policeman.

"Get out! Get out of my house!" The words still ringing in his ears, Ashby staggered down some spiral stairs into the basement of the house and stood in a half-lit corridor of doors, and behind each door, thought he heard what sounded like the whispering of children. How many had there been? Their intakes of breath. Their quivering lips. Their promises of ecstasy. He shook himself, pushing their words away, and turned the handle of a door, which creaked open revealing no girl shackled in manacles or pinned to the ground, no grinding animal, but only a tidy little store cupboard. There were brooms leaning against the wall, a smouldering grate. The voices stilled and he wondered what poor creature lived in this hovel. Ashby blinked in the rheumy light and sat on an old, neglected easy chair, the letters on his lap. He wouldn't read them again. Above him a skylight and a moonless night. No stars, just a feathering of snow. The room was warm, almost womb-like. "I'll just shut my eyes for a second," he said.

CHAPTER
TWENTY-ONE

SMITHFIELD

When the rumbling came across the yard, Monsieur Roumande was the first to hear it. He got up and walked over to the back door, but hesitated. It was late. He looked over at Hatton, who was splayed across the desk asleep, a half glass of porter unfinished by his side. Hatton had arrived covered in a layer of snow, having walked from the docks, and after telling Roumande all that he knew so far on the case, said he would take just forty winks to restore himself. That had been several hours ago, and Roumande had kept the fire well stoked and lain a tartan blanket over the Professor, which they kept for nights like this.

Roumande knew it wouldn't be one of their collectors at this hour. They usually arrived at St Bart's just before dawn, their carts laden down, having worked all night around the alleys in The Borough. The river was rich pickings, as well. Mud larks frozen solid, if they'd ventured too far across the ice, so that it was easy to chip them out, their cadavers held in readiness for the mortuary slab. But how many more months like this?

Roumande shuddered to think on it and, leaving the door for a second, moved over to the fire and threw another log on. He watched the smaller bits of wood ignite, exploding into a thousand embers. He waited for the knock to come again and when it did, looked at the body before him with genuine pity. He walked over to Hatton and shook him awake.

The Specials laid the body on a slab. Hatton put his apron on. Roumande went over to the instrument table and sharpened the knives. Neither spoke about "why" or "where". It was too late for that.

Roumande opened Hatton's surgical box, each blade cleaned and sharpened, as if somehow they had known the tools would be needed very soon again. But they hadn't seen this. The quill was jabbed in, the point perforating his trachea. A night porter heard the crash and found his body hurled down the stairs like rubbish.

"His death would have been almost instant, Albert. Adams wouldn't have suffered." Hatton took a knife and made a sharp incision, easing the quill out, which was absolutely shear, like an arrow.

Should he call the family now? Hatton thought about what Adams's last thoughts must have been after he'd followed him to the molly boy whorehouse. But that was a secret now, taken to the grave. All over and done with, and it would stay that way. A reputation pierced. A scatter of broken promises left behind. None of it mattered any more. The lies to a wife; the promises to a lover. All of it gone. So this was death then, thought Hatton. Silent like the morgue.

"Let's not cut him any more. I can't do it, Albert. It's clear what has happened, here. He has died from asphyxiation and acute blood loss. I've no need for a microscope. It's textbook stuff."

Roumande put the blades away. He stepped back and picked up an autopsy form.

"Your hand is always neater than mine. Just write the usual, Albert. Time. Weapon. Place of death. Age of victim. Overall conclusion. But none of this will matter." Hatton sighed. "I have had enough of this pointless dissection, for what have we achieved? What have we learnt that has made any difference?"

Roumande put the form down incomplete and spoke to his friend, the Professor. "Inspector Adams met his destiny, Adolphus. It's a bitter pill to swallow, but it will come to us all. Whoever did this to him has left a message. The weapon? Does it say anything to you?"

Hatton shrugged and started to rifle the dead man's pockets, lost in thought. "I thought it might be here. It's Olinthus Babbage's notebook. God knows if it's still useful."

The two men looked at the book. Roumande flicked through it. "The name of Dr Canning is here and the initials L.B., which we know stands for Lady Bessingham, and look Adolphus, here's another name we must have missed before."

Hatton took the notebook.

"Is there something the matter, Adolphus?"

"I'm not sure. Wait a minute." Hatton walked over to where they kept their microscope and pressed the notebook flat, so the entire page could be seen. "Have a look, Albert. Tell me what you see."

The apparition was clear. The ink was different, and so was the hand which wrote it.

Roumande said, "This name had been added, Adolphus. And I know this name. I read about the case in a newspaper years ago. He was up on a charge for molesting a child but it was dropped. Long before you came to St Bart's, Adolphus. But you know the rich. Nothing sticks. There was a bit of fuss at the time, but it all got swept under the carpet. The Duke of Monreith. There's a square named after him in Mayfair."

Hatton nodded, because it was all starting to make sense. The angel in the box. Property of D.W.R. Dodds. A child missing in the Fens. Violet. A dressmaker working for someone else. He asked Roumande to fetch a carriage.

CHAPTER
TWENTY-TWO

THE BOROUGH

Madame Martineau recalled when she had first come
up with her plan, sitting on the edge of his knee, doing
her buttons up. "I read all of them while she dithered
over patterns. I found them under the brushing tray.
The devil's in the detail and I am rather like one, am I
not? Don't you think? I look a little Mias, *n'est ce pas?*
So forlorn." She'd pulled a face. "And you, why you are
the very double for a great, big, dumb baboon." And
she'd laughed. But Monreith hadn't laughed. He had
gone deadly white and pushed her off him and slapped
her, very hard. And when she had stopped laughing,
he'd demanded she go back to the house sooner rather
than later, and get them any way she could.

It seemed so easy. A simple dressmaker's visit
arranged. "Yes, by all means, come late, if you must.
Just have the dress ready." The lady was bohemian and
dispensed with all convention. Even the habit of
normally having fittings in the morning. A night-time
fitting was nothing to her. A little lower, a little tighter,
a flounce here, a trimming there.

The fitting finished, the lady disappeared to try the
half-made dress on, so Ophelie saw her moment, her

fingers flying around the brushing tray, but the letters had gone.

And then who came in? The soirée queen herself, wrapped in a half-made dress, wax now smudged on her lily white fingers.

"What are you doing?" the lady said, and that Violet girl had stood open-mouthed, and then the lady said what sounded like "Thief!" And those rich ladies can really scream when they want to. Madam Martineau had her scissors in her pocket but her eyes moved to the desk, a breath away. She picked up the ammonite and brought it down.

But no time for perusal or checking the finish. Ophelie had put her palm across the girl's mouth and she warned her. "Not a word, or you're coming back with me little missy, where you came from. Back to The Borough."

And the girl had helped. As they cleaned up, Ophelie reminded Violet that she still had the smell of the brothel upon her, and if she opened her trap, well, she would cut it out. Clack, clack around the edge of her little missy tongue. Or she'd take a bodkin to her. She told the girl that's what happens to a snitch, and to get her a swig of the lady's laudanum before she left, because she had a terrible headache.

So that was that. Everything tossed in the river. But then, still she had to get the letters any way she could. But thank God, she was good on the scent and now there was a hundred more pounds on offer from the Duke to finish with this business and cover their tracks, so she wrapped herself up in a rabbit-fur muff.

And she'd dressed for the part. Madame Martineau had decided upon a dress of agate green. It lifted the colour of her skin and she'd applied a little rouge. She had her ruby earrings on and her fur-lined cloak. And it was almost Christmas, and so why not add a sense of festivity to the proceedings?

And with the money she had made — the lucre — she let the word trip around her tongue, she'd maybe run a new story, all about a Duke and his penchant for children, because time marched on and frankly, she was absolutely sick of him. Her future lay elsewhere. But first things first. She mustn't get carried away or get ahead of herself.

She pulled her fur cloak tighter against the bitter chill. A fog was lifting as she moved towards the river, and she heard no sound of the advancing steps until she saw, in the flare of a gas light, a figure moving as if stepping out of nowhere. And he was picking up his pace. That was no surprise to her. Men always did that when they saw her, the silvering shards of beaming light falling to illuminate her skin. He had a sense of purpose. She could feel it as he moved towards her. And as he moved more clearly into the beam, she knew him at once. The Duke had shown her a likeness from some scientific journal called the *Ibis* and there was no mistaking this one.

She dipped her head and caught his eye. He smiled back at her. She moved away feeling his eyes follow the curve of her back as she stepped off the pavers, lifting up her petticoat a little, thinking, men were so easy. Was this really all it took? She reached out, taking his hand,

and led him down an alley with the promise of something.

"A glass of porter?" she smiled, her hard teeth glinting. "There's a tavern at the end of this street." He answered yes, the sooner the better, because this man was the very devil. But she was not beyond giving him a little leaving present, so to speak.

"Take my arm," he said. "For I think I know you."

"I'd be happy to, *cherie*," she purred and lifted her petticoat a little higher. His breathing like a kiss.

"I know who you are," she whispered and reached for her scissors in her pocket.

She heard his sigh, or was it hers? A moan of longing and desire. Then something else. She felt the stab cut through her dress. She fell away from him.

"Do you think I would be so stupid? I've been to your workshop. I asked the girls about you. They told me where to find you. And how you would be dressed. What you would carry in your pocket. The children were not yours, Madame. They were not yours to give away. They needed protecting, but who will do it? The law? The police? They only care about money." His voice was harsh and she fell from him, clutching her side.

That she could be so weak. That she could let this creature fool her. She thought she was triumphant in that embrace, but she could see it now and her tapering hands clasped around the handles and tried to pull the scissors out, but they were stuck fast.

She staggered a little. The Borough was miles from here. She was falling with the snow. Red splatters on glistening white, and the figure walked away, without a turn or a glance at the heap of green silk stained crimson on the feathered paving stones.

The man headed for Mayfair and Monreith House. The door was shut, so he used the servant's entrance, easily forcing it open with a kick. No servants about, for they were not so loyal that they watched over the Duke, but had, the man presumed, taken to their beds. He could hear a muffled bark somewhere along the endless corridors and then a sleepy, "Shut up, you bloody hound," and then nothing.

He climbed the stairs, thinking to himself, so the old devil is asleep, then? He found the study, opened his travel bag, and took his green ledger out, running his fingers along the lines of the profit margins. A testimony to all he had become. All that drove him. *Componotus gigas.*

Everything had been neatly catalogued by Mr Ackerman. The names, the entries, the customers — companies and individuals. Sundries given as gifts, Machars whisky and the like. Some goods had been underlined because they were significant finds, and between the lines and the classifications, it was easy to make out the truth. The word mainly used being "Specimen" but there were other words, more descriptive, telling of Dayak children either sold already or due to be exported soon.

But no time to spare. He shut the ledger and as fast as an ocelot jumped up onto the desk and threw a rattan rope up and over a chandelier, making a noose, just big enough for an old man, who would be easy. Not like the other ones. Especially the Inspector, who did nothing despite all of his warnings, despite everything he'd shown him. In the end, he was as bad as the rest.

The old bugger was just next door sleeping, and there was no time for waiting. He'd show the Duke the ledger before he took his last sorry breath, so the devil could see what he really was and why justice would be done.

The door to the bedroom swung open, and Broderig hoiked the Duke from his bed, his mouth gagged, dragging him into the study. And the Duke was writhing, kicking, eyes bulging in terror, thinking this was not what he'd planned, this was not what he'd paid for, as the rope was bound tighter and tighter.

And to Broderig's disgust, he could feel the Duke's tears, and so he pulled harder, saying, "Do devils cry when they take their last breath? Well, I'll show you something to make a man cry."

Broderig opened the ledger.

"Do you see your sorry past, Monreith? Can you read the evidence?" Broderig's breath came hard, rasping. "In return for a crate of Machars whisky and ten guineas, this child was only eight when Ackerman took her for you. Not much of a cover was it, using words like specimen. And the name of your company entered over and over again. Along with the others. Mr Dodds and Dr Finch were good customers, too, from the looks of it. So, yes, sob old man, sob and repent and ask for God's forgiveness. But he's not listening, I promise you. I learnt that in the jungle."

The Duke's legs were buckling. Would no one save him? Where was Martineau? Where were his servants? And Inspector Adams? The note must be there by now, at The Yard, demanding his attention or his molly boy habit would soon be the talk of London. Where were they?

"You never met Dr Finch, did you? But I bet you read his essay, the self-justification for men like you. I made him read a little extract before he died. On his ramblings about lowering the age of consent from thirteen to eight. Is that young enough for you, Monreith? And what happens with these girls when you are sick of them? When they grow too cumbersome? Did you have them beaten, dumped somewhere, thrown in the river? Yes, I'm sure they're dead now, like you'll be soon. And don't worry, there's no one coming. Your whore is dead. And Inspector Adams, too, who did nothing, less than nothing. I warned him but he didn't listen."

"Adams?" the Duke managed to splutter through the gag, knowing it was over now.

"He should have done his job better and I hoped he might help me. I practically begged him to hunt you down in Monreith Square, but then I realised my words were falling on stony ground because I soon realised that all he cared about were the botanicals. And it occurred to me, if you want a job done well, then you must do it yourself. Well, that's it from the prosecution, M'lud. Bring the black hood. Bang the mallet down."

Broderig pushed the ledger and manhandled the accused up onto the desk. The Duke could see his future now. It was hanging before him.

"Death by hanging. It could be worse. It was worse for Finch, but then I had a little help. And it was terrible for Dodds. I pinned him down alive then cut his sullied heart out. It was better for Adams. I did it quickly. The whore, too. But for you, I want a proper hanging along the lines of Newgate. In this world without God, I'm your judge."

The Duke struggled and kicked his feet, but it was no use against the weight and youth of this man. The noose went around his neck and with a push, the body swung, flinched, then shuddered.

The makeshift gibbet worked a treat. The chandelier, an excellent hook. Broderig looked up at its crystal shards. French, eighteenth century, no doubt. There were many in London's fashionable houses all over this part of the city, and they were often stolen, taken during the Revolution and kept here in the city, like so many other thefts. This one looked extremely ornate, perhaps from a bordello. "How appropriate," thought Benjamin Broderig as he thought about a job well done.

Ashby woke up with a start. How long had he been asleep? He didn't know; the candle was almost out. But in his dreams he'd gone to a different place — a world bathed in perpetual sunshine, where people walked past, tipping their hats, saying, "Good afternoon, Mr Ashby. Lovely day!" And this dream told Ashby that he should leave by the front door. For the very last time, knowing that Mr Arnold Ashby, Esquire, was only answerable to God. And with the ease of a much younger man, he now walked briskly back to the central hallway where the spaces were vast, and the walls lined with glorious oils.

Ashby was no expert, but he took his time because why not? He had all the time in the world and so he looked at the portraits as if he were a gentleman in a gallery. And as there was no one about, he stepped into a little anteroom hung with magnificent hunting scenes. But they were not to his taste. Strung-up peacocks, their tender necks wrenched. White swans splayed out with blood on their alabaster necks. He could see that they were elegantly painted, but they were violent, yes, violent was the word.

And as Ashby walked the line of the pictures he came to the largest, which had been hung on its own. In the foreground was a magnificent stag. Ashby shut his eyes, thinking he could hear its dying bellow as its last breath ran out. He rubbed his eyes, but then it struck him like a thunderbolt. It was the very same house depicted on his own small oil. The house where his mother had worked up in Scotland, all those years ago. There was a title on the frame, "The King of Scotland Slain, Monreith House, 1802." Of course, not this London house, but the Scottish one.

And the truth dawned on him. The truth about his life. And how life was simply a set of bizarre coincidences. Like the city, a labyrinth. But at each bend and turn, in each nook and cranny, there is an interlinking of lives.

Ashby went back up the stairs. His heart was pounding, his mind racing with so many questions but less and less doubt. With the strength of an ox, he shoved the door open and it framed a broken old man. Too late for revelations. He climbed up on the desk and took the body down. And he cradled the old man's head in an old man's arms. One brother with another.

CHAPTER
TWENTY-THREE

MAYFAIR

"So, I think this is the place. Yes, look up ahead, Adolphus. I'm sure it is."

As their carriage pulled into Monreith Square, the house announced itself. It could be no other. Hatton was sure of it. The two men ran up to the main door but it was shut. They went around back to the servants' entrance.

When they left the morgue, Hatton had given the gun to the better shot, remembering the Inspector's words. Aim and fire. Adams's last, Hatton now realised. As a boy he had shot a handful of rabbits, but he had never used a weapon like this one. Roumande had looked at the gun in the carriage, caressing the metal in his bear-like hands, pressing his finger lightly on the curve of the trigger, and had asked one question. "Is it loaded?"

They were soon in an entrance hall burning with lamps and could hear servants scuttling and someone shouting, but the two friends carried on up the fanning stairs to a room where an old man lay sobbing with something dead in his arms. But where was the dressmaker? The old man was muttering something over and over again about children and letters. But

Hatton was distracted because he recognised, hanging over a chair, a well-worn travel bag, and on the desk, Broderig's ledger.

Roumande spoke to the clerk, "Do you know this man?"

Ashby looked up and answered, "He was my master, but he was dead when I found him."

"We're looking for someone. Her name is Madame Martineau. Perhaps you've heard of her?"

"Madame Martineau, you say? Did she do this, then? But that makes no sense at all, because she was making money from us. I came to ask him to stop but he wouldn't listen. She gave me these letters, but I had to pay for them." The old man looked at some letters still in his hand, which were tied with a bright-blue ribbon. Dainty in descriptive ink, the paper was flesh-coloured and run through with a monogrammed M. Hatton snatched them, read them, and as he read on, page after page, the innuendoes gave way to something more obvious. An intake of breath. An ardent tongue. The pain of love. A push, a shove. Then slashes and pricks.

Hatton put the letters down and looked at the heap before him, thinking he could have hung the Duke again, slit his throat and wielded such violence on that sorry sack of evil that it momentarily shocked him.

So had she killed the Duke for this? Or did she provide it? Hatton thought of the girls in the sweatshop. Of their sallow complexions and of Violet and the angel in the box, who he knew was not like the others. She had died by drowning and had been tucked in that orange box, her hair brushed, her hands just so, like a sign from Heaven, showing them the way, telling them something. Property of D.W.R. Dodds. And as he was trying to think about what all of this meant, the room filled with noise from the gathering of servants. Hatton watched the gun glint as Roumande pointed it, his finger on the trigger.

"We'll call the police," Hatton heard one of them cry and Roumande say, "Do it, then. It's about time, you drunks. Meantime, you'd better not come anywhere nearer if you know what's good for you."

Hatton moved back over to the windows and sat down at the Duke's huge desk. Fog and snow. The worst weather yet. The thickening vapours were yellow-tinged and murky, like the great river that snaked through London.

"What's in the ledger, Adolphus? Is there anything in that that would help us, for there's no trace of any dressmaker here."

What had Broderig said? "*Write it down, Inspector.*" The quill in his throat. *Camponotus gigas*. Forest ants and their blind sense of purpose. Hatton opened the ledger, already knowing what he'd see. The candle threw a beam of light across the owner's name. Had Broderig mentioned this man? On the train to Cambridge? The name said, "Property of Mr Christiaan Ackerman. 1855, The Malay Archipelago."

Hatton turned the pages, which were filled with goods in and out. Imports and exports. Listed commodities. And the details of customers, companies and individuals, with names that included Finch, Mr Dodds, and the Duke of Monreith, plus their addresses in London. And by the names, it said: *Specimens. Age seven, eight, six. Gender, female.*

What had the Feltwell boy said? That the Mucker's child had gone missing. That there'd been a fuss at the time but that the case was dropped. Benjamin Broderig had been at Cambridge as an undergraduate, and it dawned on Hatton that when Broderig returned from Borneo, he must have headed there, the ledger in his hand, knowing that he would find someone who'd be only too willing to help. It all made sense now. Finch, pleading for his life as he faced certain death at the hands of two men. One young and fearless, the other old but determined, as they stabbed him in the heart and cut him into pieces. And of course, thought Hatton to himself, the old porter at the lodge had cataracts. He was no watchdog. He was practically blind.

The last page of the ledger described a glorious river journey and mentioned names of the party that had travelled with this man. Mister Benjamin Broderig. It was the last entry. Hatton understood everything. "I know this ledger. Though he never showed me what it contained. It was the secret which devoured him."

By the time the two friends reached Chelsea, the sun was coming up. Swan Walk was no less elegant than the sweeping terraces of Mayfair. A topiary garden with clipped box hedges frosted with snow. Hatton could hear his own voice yelling, "Open up!"

A servant, looking bleary-eyed, did so, and beyond him, Sir William Broderig in a silk dressing gown.

"Where's your son, Sir William? We need to find him."

"I don't know. But what the devil is this? What do you mean by this unwarranted intrusion?"

"Your son has lost his way, Sir William. We must save him from himself and stop the killing," Hatton answered, knowing this was the truth.

"Killing? What the devil are you saying? He's not here, I tell you. He's been out all night. I can't keep track of him. He goes down to the river to see if his specimens have returned." Sir William was ringing his hands.

Roumande grabbed Sir William by the scruff of his neck. "And where would that be? By the river? Which bit of river, you old fool?"

"The Isle of Dogs. To the portside near the Machars Trading Company. His ship is returning this morning."

The two men headed east along the river to the Isle of Dogs. A sober grey light fell flat about them as they moved along the wharfside, and the snow was still falling in the bilious fog. The warehouses loomed up before them. A web of cobbled ditches, and cries about them, of rivermen and seagulls.

The Machars Trading Company was spectral and menacing, but they were already past it moving quickly to another place, where shadows of men and boats cracked through the ice.

But where was he? Where was Broderig?

Then Hatton saw him. Benjamin Broderig sauntering along the wharfside, one gloved hand in his pocket, the other with his gun.

"He has a pocket pistol, Adolphus. We need to be careful." Hatton called out, "Please, Ben. For your own sake, give yourself up!"

Broderig turned around, his pistol pointing directly at the Professor, and then almost as an afterthought, he turned away and sped off.

Roumande shouted, "Quick, Adolphus. I'll keep pace. But mind yourself. I'll shoot if I have to."

"Broderig. Stop, I say! We know what you did." But Hatton's voice was carried across the river, deadened by a fog horn.

Broderig vanished into the river mist.

"Which way did he go?"

Roumande answered by pointing straight ahead, where the vessels decreased in number and the fog thickened. But then a rasping cough.

"He's up ahead."

Knowing if they could corner him, they had him, because the fog was shrouding their approach. And as they drew closer, Hatton caught sight of Broderig, who stood for a second, his hand pressed to his chest, before he shot away again behind flapping sails of calico.

"Keep to my left side, Adolphus. There's nowhere to go. He's no runner, for that's an asthmatic cough. He won't get far before his lungs seize up in this weather. The land turns to marshes soon. We will have him any minute now."

Roumande was right. But what was he doing? He was heading away from the warehouses, which would have kept him hidden, and instead was moving out into the open water where the great prison hulks dominated the skyline. There was no escape this way. He must have known that. And if he had a gun and had taken other lives, why didn't he stop and face them? Why didn't he shoot?

And then Hatton saw it. Ahead, a magnificent ship, laden with cargo. And on the side of the ship, its name — *The Advancement*.

Broderig knew they were following him. But could it be that he was leading them? And it occurred to Hatton that perhaps he'd been leading them since the very beginning.

Broderig had constantly asked Adams about the welfare of the girls. In the yard at St Bart's, drinking tuak in the snow, Broderig had offered up information about Dr Finch — who he was, where they could find him, what he wrote about. But at the same time, claimed he'd never met the man. Of course, Hatton realised now it was lies. All lies.

And Broderig's constant jibbing at Inspector Adams wasn't the stuff of an overzealous young man, inclined to outbursts of temper. Hatton knew for certain now that Broderig wanted Inspector Adams to pay attention to the one thing which tormented him. An evil trade stretching to the farthest corners of the earth — children bought and sold, who were abused, beaten, and then killed by rich men like the Duke of Monreith, one of many customers in Ackerman's ledger book.

Which is why Broderig had begged Inspector Adams to visit Monreith Square and debated the issue of justice so vehemently in the carriage back to London. Of course, Broderig wanted Adams to do his job properly and arrest Monreith, ending the trade with a public hanging, which could only be secured by The Yard. But Adams didn't act. Because Adams wouldn't listen. If only he'd listened, thought Hatton, his mind racing. But he didn't, and so he had to pay the price. He had to be punished.

But why kill Adams at the museum? And then Hatton heard something. A voice in his head. Two voices. If he shut his eyes for a second, Hatton could hear them in the drawing room at Ashbourne.

"Do you have names, Dr Canning? Anyone you could specifically point to who might want to destroy these letters or bury them?"

"Not to the point of killing someone, Inspector, if that's what you mean. But when I return to London this evening, I'll talk to some of my colleagues. I'll send a note to Scotland Yard if I learn anything useful. You never know, I might find something to help."

Broderig must have hidden in Dr Canning's office, perhaps forged a note and pretended to be him. The sharpened quill through his throat? Yes, Broderig must have lured Adams to the museum, exasperated but knowing that the only way to end these crimes was to finish the job himself.

The river fog was blowing out across the brackish water. It made the great sails flap and sent an eerie sound of wailing through the vessel's timber frame. The cries of seabirds, across the choppy water, were high tones and whistles.

"He's stopped, Adolphus."

The two men hung back and watched him, half-hidden by the scaffolding which stretched along the river.

"We have to get him to lay down his gun, Albert, and then arrest him. Are you ready, friend?"

But something was holding both of them back. What was he opening? He had a crowbar in his hands, and was pulling back a lid which was slowly coming open. Roumande stepped forward towards the vessel, his hand on walnut and metal.

"Wait, Albert. Let me speak to him. He trusts me. Ben? For pity's sake, give yourself up . . ." But the wind took Hatton's voice and sent the words like bits of paper hurtling up and away. Hatton spoke again, this time shouting, "Broderig! Turn around. For pity's sake, friend. I know what you did. And why."

On command, Broderig turned around to face Hatton and was speaking, a half-smile upon his lips, but his voice was flat and disappeared in the brake of the tidal water, which was splashing against the dockside, nullified against the lee of the land.

"Stand aside, Professor! I have him in my sight." It was Roumande.

Hatton heard his friend, and shouted, "No, Broderig. Don't . . ." and heard a crack. One shot. That was all it took. Broderig fell backwards, his own gun smoking, a penny dimensional hole in the side of his head.

The two men moved forwards. Roumande first to check that Broderig was dead, his own pistol unused but still at the ready, and then Hatton, who moved reluctantly, as if he was a visitor to this place and had work to do that involved some humdrum inspection. But in truth, Hatton was in shock at the death of a friend. Because despite everything, that was what Benjamin Broderig was to him. A good man, lost. But Hatton said nothing and looked in the open crate, into which Broderig had fallen. His body bent over a great jumble of stuff. A fish, some frames, nets, and guns. But the strangest of all, at the bottom of the crate was a creature. It had arms like a man's and a face so forlorn, as if it knew something. But its eyes were not its own. They were glass. Hatton peered more closely, as if to find the creature's soul. But all that was offered was a distorted image of himself, reflected back.

CHAPTER
TWENTY-FOUR

SMITHFIELD
TEN DAYS LATER

"So, there were two killers, Adolphus? All the time, we should have been looking for two killers, not one. Which is why we could find no forensic evidence to link all of the murders. Madame Martineau was working for Monreith and killed Lady Bessingham and then Mr Babbage in order to get Broderig's letters any way she could. But the reason she wanted them was nothing to do with scientific theory."

"No, Albert. I suspect there was something in the letters which linked Monreith to Ackerman's trade in children."

"But where do you think they are now? The Yard checked every nook and cranny of that monstrosity of a house."

Hatton shrugged. "Those letters are gone, Albert. Long gone. Destroyed like the bookshop."

"I still find it incredible."

"Yes, but not impossible. So many things in life are connected. As Men of Science, we know this."

"And those other letters, Adolphus? Those vile, hateful words we took from Mr Ashby at Monreith

House. Those words scattered like tears across the swirling monogram."

Hatton nodded. "Ah, yes. *M* for Monreith. I think Madame Martineau provided those notes to Monreith along with children from the workshop. Once read, I couldn't look at them again. Did you put them in the incinerator, Albert?"

Roumande nodded. "Yes, I did as you asked and burnt them."

Hatton knew it was against police procedures. That it could be argued that the letters were crucial forensic evidence, but in the end, he decided the world was better without them, that they no longer served any purpose.

And so Hatton stood up, thinking he needed a drink, and got their usual round, as was becoming traditional after finishing a case. One double cognac for Roumande, and for Hatton, nothing more complicated than a tin mug of porter. They clinked glass against metal.

"But I sense that you are a little melancholy, Adolphus? Is it the memory of Mr Broderig?"

Hatton shrugged. "He went to a dark place in his heart, Albert. But it is done with now. Did I mention that I tried to make contact with Sir William, a day or so ago? Well, he refused it. Benjamin Broderig's body has been buried quietly in a necropolis, but I suspect that was not what he would have wanted. It would have been better if he had fled these shores and died in the jungle."

"You wanted him to escape, then?"

322

Hatton said, "He killed four people. Five if you include Madame Martineau, although we haven't found her body and I think may never do so. We shall never really know the truth about her, but yes, I think Broderig must have killed her. I think he put two and two together, as I have. Everything was connected and it all started with Broderig and so it is fitting that it should end with him."

"And there was no one at Madame Martineau's workshop to tell us anything more? No sign of life at all?"

Hatton felt in his pocket and sighed. "I went back yesterday but the place was boarded up. The girls all gone." He reached for the buckle, and put it on the table. "I still hope that I might one day give this buckle to a girl called Kitty. But this is a sprawling city."

The two men glanced at each other for an uncomfortable second, and then looked back at their dregs.

"And your trip to Cambridge, Adolphus? Forgive me for not joining you. Just nothing again, you said, but it's hard to believe you went all that way and found not a trace."

Hatton smiled. "It was as I described. The Feltwell boy and the Mucker, both gone as if they were ghosts. I asked around the villages near Wickham Fen but the people there kept quiet, little trusting an outsider like me. But there's no doubt in my mind. On return from Borneo, armed with the evidence in Ackerman's ledger, Broderig killed Finch with the Mucker's help. The Mucker's daughter disappeared the year before he set off to Borneo, when he was an undergraduate at university so he would have known about the case. And when Lady Bessingham was brutally murdered by the mantuamaker, he seized his opportunity, having a policeman and a forensic expert in his grasp. He wanted us to help him."

"To bring down the House of Monreith?"

Hatton nodded. "He took us to Cambridge, he led us to Dodds, and at Ashbourne and in our carriage back to London, he mentioned Monreith Square over and over again. He was trying to make us do our job better, but as he saw it, we failed him."

Roumande sipped his brandy. "And you were right about that little angel, Adolphus. She was never like the others. Her hair had been brushed. Broderig found her by pure chance, dragged her from the river, pricked her wrists in a perfect circle and tucked her up all cosy in the orange box. He wanted us to find her."

"Yes," said Hatton. "As I say, leading us to Dodds, the child pornographer. Property of D.W.R. Dodds? The girl was just a symbol, pointing us to others. If only we had listened to him. If only we had paid attention. It's all clear now, Albert. And although Broderig is dead, there's a message from the grave if you like, which we would both do well to take note of."

Roumande asked solemnly, "A message from Broderig? And that message is what, Adolphus?"

"*Camponotus gigas*. Being blind to everything, but our natural purpose. If Adams had listened, acted as he should have done, pursued the truth as Broderig saw it, he would still be with us."

Hatton's face clouded, and Roumande offered to buy another round, but the Professor shook his head. "Whatever you say, you are first and foremost a family man. And I'll not delay your return home to Spitalfields. Come, Albert. If you catch a carriage, you'll be back in time for lunch."

Albert resigned himself, stood up, and placed his derby firmly on.

It was a fine, crisp January day, but still cold and blustery.

ACKNOWLEDGEMENTS

Huge thanks to Susie Dunlop and all her team at A&B for publishing this book in the UK. In the US, thanks to my editor at Thomas Dunne Books, Peter Wolverton, for his smart suggestions and eagle-eyed advice, plus Anne Bensson and all the team at St Martin's. Thanks to all my early readers — Julie Major, Gaby Chiappe, Tracy Brett, Marika Lysandrou, Melanie Lanoe, Amy Fletcher, Liz Byrne, Anne Wilk. Thanks to my mum and dad, Alec and Kay Laver. Thanks also to Sarah Gordon, Claudia Daventry, Natasha Fairweather, Christine Langan, Caroline Stack and Freya Newberry — you all know why. Massive thanks to my two boys — Joseph and Rory — for their endless patience with me always disappearing to sit in front of my laptop. Writers rely on their agents for so many things, so a big, heartfelt thanks with bells on to Kevin Conroy-Scott and Sophie Lambert at Tibor Jones Associates, who have astonished me with their hard work and unshakable belief in my work. I've dedicated this book to my husband, Charlie Meredith. He also deserves my gratitude and love.

As with all historical crime novels, there was a lot of research involved in writing this book. Apart from numerous visits to the British and Natural History

Museums, The Hunterian Museum and The Wellcome Collection, I read a great deal of books. Here are the most enticing: *The Malay Archipelago* by Alfred Russel Wallace; *Charles Darwin* (Vol I & II) by Janet Browne; *London in the Nineteenth Century* by Jerry White; *Alfred Russel Wallace, A Life* by Peter Raby; *Victorian London* by Liza Picard; *The Science of Sherlock Holmes* by E.J. Wagner; and finally, *A Dictionary of Victorian England* by Lee Jackson.

I also recommend you visit my website at *www.demeredith.com* if you want to know a bit more about the wonderful world of the Victorians.

Also available in ISIS Large Print:

Death on a Branch Line

Andrew Martin

The sweltering summer of 1911. Trouble is brewing with Germany. Half the country is on strike; the other half seems to be in flames. And in his most perplexing case to date, the railway detective Jim Stringer has 48 hours to solve a murder not yet committed.

One Friday evening, a special train rolls into York station. It carries a young aristocrat lately found guilty of murdering his father. Briefly entrusted into Jim's custody, he warns of yet another murder about to happen in his home village . . .

Jim and his strong-willed wife, Lydia, take the train along the near-deserted branch line. They seek out the intended victim, who, despite their warnings, stubbornly refuses to leave. Jim has one weekend to track an ever-growing number of suspects, stop a murder, and unravel a conspiracy of international dimensions.

ISBN 978-0-7531-9196-5 (hb)
ISBN 978-0-7531-9197-2 (pb)

The Baghdad Railway Club

Andrew Martin

Baghdad, 1917. Captain Jim Stringer, invalided from the Western Front, has been dispatched to investigate what looks like a case of treason. He arrives to find a city on the point of insurrection, his cover apparently blown — and his only contact lying dead. As Baghdad swelters in a torrid summer, the heat alone threatens the lives of the British soldiers who occupy the city. The recently ejected Turks are still a danger — and many of the local Arabs are none too friendly either. The situation grows pricklier by the day. Aside from his investigation, he is working on the railways around the city. His boss is the enigmatic Lieutenant-Colonel Shepherd, who presides over the dining society called The Baghdad Railway Club. Jim's search for the truth brings him up against murderous violence in a heat-dazed city where an enemy waits around every corner.

ISBN 978-0-7531-9084-5 (hb)
ISBN 978-0-7531-9085-2 (pb)